Chasing Butterflies

Also by Amir Abrams

Crazy Love
Caught Up

McPherson High series
The Girl of His Dreams
Diva Rules

Hollywood High series (with Ni-Ni Simone)
Hollywood High
Get Ready for War
Put Your Diamonds Up
Lights, Love & Lip Gloss

Published by Kensington Publishing Corp.

Chasing Butterflies

AMIR
ABRAMS

KENSINGTON PUBLISHING CORP.
www.kensingtonbooks.com

DAFINA BOOKS are published by

Kensington Publishing Corp.
119 West 40th Street
New York, NY 10018

All Kensington titles, imprints, and distributed lines are available at special quantity discounts for bulk purchases for sales promotion, premiums, fund-raising, and educational or institutional use.

Special book excerpts or customized printings can also be created to fit specific needs. For details, write or phone the office of the Kensington Sales Manager: Kensington Publishing Corp., 119 West 40th Street, New York, NY 10018. Attn. Sales Department. Phone: 1-800-221-2647.

Dafina and the Dafina logo Reg. U.S. Pat. & TM Off.

ISBN-13: 978-0-7582-9482-1
ISBN-10: 0-7582-9482-4
First Kensington Trade Paperback Printing: October 2016

eISBN-13: 978-0-7582-9483-8
eISBN-10: 0-7582-9483-2
First Kensington Electronic Edition: October 2016

10 9 8 7 6 5 4 3 2 1

Printed in the United States of America

This book is dedicated to Triqqa Dee and his daughter, Jade. There's nothing more powerful than a father's love. May you continue to be the light in her life, and the wind beneath her growing wings.

1

The Umoja—pronounced *oo-MOE-jah*—(meaning unity)
Poetry Lounge in L.A. swells with lively chatter and fiery
energy. There are drums and congas and tambourines and
hips swinging.

We've taken the twenty-five-minute drive from Long Beach—
where I live—to be here tonight. It's a Thursday evening, and
open mic night.

I'm at my table scrambling to finish my piece. It's a last-
minute surprise for Daddy, who's sitting at the table with me.

And I'm anxious, really, really anxious.

This time.

As if it's my first time taking the stage.

My nerves are fluttering up around me.

Why?

Because I've decided at the very last moment—less than
ten, no...eight minutes before open mic starts—to change
my piece. And now I'm frantic.

Most of the people here are spoken word artists, like myself, but much older; college-age and older, but an eclectic
bunch nonetheless.

I'm one of the youngest.

An eleventh grader.

But I've earned the respect of the more seasoned poets. The poets with tattered notebooks filled with much more life experience and depth than I can possibly have at sixteen.

Still, I hold my own among them.

Being on stage is the only time I feel...

Liberated.

They embrace my innocence.

Embrace my openness about the world around me.

And allow me license to just be.

Me.

Free.

That's what I love most about poetry. The creative freedom. The freedom to weave words together. Colorful expression. A kaleidoscope of emotions, imagination, passion, hopes, and dreams. We are surrounded by similes and metaphors.

We listen.

We hear.

And tonight will be no different, no matter how anxious I am becoming. There's an uncontrollable energy that lifts me, and sweeps around the room. The feeling is indescribable. All I can tell you is I feel it slowly pulsing through my veins.

Like with all the other open mics, there are no judgments, no stones cast.

Well...not unless you are just unbelievably whacked, that is.

I am not.

Whacked, that is.

Well, okay...at least I don't think I am. So I know I should have no reason to be worried tonight.

But I am.

See. Tonight is special. I mean. It *has* to be special. It's Daddy's birthday. I brought him here for dinner. And then, I had this bright idea to surprise him with a poem. My dedication to him, my way of thanking him for being the most wonderfully incredible father a girl could ever ask for.

I am an only child. And Daddy is my only parent.

See. My mom was killed in a car accident when I was six. So for the last ten years, Daddy has been singlehandedly raising me on his own. Well, wait. Okay. He did have help caring for me the first five years after my mom's death. Nana. My maternal grandmother, she stepped in and helped Daddy provide some normalcy in my life.

But then...she died, too, from cancer.

I was eleven.

So you see, Daddy is all I have.

It's him, and me.

And, no, this isn't a sob story.

It's my reality.

My truth.

I've endured heartache and loss; more than I've ever hoped for. But I know love, too. Real love.

Daddy's love.

And, for me, there is no love higher than his. He has helped me to endure. Still, I can't lie. I lost pieces of me when my mom was killed. And even more pieces of me when my nana passed. But, over time, Daddy salvaged me. Helped put me back together. Loved me whole again. His unconditional love has been my soothing balm. It heals me. It protects me. It gives me promise.

That there's nothing I can't get through.

And I love him for that.

I know there are no coincidences. Everything that happens to us in our lifetime happens for a reason. And sometimes that reason is much bigger than us. We can't see it. We can't always understand it. Still, it happens because that's the order of destiny.

Daddy taught me that.

That we live, we love, we—

Daddy must sense my trepidation. He reaches for my hand and gently squeezes it. I look at him and smile. No words are needed. His touch is all I need. But he gives me more. He always does. "You've got this, sweetheart. This is your world."

I smile wider.

Instantly, I calm enough to focus and write a few more verses.

Maybe I should just speak from the soul.

Let words flow from my lips in synch to what I feel in my beating heart.

I quickly glance around the dimly lit room. Candles flicker on the tables.

Suddenly, I am feeling nervous again.

I try to calm myself, to no avail.

I try to—

"Peace and blessings, my beautiful people," I hear the emcee say. I look over toward the stage. She's a beautiful brown-skinned woman, the color of milk chocolate, wearing a fire-engine-red halter-jumpsuit that complements her curves and her complexion.

Her skin shimmers under the glow of the light.

She stands at the mic, confident.

Proud.

Graceful.

Her presence is electric.

"Peace and blessings," the crowd says in unison.

"Y'all ready to get lifted?"

The crowd raises their arms, fingers snap.

"I am Sheba, your host tonight. And trust me. Tonight you are in for a real treat. We have a lineup of some of the west coast's finest spoken word artists slated to take the stage and stimulate your mental. So sit back, relax, and enjoy the prose. First up to take the stage is Nia..."

I am taken by surprise when the emcee introduces me.

Oh no.

That can't be—

I think I am hearing things, but then she announces my name again.

Nia Daniels.

I hoped to be somewhere in the middle. Not first.

Never first.

Daddy must sense my hesitation. "Go do your thing, But-terfly," he says beaming. I smile back nervously, then lean over and kiss him on the cheek. Daddy has been calling me *Butterfly* since I was three years old. He says it was because I would get excited every time I saw one in our yard, and that I re-minded him of one because I was light on my feet and always flitting about as a child, never settling on one thing for any length of time before moving onto something else, like a but-terfly.

I push up from my chair, grab my book, and head toward the front of the lounge. I slowly take to the stage, the glare from the lights blinding me.

I blink. Blink again.

My nerves are getting the best of me.

I am literally trembling.

My piece isn't finished.

I'm never unprepared.

Never.

But tonight...tonight I'm feeling mentally disheveled.

I stand at the microphone, head bowed, hands clasped, trying to collect myself, trying to gather up my anxiety.

I clear my throat.

Take a deep breath.

"Hi, everyone. Tonight I'm sharing a piece I've written for the most special person in my life. My rock. My anchor. My world. My one constant. Since birth, he's been everything to me." I glance over at Daddy. He leans in, his attention fixed on me. "And, tonight, I want to share with all of you a piece of who he is, who he has been, to me." I glance over at Daddy again. "Daddy, this one's for you."

He smiles.

I look out into the crowd. "Y'all please bear with me. I didn't get a chance to finish it, so I..."

Someone says, "Take your time, little sister."
"That's all right," someone else says. "We got you."
I smile.
Glance over at Daddy one more time. Then grab the mic,
and close my eyes.

Mother
Father
Protector
Provider
Best friend
Wrapped into
one
beautiful gift.
You are...
Pancakes
smothered
in warm maple syrup,
eggs scrambled hard,
grits with lots of cheese.
You are...
Sugar cookies
and
ice cream cones,
lemon pound cake
and
painted toes...
tree houses
jump rope
hopscotch
hide 'n' seek
and Barbie dolls.
You are...
Easy-Bake Ovens
crayons

and
Play-Doh;
Rollerblades
carousels
and
no-hand
roller coaster rides.
You are...
Saturday morning
cartoons
and
hot fudge sundaes.
Sandcastles
and seashells;
rushing waterfalls
and Venice Beach.
You are...
Gershwin piano keys
Bach French Suite
No. 1
in D-minor;
toothy grins
crooked parts
lopsided ponytails
and
colored barrettes;
that's what you are to me.
Bedtime prayers
and
nursery rhymes;
candy-coated rainbows
sweet dreams
and lullabies;
shiny trinkets
and glass slippers.

Pixie dust
and
scraped knees
drenched
in kisses;
gentle
warming
so full of love;
that's what you are.
Tea parties
And dress up.
My inspiration
My hero
No
No
My super hero
Always there
to save the day...
sunshine in the rain.
The gentle breeze
beneath my
fluttering wings...
Morning hugs
and tummy tickles;
vanilla skies
and butterfly kisses...
That's what you are.
Mother
Father
Protector
Provider
Best friend
wrapped into
one
beautiful gift
That's what you are.

"And I'm the luckiest girl in the world," I say, so full of joy. "Happy birthday, Daddy. I love you."

The room erupts with applause. Then everyone joins me in singing "Happy Birthday" to the world's greatest dad.

With my heart full and my soul fed, I step away from the mic and glance over at Daddy. The look on his face says it all.

He is so very touched.

And I am loved.

2

"So how was last night?" my best friend, Crystal, asks in her hoarse, raspy voice. If you didn't know Crystal, you'd swear she'd gotten her voice from drinking jugs of moonshine and smoking packs of cigarettes a day since birth.

However, she doesn't drink or smoke.

But she sort of looks and sounds like the late singer Amy Winehouse. Bless her heart. But don't tell Crystal I told you that. She'll beg to differ. Ask her, and she'll tell you she's Etta James all the way. But everyone, anyone, who knows anything about Amy Winehouse also sees the uncanny resemblance.

And they hear the similarities.

Crystal even has a mole over her lip like her. She's just a browner, thicker—not much thicker though—version of Amy sans the grungy beehive hairdo, and the smoking, drinking, and drugging.

Crystal cringes every time someone tells her how much she resembles her, but then she'll break out in song, singing, "I say...no, no, no..."

All I can do is laugh.

Because she really does sound so much like her.

It's eerie.

Rest in peace, Amy...

"Ummm, *helllllllo?*" I can hear her snapping her fingers. "Earth to Nia. Are you there?"

I chuckle. "I'm here."

"Oh, good. Welcome back," she says sarcastically. "I thought you might have been kidnapped or something."

I playfully roll my eyes. "You're so theatrical."

"Uh-huh. What. Ever."

I laugh again. "Soooo, why weren't you in school today?"

She blows out a long, exaggerated breath. "Please, don't get me started. My mom had this bright idea that *I* should spend the day riding with her to San Diego to drop things off to my brother..."

Crystal has three brothers, and is the only girl. She's also the baby in her family. Need I say more? Nope. The youngest of her brothers, Christian, is a junior at San Diego State. Her brother CJ recently finished law school and lives in Miami. And her brother Cordell is in the marines.

She always says she wishes she were the only child.

And I'd give anything to have older brothers.

She huffs. "...I mean, like *really*? She needs a new hobby besides ruining my life. Like I have nothing else better to do than miss a day from school, while she prattles on—the *whole* drive—about how awful her cuticles look, and how she needs her edges touched up, and how much weight she thinks she needs to lose. For Christ's sake, she only weighs a hundred and thirty-seven pounds, and she's stressing over having gained seven pounds! I can't with her sometimes. She's going to be the reason I OD on Kit-Kats and gummy bears."

I laugh at that. "Crystal, you're hilarious. You know that, right?"

"No. But I *know* my mom is determined to drive me crazy with her fresh-fruits-and-vegetables speeches. It's overkill, Nia. Geesh! I get it. She wants to see me starve to death."

I can't stop laughing at Crystal's overexaggeration of her mom. I mean, Mrs. Thomas is really, really cool. But she *is* kind of obsessive when it comes to *her* weight, healthy eating, and always looking *her* best. Mrs. Thomas is always in the gym, or doing yoga, or taking Pilates classes. And she always tries to drag Crystal along. But Crystal's so not interested. But I have to give it to Mrs. Thomas. She looks *sooo* good for her age. When people see Crystal and her mother together they automatically think that she's Crystal's older sister.

Crystal hates that.

But I think it's cool.

"...Nia, girl, my mom acted like that little road trip couldn't wait until Saturday. I asked her why she couldn't go by herself, and she just stared at me, then narrowed her eyes. No explanation. Nothing. Just glared at me. Like who does that?" I can see her shaking her head and rolling her eyes in my mind's eye. "I swear, she's going to drive me to drink dark sodas just for the sugar high."

"Hahahaha. You're comical, Crystal."

"I'm serious, Nia. But, annnnyway. Let's get back to *you*. I asked you how last night was, and you *still* have yet to give me details."

"Well, that's because your mouth has been going nonstop since we've been on the phone. You haven't stopped talking long enough for me to get a word in."

She sucks her teeth. "That's beside the point, Nia. I need details. Starting with the cutie alerts. Were there any cute boys there? I'm dying over here."

I swear I love her.

But the older she gets, the more boy crazy she gets.

When we were like ten, Nana would say every time Crystal came over, "Somebody better watch that one. She's gonna be hotter than a firecracker."

I used to beg Nana to not say that. But she'd say it every time. Truthfully, I don't think Crystal's going all the way with boys, yet. Well, wait. I know she isn't. Well, I hope not.

She would have told me.

Wouldn't she?

I mean. We tell each other everything.

Crystal and I have been friends since kindergarten.

Thick as thieves.

The dynamic duo.

That's what we are.

We've shared every milestone together.

Shed tears together.

Laughed together.

And explored the world together.

Like sisters, we share a very special bond.

She's traveled with me on vacation with Daddy. And I've gone places with her and her parents as well. Two summers ago I spent a month in Paris with her and her parents.

It was amazing!

And this summer, she'll be going to Vienna, Austria, and Hamburg, Germany, with Daddy and me.

Why those places?

Because Daddy let me choose where I wanted to vacation this year. And I chose those countries because I love, love Europe and they are both musical capitals—considered home to classical music, and I want to experience everything each country has to offer from classical concerts and opera houses to the ballet.

I love the arts.

And so does Daddy.

Unlike most kids my age, I've been listening to classical music for as long as I can remember. Thanks to Daddy.

And, when my mom was alive, the sounds of Motown could also be heard playing through the house on any given day.

She'd sing to me.

And when I was old enough to learn the songs, I'd sing along.

Then when Nana moved in to help Daddy raise me, she'd play nothing but jazz. The sounds of Nina Simone and Billie Holiday and Etta James caressed my ears religiously.

So music has been all around me.

Good music, that is.

Music that makes the spirit come alive.

Umm, I guess you can say I kind of have an old soul.

I don't think like most kids my age.

Nor do I see the world like most of them, either.

I do not think I am better than them. I've simply been exposed to more cultural experiences than most that have broadened my perspective on life and the world around me.

Still, I am the first to admit my own truths.

That I am spoiled.

That I am well traveled.

That I am very much sheltered from the harsh realities of many kids my age.

The disenfranchised.

The impoverished.

The misunderstood.

The underserved.

The trapped.

The less fortunate.

And no matter how many times I volunteer at shelters and soup kitchens, there's still a disconnect. No matter how many bags of clothes or toys I donate to homeless centers, I am still standing on the outside looking in. No matter how much empathy I have, or compassion I feel, I can and will never truly understand their struggle until I've slipped into their shoes and walked in their footsteps.

Shoes I'm too ill prepared to step into.

I know that.

And I also know how blessed I am. How very grateful I am.

"I soooo wish I could have been there," Crystal says, slicing into my thoughts before I can answer her question. She does that sometimes.

Okay. Most times.

"It was incredible," I am finally able to say. My smile widens as flashes of last night replay in my head. Daddy was so moved by my poem to him that he was practically in tears by the time I returned to my seat, although he smiled the rest of the night—and beamed with pride—every time someone came to our table to wish him happy birthday, or tell me how much they enjoyed the piece.

I tell Crystal all about it.

"Ooh, it sounds so beautiful," she says excitedly. "Did you do that piece on fatherhood?"

My forehead creases. Was she not listening to a word I said? I could swear I told her I wrote a birthday poem specifically for Daddy last night.

I blink.

"Umm, why are you Facebook stalking, instead of listening to *me*?" I say, feigning annoyance.

"See. There you go assuming. I'm not even on Facebook. Now apologize."

"Then stop Twitter stalking."

She laughs. "Oops, busted. I'm sorry. Wait. Didn't *you* zone out on *me* just a few moments ago? You were probably on social media yourself, which is how you probably knew I was."

I laugh. "Nope, I wasn't. Try again."

"Mmhmm. Anyway. Go 'head tell me again."

"Nope. It's obvious I'm not that important to you. Twitter is."

"Ohhh, Nia-pooh," she whines, "don't be like that. You know you're my bestie for life."

I suck my teeth. "I can't tell. So you might as well tell me who tweeted what."

"Oooh, I thought you'd never ask..."

3

"Ohmygod, I still can't believe what you told me last night," I stage whisper to Crystal as she swings open the glass door, and we step through the school's entrance. She'd told me last night that some boy she's following on Twitter tweeted that Naomi Pitts, one of the varsity cheerleaders here, gave him and two of his friends an STD.

Chlamydia.

Yuck!

In Twitter news, from what Crystal told me, the three friends shared in a game of naughty tag-team, passing a very naked Naomi around like a football.

I know, scandalous, right?

No, more like gross.

"I know, right," Crystal says, frowning. "She's so, so nasty for—"

"Who's nasty?" Cameron cuts in, sliding in between Crystal and me, startling both of us. Cameron is one of my best male friends here at Colgate High, the private high school we attend. And he's, um, well—for a lack of a better description, he's the thorn in Crystal's ultra-toned side.

She punches him in the arm. "Dang, boy. Stop doing that."

He feigns ignorance. "Doing what?"

She punches him again. "Scaring us with that ugly face."

Cameron laughs, rubbing his arm. "That tickled."

She hits him again, this time a little harder, in the shoulder. He brushes it off. "You hit like a girl."

Crystal sucks her teeth. "I *am* a girl, stupid." She pushes him. "Now get out the way."

He glances over at me. "Nia's a girl, *too*, but she *hits* like a guy."

Crystal huffs. "Well, I'd hit like a boy, too, if I knew how to fight like one."

"Umm, *hello*?" I say, waving a finger to stop them. "The two of you, leave me out of your little sparring match. It's way too early to play referee."

"Yeah, Crystal," Cameron says, pinching her cheek, "play nice."

"Oww, boy! I can't stand you."

Cameron grins. "Okay. You should work on your lying."

"And you should work on your face," Crystal shoots back.

I roll my eyes.

She knows his face is just fine.

Cameron dismisses her. "Sooo, who wants to tell me who's being nasty? I like nasty talk."

Crystal huffs. "Boy, stay your nasty butt out of adult conversations. This has nothing to do with *you*."

I shake my head, maneuvering through the crowded hallway. I don't know why Crystal just won't admit that she has a *thing* for him. Cameron is a really, really nice guy. And he's cute, too.

No, really super cute.

He has these light brown, slanted eyes—courtesy of his Japanese mom—and thick curly hair. He looks exotic thanks to his mixed heritage. His dad is black—excuse me, I mean African-American. Both of his parents are in medicine.

His mom is the head of neurosurgery at UCLA Medical Center.

And his dad is an OB/GYN doctor at Cedars-Sinai Medical Center.

So, as my nana would say, Cameron comes from "good stock."

And at almost six feet, he's not only athletic, but he has a quirky sense of humor and he's really easy to talk to, which makes the girls at school like him even more—including Crystal.

But she's too stubborn to admit it.

He laughs. "I'm a grown man, little girl. Respect your elders before I put you over my knee and spank you." He snaps his finger. "Oh, wait. You might like it."

Crystal gags and fakes choking. "Ugh, ugh. Eww, gross. You're such a pig."

Cameron chuckles. "The only thing gross is your breath." He waves a hand over his nose then pulls his Morehouse T-shirt up over his nose, exposing a sliver of his flat, hard stomach.

Even I notice little things like that.

I mean, c'mon. He might be my best friend, but he's *still* nice to look at.

Eye candy, that's what they call it.

Right?

"So what—or should I say, who—were you two gossiping about?" He keeps his mouth and nose covered for effect. "You need to brush your tongue," he says to Crystal.

She sucks her teeth, ignoring him.

"Nothing," I say, still reeling from the thought of one of the school's most popular girls having sex with not one, not two, but *three* boys—friends, no less, spreading around a sexually transmitted disease.

"And for the record," Crystal corrects, "we don't *gossip*. We share news."

Cameron snorts, then slings an arm around her shoulders. "Yeah, okay. It sounded like a whole lot of newsy gossip to me. And I want in."

"Well, too bad." Crystal shrugs his arm off and shoves him away. "Your big mouth won't ever find out."

He pretends to be insulted. "Dang. Low blow. I didn't know you really felt that way."

She smirks. "Whatever."

"Well forget you then, pickle head," Cameron says. I shift my backpack to my other shoulder as he comes around to walk on the other side of me. He sidles up closer to me and puts his arm around my shoulder. "We should just run off and elope," he says with a grin, "and leave this"—he gestures with his head—"stank-mouth gremlin over there to fend for herself."

I just laugh.

Cameron's such a big tease.

4

By the time the bell rings to end third period, everyone in the school is talking about Naomi Pitts. And the rumors are swirling around the halls like a bad case of the bird flu. No one seems immune to getting sucked feverishly into the gossip.

Crazy thing is, she has a boyfriend.

Super jock Connor Greene, who plays on the varsity wrestling and football teams.

Annnnd...

Drum roll, please.

Is rumored to have given the disease to Naomi *first*, which she supposedly passed on to three other boys.

Yuck.

How disgusting is that?

And they're supposedly *still* together.

They cheat—excuse me, *allegedly*—on each other, then act like they can't be without the other.

Makes no sense to me.

However, I'm smart enough not to engage in any dialogue with anyone—except Crystal, about Naomi—or anyone else, for that matter.

Nia Daniels's middle name is Switzerland.

I stay neutral.

Still, Naomi is a straight-A honor student and member of the National Honor Society, so you'd think she'd be smarter than that to let a bunch of boys have their way with her without using protection.

I guess not.

Apparently, intellect has no bearing on one's level of common sense and overactive hormones.

But, if the rumors are in fact true, why wouldn't she get treated?

Aren't there symptoms for chlamydia, as with any other STD?

There have to be, right?

And why the heck would she purposefully give it to someone else?

None of it makes any sense.

Oh, well.

Anyway, thank God for Daddy, and his openness and his relentless conversations with *me* about safe sex and making healthy decisions.

He always says, "I'd hope that you'd wait until you're married to have sex. But I know I can't stop you from having it if that's what *you* choose to do—when you're ready. But I can arm you with a box of condoms and information. And, hopefully, instill in you that your body is your temple. If you don't respect it, no one else will."

That, my body being my temple, is stamped in my head.

Forever.

And ever.

Amen.

That, along with having common sense, keeps me focused on more important things than sex, let alone having unprotected sex.

No, thank you.

No boy is worth risking my life, or my health.

Ever.

Sorry.

I blink when I see Naomi and Connor coming out of class across the hall together, hugged up. He has his arm draped around her shoulders, kissing her on the neck.

"Hey, Nia," she says, waving a hand at me; her signature oversize handbag is hanging in the crook of her right arm.

The three of us pause in the hallway as students scurry past in all directions.

She's wearing a short, expensive-looking crimson red dress—designer, of course—and a pair of multicolored Christian Louboutin sandals. And, um, for the record, the red soles of her heels are the *only* reason why I know which designer shoe she has on. Otherwise, I never have a clue.

Naomi has an incredibly vast wardrobe of extremely expensive clothing. She's always a little too flashy and overdressed for me, but that's her.

Always stylishly dressed, and runway ready.

For some odd reason, seeing her in all this red makes me think of that book, *The Scarlet Letter*. I so loved reading that classic tale. Like the character Hester who was publicly shunned for her infidelity, I suspect Naomi will be ostracized for her own sin.

They are both guilty of infidelity.

The only difference is, Hester had a baby by her lover.

Naomi has chlamydia from hers.

I zero in on the big LV logo on the front clasp of her red bag, then flutter my gaze up to meet hers.

"Oh, hey, Naomi," I say, doing my best to sound casual, as if I hadn't just heard all the scandalous little details of her behind-closed-doors proclivities.

I hear Nana saying, *"Just look at her. Poor child. She's hotter than a bowl of habañero chili peppers. Letting all them boys plow through her field. She should be ashamed of herself. Ole nasty heifer."*

I stifle a giggle. *Get out of my head, Nana.*

Connor gives me a head nod. "What's up, Nia."

"Hey, Connor."

"Girl, cute boots," Naomi says, tilting her head as she speaks. "You always look so cute in pink."

I do? That's news to me.

Subconsciously, I glance down at my feet. My Ugg boots. Then back up at her. "Um. Thanks."

Connor pulls her in closer to him. "C'mon, bae. We're gonna be late."

She gives me a two-finger wave. "See you, Nia."

"Bye," I say as the two lovebirds stroll off down the hall. Truthfully, I've always liked Naomi. She and I were in a few accelerated classes together sophomore year. And she always seemed nice. She still does, although everyone says she's stuck up and materialistic.

Not my problem.

But, um, this latest news right here has me looking at her sideways.

"Ohh. Emm. Geee," Crystal gushes, rushing up to me breathlessly. "Did you see those two nasty horndogs, practically licking and pawing each other down the hall?"

I giggle. "Um, Crystal. I don't think girls can be horndogs, silly."

She snorts. "Well, then she's a horn puss. And they're both nasty. I need a Pepsi and a cigarette just looking at those two. And I don't even smoke."

I laugh. "You're so silly."

"No. I'm serious. I feel dizzy."

"Come on, bestie." I shoulder my backpack, then loop my arm through hers. "Let's get to next period before you have a meltdown."

5

"Why is it boys and girls can't have platonic relationships?" Cameron wants to know, lifting two French fries from off of Crystal's plate.

The three of us are hanging out downtown at one of the local hot spots. Today it's Arcadia, a really neat hangout for teens that has lots of vintage, coin-operated video and pinball arcade games, like Pac-Man, Asteroids, Defender; games none of us ever knew about until coming here; well, except for Pac-Man.

Everyone knows, or has heard of that game before.

Anyway...

There are also several pool tables in the back area, along with a huge flat-screen TV and one of the latest gaming systems. And what's really cool about this place is the thick glass floor that houses a ginormous aquarium of tropical fish and other sea life.

I really love coming here.

For selfish reasons, truthfully speaking.

Daddy's architecture firm designed this place. So it makes it that more special to me.

Yup.

Daddy's an architect. A well-sought-out one, I might add.

Daddy designs mostly commercial buildings. But his firm has designed most of the elaborate homes in Naples, Belmont Shore, and Spinnaker Bay, all exclusive sections of Long Beach.

Anyway...

Crystal smacks Cameron's hand. "Hands off my fries," she warns, pointing a finger at him.

"Ow," he yelps.

"Next time it'll be your face," she warns, pointing her fork at him.

He laughs. "Slap me, boo. I like it when you talk dirty."

Crystal grunts. "Oh, brother. Someone come put this lecherous boy out of his misery. Please. Before I stab him with my fork."

"Go ahead. I dare you." He takes a sip of his Mountain Dew. "I bet you'll look real chic in shackles and a Lynwood jumper," he teases, referring to the Lynwood Jail for women.

She sucks her teeth. "First of all, I'd probably get off on a technicality."

"Yeah, because you're *technically* crazy," he says. "Your next point?"

She rolls her eyes. "And, secondly, Dumbo, I'm not old enough to go there."

Cameron furrows his brows. "Are you serious? Dang, Crystal." He shakes his head, giving her a pitiful look. "Have you looked at yourself in the mirror lately?"

"*What?* Excuse you?" she says, indignation rising in her tone. "Have *you?*"

"Yup. Every day. And I love what I see. But you..." He pauses, shaking his head again. "Sorry, babe, you look *old*, like Social Security, pension-collecting old."

Crystal feigns a yawn. "That was so lame."

These two are ridiculous, I think.

Swallowing a sip of my iced vanilla latte, I slide a look over at Cameron. "To answer your question..."

He gives me a puzzled look. "What question was that...?"

I sigh. "Jeez. Why boys can't be friends with girls."

"Oh, yeah, right. Yeah, what's the deal with that?"

"Oh, I can tell you the deal with that," Crystal offers, pushing her plate back, and wiping her mouth with her napkin. "Because instead of just being BFFs, boys are always trying to be FWBs. They'd rather have the perks of a *boo* without the title. They'll say she's just a friend, but we know what that really means." She narrows her eyes at Cameron, who steals another French fry. "They're such douchebags."

Cameron ignores her, gazing at me with those amazingly cute eyes of his. "Feel free to chime in, Nia-pooh."

"All boys aren't jerks," I say, eyeing Crystal, who's sitting across from me with her arms folded over her chest and staring at me with her puppy-dog eyes. "Some are actually really nice, if you just give them a chance." I gesture with my eyes from Crystal to Cameron.

She frowns. "Oh, puh-lease. Try nice *and* horny."

Cameron rolls his eyes up to the ceiling. "You know this angry black girl syndrome you're struggling with has to stop. You sound real bitter."

"I'm not *bitter*."

"Okay, then. Try sour. You're real tart, Crystal. You need Jesus. And you still need a breath mint."

I chuckle, shaking my head. "Crystal, ignore his silly butt." I bring my attention to Cameron. "I agree with you, though. Most boys are guided by their hormones, but not all of them act on them. There are some who know how to exercise restraint."

I am simply regurgitating what Daddy once told me during one of our many *talks*. And I believe him. And I trust him.

Because he said I could.

Because he promised to always give me the best advice he possibly could.

Crystal grunts. "*Mmph*. When? Where? And who? Because I haven't met one boy yet who isn't trying to hump and grind up on something."

Cameron waves his hand as if he's trying to get her attention. "Umm, hello. I'm right here."

She scowls. "Yeah, okay. And you're still ugly as ever."

Cameron rolls his eyes up in his head, flicking a thumb over at Crystal. "See. *Angry*." Yeah, she should be, I think. Angry with herself for not seeing what a great catch Cameron is.

I sigh inwardly. "Crystal's entitled to her opinion," I offer, glancing over at her. "That doesn't mean she's right. Or I'm right. Or you're right. It simply means we all have differences of opinion."

"Exactly," Crystal says, shifting in her seat. "Didn't you read that book, *Boys Are Martians, and Girls Are*—"

"It's *Men Are from Mars, Women Are from Venus*," Cameron says, cutting her off. "She's such a bubblehead. And, by the way, good book."

"And I saw the movie," Crystal retorts.

Cameron laughs. "No you didn't. That isn't even a movie. See. I keep telling you to work on your lies."

She snorts. "Boy, I did see it. So now. I saw it with Nia. Isn't that right, Nia?"

Wrong. "That was *He's Just Not That into You* with Scarlett Johansson." I tilt my head at her. "*You* wanted to see it, remember?"

She shrugs. "Oops. As you were saying?"

I wave her on dismissively.

"Yeah, Nia," Cameron repeats. "As you were saying. Please and thank you."

"Well, I was getting ready to say that girls just think differently than boys," I reason, spearing a cherry tomato from my salad with a fork.

Cameron takes a bite of his sandwich. "True. But that doesn't mean he can't have boundaries. Take me for instance. I'm friends with two of the"—he looks over at Crystal and frowns—"on second thought. *One* of the prettiest girls, *and* one of the ugliest..."

I chuckle to myself.

Cameron loves instigating Crystal.

She hits him. "Boy, whatever. The only ugly one in the room is *you.*"

"Yeah, okay. But you don't see me trying to hammer either of you. Do you?" He glances over at Crystal. "Well, I'd have to put a bag over your face to even consider it. Sorry."

"Ohmygod, Cameron. Stop!" I say, trying to hold back a laugh. "That's so not nice. I told you to play nice."

"I *am* playing nice," he insists, grinning sheepishly. "Being ugly and having bad breath is a bad combination." He places a hand over Crystal's. "My heart goes out to you, Dragon Girl."

Crystal sucks her teeth, snatching her hand from beneath his. "Forget you, boy. I can't stand you."

"Stop lying," he says.

I sigh, shaking my head. "Cam, you wouldn't try anything with Crystal or me because you were taught to respect females. And you respect us."

He nods his head. "True." He grins. "That doesn't mean I don't fantasize."

I ball up a napkin and throw it at him. "Ugh. TMI."

He swats the napkin away. "Hey, what's the problem? I'm being honest here. Even ugly girls with bad breath need love."

Crystal rolls her eyes. "Boy, you couldn't hammer me if you tried."

Cameron shakes his head. "I'm not that interested, Box-troll. Try again." He looks at me. "But..."

I arch a brow. Tilt my head. "But what?"

I hold my breath, waiting.

You never know what'll come out of Cameron's mouth. The boy has very little filter.

"We've been friends since fourth—"

"*Fifth* grade, idiot," Crystal snarls.

"Right, right. I stand corrected. Since fifth grade." He smiles thoughtfully. "I wouldn't want to do anything that would jeopardize our friendships."

"Aww," I say, reaching over the table and squeezing his hand. "I love you, too."

"Can I get a kiss then?" He wiggles his brows up and down. "I won't tell anyone." He puckers up his lips, then makes a loud kissy noise.

I snatch my hand back. "*Ill*. Nooo." I laugh. "You're pathetic."

"Marry me, boo."

Crystal tilts her head, giving me a look. "See. Horny."

I wave her dismissively. "I don't pay Cameron any mind. You know he's a play fiend."

She gives me an incredulous look. "No. Just *fiend*. That's what he is."

Cameron smirks. "Says the girl with the dragon breath." He reaches for her plate and grabs more food. "Dang. All this foreplay has me starving."

Crystal pulls her straw from her glass and playfully flicks water on him.

"Do it again. I like it wet," he mock-groans, before shoveling French fries into his mouth.

Crystal gives me a look. "*See*. He's a freak for all things vulgar."

6

"Hey, Daddy," I say a few days later, popping my head into his bright, airy office with the glass wall that offers him a picturesque view of our infinity pool and our enormous backyard lined with beautiful electric-blue jacaranda trees.

He's hovered over his desk, glasses on, pen in hand, sketching. He looks up from his blueprints and smiles. "Hey, Butterfly."

I step across the threshold, smiling inside. Every time he calls me *butterfly* I can't help but smile inside. I feel so loved by him. "Are you busy?"

He leans back from his glass-top drafting table and removes his glasses. "I'm never too busy for my favorite girl."

"Oh, Daddy, stop," I say lightheartedly. "I'm your *only* girl."

He smiles. "That you are. And you're still my favorite."

I smile back at him.

Daddy is the most handsome man I've ever seen. And I'm not just saying that because he's my father. I'm saying it because it's true. He's thirty-nine, but he looks like he's younger. And he has a reddish-brown complexion that always looks as if it's been kissed by the sun. When he's dressed in his suits, he always looks as if he's stepping off a photo shoot for *GQ* magazine.

And ladies are always looking at him, or trying to catch his eye when I'm out with him. But he doesn't really pay them any mind, maybe because he's out with me.

I know I probably shouldn't say this. But I think it's time for Daddy to start dating again. Mommy's been gone for ten years now, and he deserves to be happy with someone. He says when the time is right, he will. But for now he always says he's already happy.

"So what's up, sweetheart?" Daddy asks, cutting into my reverie.

"Nothing really." I clear my throat, and saunter further into the room. "I didn't know you were working from home today."

Daddy's firm is located in the heart of downtown L.A., and—with close to a hundred architects, interior designers, and urban planners—is ranked among the top five design firms across the state. Ohmygod! Wait. They also have a spectacular studio in Dubai!

And I got to spend the whole summer there last year while they opened it.

It was super cool. No, stupendously awesome!

But that's another story, for another time.

"I decided not to go in today," Daddy says, folding his arms across his chest as he leans back in his chair. "Figured I'd get more done being home."

"Ahh, playing hooky, eh?"

Daddy chuckles. "Something like that."

I give him a hug. "So how was your day?"

"It was good. Better now." He kisses me on the side of the head. "How was school?"

I let out a long exaggerated sigh, releasing him from my hug. "Oh, you know. The usual. Boring." I slink around his desk, sliding a finger around the edges of the tempered-glass, then lifting one of his architectural scales from his desk. "But I only skipped four classes instead of my usual six today."

Daddy knows I'd never cut classes, but he plays along anyway.

He considers me thoughtfully. "Hmm. Is that so?"

I nod. "Yup."

"Well, did you get caught?"

I shake my head vigorously. "Nope." I set the scale back down and glance over at the large rolls of tracing paper, then sweep my gaze over toward the rows and rows of architectural reference manuals and books in the mahogany wall-to-floor bookcases that line the wall in back of Daddy, before my eyes land back on him.

He eyes me with amusement.

"I'm too sly to get caught," I tease.

"I see. So, tell me. What would your father do if he ever found out you were skipping out on your classes?"

I shrug. "Ohhh, I don't know. Probably ground me for a week or two."

"Hmm. I see. How about until you turned eighteen?"

I feign shock, placing a hand up to my chest. "Oh, no. That's too harsh. That would be cruel and unusual punishment."

His eyes flicker. "Is that so?"

"Unh-huh. But lucky for me, I don't have a daddy who would do such a cruel thing to his only child. His *favorite* girl."

He smiles. "Well, lucky for *you*, you have a father who trusts you immensely. And I have a daughter who gets straight As and who'd never run me ragged, skipping her classes, going out doing God knows what."

And he's sooo right. I wouldn't. School—next to piano and poetry—is one of the most important things in my life. I want to go to college when I graduate, so I am not about to mess up now.

"But would you be mad *if* I did skip classes?"

He considers me for a moment, rubbing his smooth-shaven

chin. "No, sweetheart. I wouldn't be mad if it were only an isolated incident. Now if it became a pattern, I'd probably still not get mad. Surprised, absolutely. Disappointed, most definitely. But definitely not mad. Like I always tell you. I can't be everywhere all the time. And I'm not going to always be around to gauge your choices in life. That's where integrity comes in. You're a gifted and talented student, Nia, who's always been disciplined. That's all your doing, not mine. You've been primed and prepared to be, and do, your very best. So I'll always trust you'll do the right thing, even when I'm not around. Your destiny is in your hands, Butterfly; not in mine."

Daddy is so wrong, though.

He has *every*thing to do with whom I am, with how I am. And with whom I'll potentially become.

I know who I am.

I know what I want.

Because of him.

I smile proudly, walking over and throwing my arms around his neck. "I love you, Daddy."

He hugs me tightly. "I love you, too, Butterfly."

Later on in the evening, I'm downstairs in the family room with Daddy, painting my toenails and watching the latest episode of *Empire,* while eating popcorn and drinking orange cream floats.

I love, love, love this show.

And I love my time with Daddy.

There's no other place on earth I'd rather be than right here with Daddy.

At least two nights a week we watch one of our favorite shows together. Or we hang out all day Sunday watching whatever we missed during the week on DVR.

Chicago Fire—Daddy's

Rookie Blue—mine.

Mistresses—mine.

Pretty Little Liars—mine, of course.

Dance Moms—mine.

Extant—Daddy's. I always tell him I know he only watches it because of Halle Berry. He always denies it and laughs. But I know better.

Vikings—Daddy's and mine. I always love the shows on the History channel.

Stalkers—Daddy's. Ohmygod! This show right here really frightens me. There are some really crazy people out there doing crazy things to people. Any time I watch this show with Daddy, when it's over he has to keep his bedroom door open and go through the whole house making sure all the windows and doors are double-locked and the alarm is working properly before I can go to sleep—with a baseball bat in the bed with me.

Daddy always tells me he's here to protect me.

And I believe him.

Still, I feel safer knowing the alarms are set.

Daddy belches, and I laugh. "*Ill*, Daddy."

"Excuse me." He rubs his stomach. "You have me gorging myself on all this junk. All that butter and ice cream doesn't agree with me."

I smirk. "Uh-huh, Daddy. No one told you to be a pig and eat it all."

Oops.

I cover my mouth.

I've accidentally belched.

"Oh, who's the pig now, huh?" Daddy teases, reaching for a throw pillow and playfully hitting me with it. We have an impromptu pillow fight during the commercial break. Something we've done ever since I was a little girl, along with having water balloon fights.

I'm a girlie girl, but I also have my tomboy moments. I can throw a football; enjoy hiking, boxing, and riding dirt bikes... all thanks to Daddy.

Sometimes I tell Daddy I know he secretly wishes he'd had a boy. He tells me never. But I think he only says that because he knows he has to.

Still, Daddy is a lot of fun.

"Okay, okay," I say, laughing. "Pause, Daddy. *Empire*'s back on."

"Oh, aren't you the lucky one," he says, tossing the pillows back on the sofa, then plopping back in his recliner. "Saved by the television." He reaches for his glass mug and slurps out the rest of his orange float, before reaching for the bowl of popcorn.

Ten minutes later, I look over and Daddy's reclined all the way back in his chair, asleep—mouth slightly ajar, drooling.

Shaking the nail polish bottle, a devilish grin spreads across my face as I glance at his bare feet.

I ease up from the floor and tiptoe over to him—even though I know a herd of elephants could stampede through the house and Daddy still wouldn't hear them.

I unscrew the polish and carefully paint his two pinky and big toes.

Pink.

7

"**O**hmygod! Daddy!" I squeal the following morning, looking down at his feet. He's wearing a pair of Cole Hahn sandals, showing off his four pink-painted toes. "What do you *think* you're doing?"

He feigns ignorance. "What? I thought you wanted to spend the day with me at the mall, then catch a movie."

I blink. "I do. *But*—"

"So what's the problem?"

There go my eyes again.

Back down at his feet.

His eyes follow my gaze. "What, you don't like my sandals?"

I shake my head vigorously. "No. I mean, yes. But you can't go outside like that." And I can't be seen walking around the mall with you and your painted toes.

He gives me a confused look. "Like what, Butterfly?"

"Like *that*." I point at his feet. "With your toes painted."

He arches a brow. "Why not? *You* painted them."

Now he's smirking.

I swallow. "I know I did. But it was a joke."

Daddy lets out a loud *ha*. "So the joke was on me last night, but now it's no joking matter, huh?"

"Well, no. I mean. It's still funny. Behind closed doors. Not out in public."

He shrugs. "I kind of like it, though. The color looks great on my skin tone. Don't you think?" He doesn't wait for me to respond. "I think I'll wear a pink T-shirt, too, in support of Cancer Awareness month."

I give him a mortified look.

He glances at his watch. "C'mon. You better get a move on it. I'll be downstairs when you're ready."

Ohmygod! I can't believe him!
Daddy has officially humiliated me.
I'm the town laughingstock.
Okay, okay. Maybe I'm exaggerating just a teenie bit.
He hasn't shamed me *that* bad.
But he's definitely made me uncomfortable walking through the Grove on a Saturday afternoon baring his pink toes for ALL to see.
Oh, how shameless he is.
And, now, here he is.
Standing in line in Banana Republic all decked out in his pink T-shirt and pink toes with his wallet out, ready to pay for my purchases. Crazy thing is, no one else seems fazed about what he has on, except for *me*.
So I need to just get over it.
Huh?
Yeah. I guess.
Daddy is simply proving a point, I think as I eye the lady who has inched herself close enough to engage Daddy in small talk while we wait in line. The point being, be comfortable in your own skin. Something he's always instilled in me.

I find it quite interesting how I've spotted several women smiling and trying to catch Daddy's eye, but once again, he's acting like he's too blind to see that he has admirers.

A few brazenly flirt with Daddy.

Others tend to be coy about it.

But I notice everything.

Like this lady now in her black-and-white sundress and white strappy sandals. She looks really nice. And she seems really, really smitten with Daddy.

"Mm. Excuse me. What's the name of that cologne you have on? It smells so good. *You* smell so good."

Daddy smiles. "Oh, thanks. I can't remember the name of it right off the top of my head. It's something my daughter picked up for me." He looks over at me. "Nia, sweetheart, what's the name of that cologne you bought me last Father's Day?"

The lady sweeps her gaze over at me.

I shrug. "Um, I—"

"She's your *daughter*?"

"Yeah. This is my beautiful butterfly, Nia. She's sixteen," he tells her.

"*Sixteen*? Oh, my. I wouldn't have guessed. You look too young to have a teenage daughter," she says teasingly. She touches his arm.

Daddy's grin widens.

Oh, Lord.

I silently roll my eyes up in my head.

I can't remember a time when Daddy's ever gone out on a date. If he has, he's never mentioned it. "I'm keeping it easy, breezy; light and easy," he always says.

He says I'm his number one priority.

"What do you think about my pink toes?" Daddy asks her, the question slicing into my musing.

My eyes widen.

I can feel the floor opening and slowly swallowing me in.

She tears her starry-eyed gaze from his and glances down at his feet. Her eyebrows rise. "Oh. Different," she says coolly.

Daddy chuckles. "Yeah. I thought so, too." He gestures with his head toward me. "My lovely daughter here decided to paint my toes while I was asleep."

"Daddy," I say shamefacedly.

She chuckles, touching his arm again. "Well, she did a fabulous job, I might say. I'd love to have a daughter who painted my toes."

Daddy proudly throws an arm around my shoulder. "Yeah, I'm a real lucky guy." He kisses me on the temple. "I think I'll keep her around for a while."

My heart melts.

I want to tell him, no. I'm the lucky one.

Instead, I squeeze him back.

And for the rest of the day, Daddy spends every chance he gets drawing attention to his feet and telling random women the story behind his painted pink toes.

I can't help but smile.

And love Daddy even more.

8

In my dreams
Nothing else ever matters
But the fire in his eyes
And the desire in his touch
As our
hearts meld
into
one heartbeat;
Lips press
Passion ignites
I am all hands
He is all hands
Hands on bodies
We are in sync...
Motion.
Breath.
and
Heat.

I close my journal.
Shut my eyes.
Take a deep breath.
Exhale.

Inhale.

Then slowly open my eyes.

Don't ask me why I wrote that.

It's not like I'm in love, or have a boyfriend.

Nor am I looking for one.

Not now, anyway.

Boys are distractions.

They require time and patience I don't have.

I shake my head, a smile slowly spreading across my lips.

Okay, okay...

If I'm really, really honest with myself I sometimes fantasize about having the kind of love that Daddy had with my mom before she passed away.

They always looked so happy.

You saw his love for her.

You felt it.

It was in the way he looked at her.

In the way he spoke to her.

In the way he held her hand.

There was never any question what was in his heart for her.

Real love.

Unadulterated.

Unwavering.

He always made her feel special.

And appreciated.

I can remember my mom's eyes lighting up every time Daddy stepped into the room. He'd lean in and kiss her on the lips. And she'd smile. And then he'd scoop me up in his arms and smother me with kisses. And tell me how much he loved me.

Mommy would watch him with me, her smile widening. Then she'd wait until Daddy left the room and say, "I love the hell out of that man."

"Oooh, Mommy," I'd squeal, "you said a bad word. Don't say that."

She'd pull me into her arms, then she'd sweetly say, "I'm

sorry, sweetheart. But my heart dances and skips a beat every time I see your father. When you're old enough, hopefully, you'll be blessed to have a man whom you love as much as I love your father. And, if you're fortunate enough, he'll love you back. And make you feel like you are the most important woman in the world to him."

And I'd say, "When I grow up, I'm going to marry Daddy."

She'd laugh. Tell me I couldn't marry him, because he was hers.

And I'd say, "It's okay. I can share him."

She'd burst into laughter every time. Tell me I'd have to find my own knight in shining armor.

So, let's try this again.

Why did I write that?

I wrote it because I hope to one day have a husband like Daddy—a man who is full of love for me, who makes my heart dance and skip beats the way Mommy's once did.

Mommy's face, her smile, her wide bright eyes, flash in my head, and I find myself becoming nostalgic.

Not a day goes by that I do not think of her.

That I am not wishing she were still alive.

Emotions welling up inside of me, I fight back tears.

It's been ten years, six days, and almost nine hours since her passing. And, for me, it still feels like yesterday.

They say time heals, but I am still waiting.

The pain is not as intense as it once was.

Maybe because I was too young to really understand the impact of her death.

Still, it left a hole in my heart.

But I had Daddy and my nana to fill it with their love.

And eventually the hole closed.

The pain of being motherless subsided.

And I learned to move on.

Still...

She's always in my heart.

Forever.

Infinitely.

When Mommy first died, I cried every day, and I'd ask my nana why she had to die, why that man in the truck had to hit her car?

And Nana would say, "Because Heaven couldn't wait for her, baby. God called your momma home to be with His angels."

Nana's voice floats through the room. *"When God looks to place flowers in His garden, my sweet baby, He always picks the prettiest ones... your beautiful momma is amongst some of the most beautiful flowers in His garden. So breathe in your momma's sweet scent, knowing she will always be in bloom..."*

I inhale deeply.

Breathe in my mother's presence.

Then glance up at the sixteen-by-twenty-inch portrait of her hanging on the wall.

I love you, Mommy...

Needing to feel close to her, I place my journal down on the sofa, then climb the basement stairs to the main level of the house.

I walk into our formal living room, with its white Persian rug and crisp white walls. There's only one piece of furniture in here, positioned in the center of the room.

A Steinway.

My mother's prized possession.

And gift from Daddy.

I saunter over to the baby grand piano.

Pull out the bench.

Slide onto it.

Then lift the fallboard.

My fingertips graze the piano keys, and I close my eyes.

Breathe in.

Conjure up the sweetest memories of my mother.

And then I am transported back in time.

I am five again.

Mommy is sitting beside me, close, so very close.

Her leg brushes mine as she gently rests her hand over my right hand.

"Okay, sweetheart. What will it be today? Mozart or Beethoven?"

I'm shaking my head. *"My favorite* Little Mermaid *song."*

She is smiling at me. *"Okay. Just this once."*

I giggle, knowing she doesn't mean it. She always says that.

I go into character.

I am Ariel.

The Mermaid.

Then her hands swoop down on the piano keys, her slender fingers, flying over the keys, graceful and almost balletic as she belts out "Part of Your World."

I can hear every word.

Feel every note.

The song ends, and I open my eyes.

Exhale.

Then allow my fingers to settle on the keys, my feet on the pedals as I play one of my mother's favorite tunes.

A song that speaks to the heart. And to the love she and Daddy shared. "The First Time I Ever Saw Your Face" by Roberta Flack.

The music comes alive.

The melody takes over.

And I get lost.

Lost in my mother's love.

Lost in her love for Daddy.

Lost in his love for her.

Lost in her memory.

So wrapped up in the music, I am oblivious to the fact that I am not alone.

It is not until I reach the end of the song that I realize Daddy has slid onto the bench beside me.

And I am crying.

9

Two days later, Daddy and I are sitting at the breakfast bar. He's sipping a cup of his favorite vanilla bean coffee, and reading the *Los Angeles Times*, which he has delivered every morning. I'm eating a bowl of vanilla Greek yogurt and sliced strawberries. I never like eating anything too heavy in the morning; well, not on school days, that is.

I'm on my phone, scrolling through my Facebook news-feed and accepting new friend requests, when Daddy looks up from his paper, and—right out the blue—asks me who the first African-American poet is, as if this is some difficult trivia question.

He *knows* I know.

I smile.

Set my phone down on the table.

And indulge him anyway.

He grins. "Now before you answer, Butterfly, I want you to think about it carefully. There's a fifty dollar bill riding on this."

Ooh, yeah. I clap my hands. "Ooh, easy money, Daddy. You might as well just hand it over to me now." I laugh. "Please and thank you."

He chuckles, his brown eyes lighting up. "You sure?"

I raise a brow.

Am I sure?

Of course I am.

Everyone *knows* anything about African-American history knows Phillis Wheatley *is* the first African-American poet.

I tell him so.

Then extend my hand out. "Pay up, Daddy."

"Ahh, not so fast, young lady." A smile eases over his lips, as if he knows something I don't. "Are you one hundred percent certain?"

"Yes, Daddy. I'm sure. Why wouldn't I be?"

"So Phillis Wheatley is your final answer? Is that what you're telling me?"

Um. It's the only answer. Isn't it? "Yes. Final answer. There is no other answer."

I hold my hand out and wiggle my fingers. "Money, please."

"And if you're wrong?"

"Daddy, stop playing," I say, laughing. He's so silly. "You know I'm not wrong."

He grins. "But if you are?"

I furrow my brows. "Okay, hypothetically speaking, if I *were* wrong—which I'm *not*, by the way—then I'd make you breakfast in bed for the next two weekends."

Now he lets out a hearty laugh. "What, a bowl of cereal and two slices of toast?"

I keep from laughing myself. I can't cook. Can barely boil water.

Daddy knows this.

But I'm okay with telling him I'll fix him breakfast, knowing I won't have to because I've given him the correct answer.

"Nope. Pancakes, eggs, and bacon, and grits."

He smiles wide. "Oh, I'd like to see this. And I get to take pictures and post them up on Facebook, right?"

"Daddy!" I squeal. "No one really posts pictures up on Facebook anymore. That's *so* last year."

"Oh, is that so? Well, then, how about I post them up on Facebook *and* Instagram? Or is that still *so* last year?" he teases.

I giggle. "I'm not telling."

He shakes his head and takes a sip of his coffee. Then he sets his cup down, before saying, "I want you to look up Jupiter Hammon."

"*Jupiter* what?"

"Not what. *Who*."

"Okay. Who?"

"Jupiter H-a-m-m-o-n. Hammon."

He pushes back from the table and stands.

I give him a perplexed look. "Now?"

"By all means." He starts whistling toward the sink with his breakfast dishes, rinsing them in the sink.

I reach for my cell. Type in my password, then click onto the Internet and Google this Jupiter Hammon person.

I click the link for Wikipedia.

I blink.

Crinkle my forehead.

It says he's a black poet who, in 1761, became the first African-American writer to be published in the United States.

"See anything interesting?" Daddy says.

I look up from my phone to catch him smiling.

Sigh.

"This is so not right. Everybody knows Wikipedia can be manipulated by anyone. Half of the stuff on there probably isn't even true."

He laughs, shaking his head. "Okay, if you say so. Keep browsing the search engine, then."

I do just that as Daddy stacks the dishwasher.

I find something else on him that calls him the "Father of African-American poetry." That says he was born in 1753, *before* Phillis Wheatley. That he is believed to be the *first* published male African-American poet and essayist.

Wow.

"So who was the *first* African-American poet?" Daddy probes, grinning.

I playfully roll my eyes at him. "I *still* think it was Phillis Wheatley," I say as I keep reading. "But, for argument's sake, I'll go with this for now. But the verdict is still out."

He laughs. "Whatever you say, Butterfly." Daddy walks back over to the table holding something rolled up in his hand, a shirt or something. "Here." He hands me what's in his hand. "You'll need this."

"What is it?" I take it from him.

Daddy chuckles. "Your apron."

My jaw drops. *"Apron?"*

"Yes. You'll need it for Saturday." He leans over and kisses me on the forehead. "And I like my eggs scrambled hard. But you already know that."

Oh joy. "Hey, how about I take you out instead?" I say as he heads out the kitchen.

"Fat chance," he says over his shoulder. "I want blueberry pancakes, too."

I suck my teeth and turn my attention back to my phone. "Love you, too, Daddy."

"I know you do. Don't be late for school."

"I won't," I say, opening another link about the life of Jupiter Hammon.

"See you tonight, Butterfly."

"Bye," I say absentmindedly, reading more about this eighteenth-century poet.

The security alarm chirps.

Daddy has opened the door.

It chirps again.

He's gone.

I know without looking at the clock on my phone what time it is: 6:30 a.m.

And time for me to get ready for school.

10

"Soooo, are we hanging out after school?" Crystal wants to know as we climb the stairs toward our lockers on the second floor.

I shoulder my backpack, shrugging. "I don't know. I guess."

Crystal stops walking and places a hand up on her narrow hip. She's wearing her WTH face. "Umm, you *guess*? That is sooo not the answer I was looking for, Nia. You do not get to ditch me today, girlfriend. I need a friend."

I shake my head, smiling. "Sounds like you need a hug more."

"Well, I'll take that, too." She spreads open her arms and gestures with both hands for me to come to her. "Bring it in, Nia-pooh. Give me hugs."

I laugh. "You're so silly, girl." I give her a hug, then grab her right arm and pull her along. "C'mon, before we're late."

She groans. "I have calculus first period. You know my brain doesn't fully awaken until after twelve. I should have never chosen that class so early in the morning. It's slowly killing my brain cells."

"Oh, well," I say, still dragging her down the hall. We're almost at our lockers when we run into Cameron and two of his basketball friends, Nate and Cole.

Oh, did I mention that Cameron is a starter on the team? Well, he is.

Crystal grunts. "Oh, God. Not him. It's too early in the morning for his foolery."

"Oh, Crystal stop," I say out of the side of my mouth. *You know you like that boy*. I keep that to myself, as usual. Daddy always says playing matchmaker is a bad thing between two friends you really like. Then if they break up, they'll both be trying to pull you into their drama. So, because I value Daddy's opinion, I'm keeping my Cupid's arrow tucked away in my locker—for now.

Cameron and Nate are laughing and chest bumping each other, then quickly stop goofing off the minute they see an underclassman in a short skirt walk by. They start grinning at her and licking their lips.

"Just look at 'em," Crystal snorts. "A bunch of horny toads. All testosterone-charged."

I pretend not to hear her.

Cameron gives his teammates fists pumps, then heads are way when he spots us. He speaks first the minute he approaches us. "Hey."

"Hey," I say back.

"Hey," Crystal mutters, hardly moving her lips, as he sidles up beside us.

"Oh, you can't speak, peanut head?" Cameron says, stopping. "Please don't tell me today's the day that you think you're too *cute* to speak."

She rolls her eyes. "Nia, please tell that freakazoid that I said I *am* cute."

Cameron grabs her in a headlock and playfully rubs his knuckles over her scalp vigorously. Crystal pretends to be pissed, fakes protest, but I see something else in her face.

She likes it.

When Cameron finally releases her, her hair is now all over her head. She hits him. "Boy, you've messed up my hair. I can't stand you." She runs her hand through her hair trying to smooth it down.

Cameron laughs. "You look better with it tousled. Now you sort of look like a chinchilla instead of a mangy mutt. You can thank me later."

She flicks him a dismissive hand. "Whatever, dumbass. I'm so done with you." She stops at her locker, and I wait with her while she opens her locker and pulls out her calculus book. She slams it shut. "Ohmygod! Why is he *still* standing here?"

"By the way, Nia," Cameron says, "you're looking real pretty today." Then he smiles. Flirtatious as usual, because that's what he is.

A big flirt.

"So where are we hanging after school?" he wants to know when we get to my locker.

"I—"

"*We'll* be hanging out without *you*," Crystal cuts in. "You're officially on a lifetime ban. We need a permanent break from you, boy."

He laughs. "Nah, *we* need a break from your breath."

Crystal sucks her teeth. "What a lame."

"And you're the fricking best," Cameron answers back, turning his head to smirk at me and roll his eyes subtly in Crystal's direction.

That's when the bell rings. Dang!

"I have to go," I say abruptly. "See you both fourth period."

"Nooooo," Cameron cries. "Don't leave me with this man-eater. If I end up missing, check her stomach."

Crystal plucks him. "Oh, shut up, boy. You're the last thing I'd ever eat."

Ugh.

I wish they'd just kiss and get it over with already.

* * *

When the last period bell finally rings, everyone gathers their things and quickly spills out into the hallways. As usual, I'm the last to leave Mr. Ling's physics class. Most kids find Mr. Ling's honors class to be extremely hard. I see it as a challenge. It pushes me to be more perceptive. It's a whole-brain subject that really requires you to use both right and left-brain regions. Most people don't know that. It really hones your thinking skills.

So I enjoy it.

I step out into the hallway and run smack into Cameron. "Oh, hey," I say, surprised.

"Hey," he greets me, walking alongside me. "I was waiting for you."

"You were? *Why*?" I give him a curious look. Or maybe it's a confused one. It's hard to tell since I'm not exactly looking at myself in a mirror.

"I wanted to see if..." he begins. Then pauses, glancing around at students hurrying past in all directions.

"You wanted to see what?" I ask as we maneuver through the crowded hallway.

Cameron stops walking. He digs into the outside pocket of his book bag and pulls out a small tin of Altoids mints.

"Want one?" he asks, holding the tin out to me.

I hold a hand over my mouth and blow out a breath. "Wait. Does my breath smell?"

"Nah. Your breath always smells sweet," he says.

For some reason, I feel my cheeks heat, and I blush. "Boy, stop."

"Nah. I'm serious. Smelling your breath makes butterflies flutter in my stomach. Your breath makes my knees go weak, Nia."

He says this with a straight face. But I can't help but burst into laughter. "Ohmygod!" I cry, clutching my chest as if I'm on the verge of cardiac arrest from laughing so hard. "You are sooo dang silly, Cam!"

"Yeah. I'm silly for you, boo." He waggles his eyebrows. Then smiles.

He plays too much.

For a split second we're both just smiling at each other.

Awk. Ward.

I tuck hair behind my ear. And then Cameron frees us from this uncomfortably weird moment that passes between us and says, "So you want a mint or not?" He shakes the tin in my face.

"You just said my breath smelled sweet."

"Yeah. It does. But it'll smell sweeter with a mint."

"Ohmygod! You're so full of BS." I take a mint. "Thanks."

"Anytime." I eye him as he pops a mint into his mouth, then tosses the tin back in his bag. "Where's Cruella, walking her Dalmatians?"

"Boy, leave Crystal alone," I say, punching him lightly on the arm as we leisurely stroll the hallway. I wipe a tear from the corner of my eye from laughing so hard. "Why are you always picking on her?"

"On who? Crystal?"

I suck my teeth. "Yes, silly. Who else?"

"Oh."

I sigh. "Well?"

He shrugs, shoving his hands into his front pockets. "She's easy prey." Hmm. Why can't boys just be honest?

He likes her.

We walk in silence for a moment as he walks me to my locker. I suck on my mint, allowing the sharp peppermint to melt over my tongue as an idea of a poem slowly takes root. A boy having a crush on a girl, but doesn't tell her until it's too late. When she's finally stopped holding her breath and moved on because she never got the memo.

Maybe I'll call it "Secret Crush," or something like that.

"So where is she?"

"Huh?" I say, confused, turning to look at him.

"Crystal?"

Oh. I smirk. "Why, you miss her?" I open my locker, tossing my physics book back inside my locker.

"Nope," he says, leaning up against the bank of lockers. "I'm actually glad she's not around. She's annoying."

I give him a look. "That's the same thing she says about you."

He grins. "It's the one thing we have in common. Besides you."

I playfully roll my eyes up in my head, shutting my locker. "Oh, lordy. Denial, I see."

He gives me a puzzled look.

I tilt my head, shouldering my book bag, while giving him a critical once-over. "Cam, admit it. It's okay."

He frowns. "Admit *what*?"

Ohmygod!

So he wants to play stupid.

Boys.

I sigh. "Admit that you like her."

He rapidly blinks his eyes, then pops them open wide. "That I *like* who? *You*?"

"I said *her*. Not *me*, silly. Crystal."

"Crystal?" He bursts out laughing, clutching his stomach. "Hahahahahahaha. You're joking, right?"

I frown, not seeing the humor in any of this. "No. I'm serious," I say, arching my brows. "You can tell me. I promise. I won't tell her."

He gives me a serious look. One he rarely gives. "Nia. I hate to disappoint you. But I don't like Crystal. Not like *that*."

Now I'm confused.

"Are you sure you don't like her"—I gesture with my forefinger and thumb—"just a teensy bit?"

"Not even." His eyes never leave mine when he says this.

Still, I'm not fully convinced.

"But you're always picking with her, like you do."

He shakes his head. "I tease her because I *like* ruffling her feathers. Not because I *like* her, like her. She's my *amiga*."

"I'm your friend, too, but you don't tease *me*."

He shifts his stare from mine. "You're different, Nia."

Different?

How?

He quickly looks away, then glances down at his watch. "Hey, I gotta run. I have study group in the library. Big chemistry test tomorrow."

"Oh, okay."

He hoists his backpack onto one shoulder, then turns and scurries away without a backward glance.

Hmm.

What's up with that?

Then it dawns on me.

He never told me what he wanted to see.

11

Saturday morning.

Six-thirty a.m.

I'm in the kitchen.

Apron on.

Hair pulled back.

Hands and face covered in flour.

Watching a homemade buttermilk pancake-making crash course on YouTube, for the third *time*.

I've been up since the crack of dawn trying to figure out how to make these stupid pancakes for Daddy.

And I only have—I glance up at the clock—another hour and a half before Daddy comes down for his morning coffee. He usually sleeps in late—until eight—on weekends.

Anyway, I'm scrambling.

And there's probably more baking powder and baking soda and sugar and salt all over the counters than in the bowl.

Dry ingredients in one bowl.

Wet ingredients in another.

The recipe says it makes six six-inch pancakes.

I keep cracking eggs and getting the shell pieces into the bowl. So I have to keep trying until I get it right. So far, I've gone through six eggs because I keep pouring them down the sink and starting over.

Oh, no!

I'm supposed to separate the egg yolks from the egg whites.

The YouTube host says adding the egg whites later makes the pancakes light and airy.

Umm.

Is that same as being light and fluffy?

God, this is awful.

Cooking is surely not going to ever land me a husband. Then again, if I'm fortunate enough, I'll marry a man who loves to cook.

Or eat out.

Or, maybe, if I'm really, really lucky, I'll hire a cook.

Yeah. I like the sound of that even better.

Who needs to cook when you have a cook?

Exactly.

Not me.

But in the meantime, I need to get these pancakes made.

Wait. I know what I need.

Music.

Walking over and turning on the kitchen's stereo, I start humming Bob Marley's "One Love" as his voice seeps through the speakers.

By the time Kem finishes singing, "You're on My Mind," I finally get it right. The egg cracking, that is. Now I'm mixing the wet ingredients in with the dry ingredients. I whisk, being sure to leave some lumps in the batter.

I forget why.

I just do.

Now comes the moment of reckoning.

Pouring the batter onto the girdle. I mean griddle.

The griddle's hot. Greased. And ready.

I scoop a half-cup of batter out and pour it onto the griddle, then watch it bubble.

Oh, wait.

Blueberries.

I race to the refrigerator and pull out fresh blueberries

bought from the farmer's market, then quickly rinse them, but I'm not fast enough.

Something's burning.

Oh no!

My pancake is smoking.

And now the smoke alarm starts going off.

I open the windows and slide open the glass door that leads out to the deck, then glance over my shoulder to make sure Daddy isn't coming into the kitchen holding a fire extinguisher in his hand.

I look up at the clock. It's five minutes to seven, and I still don't have the grits—which I don't know how to make—cooked. Not one egg is scrambled and the turkey bacon is sitting in the sink, soaking in water.

Bacon is supposed to be washed, right?

I take in the kitchen. It looks like a war zone.

Oh boy, Ms. Katie's going to have a fit when she sees this mess. She's our part-time housekeeper. But I can't think about that right now. I have to get Daddy's breakfast done. A deal's a deal.

Right?

Right.

I dump blueberries into the batter and stir.

Then try again.

And again.

And again.

Until I finally get it all done.

Seven fifty-eight on the dot!

Whew!

I'm exhausted.

I never knew cooking was so much work. But I've survived my first kitchen experience. And I'm pleased—okay, okay, *half* pleased—with my results.

Fresh coffee brewed.

Grits done.

Eggs scrambled.

Bacon cooked.

I've really outdone myself.

I set everything on a serving tray, covering Daddy's plate with a silver cover. Then I make my way up the stairs.

"Rise and shine!" I sing, opening his door and walking across the threshold.

Daddy is coming out of his bathroom, drying his hands with a hand towel, when he sees me. "Good morning, Butterfly." He walks over and kisses me on the cheek. "What's this?"

"Breakfast," I say gleefully.

"Aww," he says, grinning. "You didn't forget."

"Nope. Now get in bed so I can serve you."

He rubs his hands together, smiling in anticipation.

"I made your coffee just how you like it. Dark." Well, it looks more like mud, but that's okay. It's nothing a little— okay, a lot—of cream can't fix.

"You're spoiling me already," Daddy says, climbing onto his king-size bed. He props two pillows in back of him.

"Hope you enjoy," I say, my smile widening.

He looks at me. Really looks. Then points. "What's all this?"

I glance down at the apron he'd given me to wear. It's covered in caked-up batter and egg yolks.

I giggle. "Oh, it's not as bad as it looks." I thrust his tray in front of him. "Here, eat up."

Daddy doesn't lift the cover from his plate right away. He lifts his mug, and takes a slow sip of his coffee. He makes a face.

"What's wrong?"

"Oh, nothing, Butterfly. It's a bit strong; that's all."

"Oh."

"But that's fine," he says. "Let's see if you're going to be the next *Top Chef*."

He lifts the cover and blinks. Then he narrows his gaze down at his plate. "Umm, sweetheart?"

"Yes?"

He takes his fork and sticks it into his grits. "Um. What's this?"

"Grits," I say proudly. "With cheese." Okay, they're a bit lumpy. Well, a lot lumpy. But they're real cheesy, the way he likes them.

His fork points at his eggs. "And this?"

I giggle. "Daddy, stop. They're eggs. Scrambled hard." Okay, okay, they're looking kind of crazy. But I get an A for effort. Don't I?

"I see," he says. "And these I'm guessing are blueberry pancakes."

"Right again, Daddy." They sure are, even if they do look like little round hockey pucks.

He picks up a piece of bacon. "And...?"

"That's turkey bacon." Okay, okay, okay...the bacon is rubbery. How was I supposed to know you don't soak it in water?

"This was a really sweet gesture, Butterfly. But..."

Uh-oh.

Here comes the ax.

"What? You don't like what I've cooked?"

"Well, sweetheart," he says, clearly choosing his words carefully, "let's just say you won't be winning any cooking awards any time soon."

And with that I am laughing.

And so is he.

12

I am on the open mic list, waiting my turn.

Poets talk and laugh and prepare to peel back layers of who they are.

Pour open their hearts and souls up on one single stage.

The energy is high.

But I am eerily calm.

Anyone who knows me knows I live and breathe poetry. It is the key to my soul. It lives inside of me. Sometimes I think it's more real than my own existence.

More real than the air I breathe.

So it's no wonder that I am floating from the energy in the room tonight.

The Poetry Barn is flooded with positivity.

And it's one of my favorite places.

Not only do I love the atmosphere, the décor is so chic. The Barn—which looks nothing like a barn in the traditional sense, but more like an upscale lounge—has sleek white leather sofas and large square white leather coffee table ottomans that double as tables or extra seats. There's also a glass DJ booth in the back. And a bar that serves all nonalcoholic beverages, named after some of the world's greatest poets.

I sweep my eyes around the space, my gaze landing on the

Wall of Poets—black-and-white framed photographs of many of the great African-American poets, past and present, that line the wall.

Audre Lorde.

Nikki Giovanni.

Gwendolyn Brooks.

Maya Angelou.

Paul Laurence Dunbar.

Countee Cullen.

Sonia Sanchez.

Langston Hughes.

Alice Walker.

James Weldon Johnson.

This place is filled with the souls of poets.

I smile when my eyes lock on the black-and-white framed image of Phillis Wheatley.

"Who is the first African-American poet...?"

The emcee calls up the next spoken word artist, one of the regulars: Legacy. He's like twenty-one, twenty-two, I think, but he has a presence of someone with much more life experience.

He's a little under six foot, the color of fudge chocolate with a rich, deep voice.

And from Brooklyn, New York.

I love when he steps up to the mic.

He always delivers his pieces with so much intensity.

A staccato filled with passion and vulnerability.

And sometimes anger.

I watch as he moves through the crowd toward the stage.

Crystal leans in and says, "He is sooo cute. I mean really *cuuuuute*."

That he is. "And he's too old."

She sucks her teeth. "Dang. I can still look."

"Uh-huh. And lust," I tease.

She feigns insult. "Who, *moi*?"

"Yes. You."

"I beg your pardon." She laughs. "I don't lust. I admire."

"Oh, that's what you call drooling at the mouth? Admiration? Oh, okay. I'll keep that in mind the next time I have to hand you a napkin."

She gives me a dismissive wave. "What. Ever."

I smile, shaking my head.

Every other week Crystal has a new crush on a poet. She isn't a poet; however, she enjoys the art. But I think she enjoys coming just so she can look at the male poets who grace the stage—the cute ones, that is—more than anything else.

Legacy takes the stage.

The room falls silent before he opens his mouth.

He stands there, looking out into the crowd at no one in particular, I don't think, since it's his MO just before he gives the mic his signature one-hand caress.

His jeans hang low on his waist, the waistband of his American Eagles showing.

He motions with his hand for the DJ.

And then...

The lights dim, the spotlight going from a bright white light to a reddish glow.

"Peace and blessings," he says, coolly, into the mic.

"Blessings and peace," the crowd says in unison.

"I'ma just get right into it. I was called the *N*-word the other night..."

The room grumbles in disgust.

A few grunt their dismay.

Others want to know what he did.

I shift in my seat.

Lean forward.

Wanting to know, too.

"I'm not gonna lie. It had me tight. I wanted to crack his jaw..."

"I know that's right," someone says.

"But instead of using my fists, I chose to put it on paper. Chose to filter my erupting anger into something much greater, much more meaningful than his ignorance.

"This piece tonight, 'The Black Man I Am,' is my response to being called the *N*-word." He clears his voice, then begins, allowing words to flow from his lips like molten lava as he bares his soul.

When he finishes, he says, "May we have a moment of silence for all those before us who have shed tears and spilled blood and died so that we may see a better day." He bows his head.

A hushed silence sweeps over the room.

Everyone bows his or her head, including me. But I do not close my eyes. I keep them on him. Legacy.

The prince of poetry.

After several moments, his voice slices into the quiet. "Thank you."

And then comes the clicking of tongues, and the snapping of fingers, and a thunderous roar of applause. People stand and clap and shout.

I smile, swept up in the energy.

And then it's my turn.

The emcee calls out for me, and I get up from my seat, making my way up to the stage.

"Yeah, Nia," I hear Crystal call out.

Someone else whistles.

I grab for the microphone. Then I say, "Hello. This piece is inspired by Legacy. And to all the forefathers and foremothers." I close my eyes. And begin...

> Stolen from the Motherland
> Dragged on slave ships
> Deafened by the sounds
> Of the Kings and Queens
> Who cried

And died
At the bottom of the sea

Shackled
Whipped
Across the back
Dragged by the feet
Hung from a tree
Robbed of a native tongue
That belonged to me

Bought and sold
Like property
Became enslaved
Families torn apart
Women raped
Men burned
And beaten
Babies snatched
From the arms
Of wailing mothers
Whose milk still drips
And wombs still ache
And bleed
From your misdeeds

Forbidden to speak
So I spoke in codes
To the beat of drums
And looked toward the sun
And the moon
And the stars
To guide me
Toward a freedom
You tried to keep from me

Spit on

Stepped on
Hosed down
Bit by dogs
Jim Crow laws
Burning crosses
Segregation
Degradation
Plagued by the horrors
Of a past
Fueled by hate
And bitterness
Because of the color of my skin
Still I rise
Despite your sins

From
Imhotep
Hatshepsut
Nerfertiti
Akhenaton
Makeda
And
Cleopatra
To
Aesop
Cetewayo
Bambata
Menelik
Chaka
And now Obama
We have been mighty warriors
Since the beginning of time
Fighting for a cause

Behind the cold glances
I know you want to be like me
But will never be me

Imitate my swagger
Bite off my dances
Profit from my lyrics
Yet
You fear me
That's why...
Despite my emancipation
You still try
To keep me on a plantation
Chained
To discrimination
Humiliation
Substandard education
And
Incarceration

You think labeling me
Hostile
Dangerous
Endangered
Keeping me behind
Concrete walls
And
Razor wire
Will prevent me
From becoming who I'm destined to be

You try to inject me
And infect me
With your drugs
And diseases
And pour guns into my community
In order to commit
Homicide
Suicide
Another form of genocide

Behind the smiling
You disguise your contempt
Through racial profiling
And media lying
But your sick
Twisted ploy
Will never get the best of me
There's nothing you can do to me
That hasn't already been done to me
You can't hurt me
Can't break me
Will never destroy me
I'm a survivor
I rise
I rise

"You better talk about it," someone shouts out.
"Go 'head, li'l sister. You spitting nothing but the truth!"
I continue...

And despite your lies
And distortions
Of who I am
I rejoice
In celebration
Of a rich history
You've tried to hide from me
For I am the descendant
Of great achievers
And believers
Founders of civilization
Who have paved the way

Great men
And women
Who have shed tears

And sweat
And blood
To build this nation
And give birth
To a new generation
Of
Leaders who rest
On a solid foundation

So in spite of
Everything you've done to me
I will continue to stand
With my head held high
And rise
And rise
And rise...

13

A few days later, Daddy is steering his Mercedes truck into the drop-off zone, dropping Crystal and me off for school. "All right," he says, shifting the gear into neutral. "You girls enjoy your day."

"Thanks, Mr. Daniels," Crystal says, opening the rear passenger door. She climbs out and shuts the door behind her.

I lean in and give Daddy a kiss on the cheek. He smells of cologne and Dial soap. I breathe him in. He always smells so nice. "Thanks, Daddy. Love you."

He smiles. "Love you, too, Butterfly. I'll see you tonight."

"Wait. What time will you be home?" I ask, opening the SUV's door.

"Hopefully before seven thirty," he says. "Do you want me to pick up dinner?"

"No. That's okay. I'm going to go over to Crystal's after school, then maybe grab something to eat down at the Poetry Café. Is that okay?"

"That's fine. Do you need me to pick you up?"

I shake my head. "No. Crystal's mom will pick us up, then drop me off later." He wants to know what time I'll be home. I tell him before curfew. By ten.

"Okay then." He smiles at me. "Call me when you get out of school."

"I will." I shut the door, then wave good-bye as he pulls off.

Crystal loops her arm through mine. "How much you want to bet Cameron's somewhere lurking by the lockers waiting for us?" She sucks her teeth. "Ugh. He's so annoying."

Uh-huh. More like annoyingly cute.

But okay. If she says so.

"Um, no," I say, shaking my head. "He's waiting for *you*." I know, I know. He swore up and down he doesn't like her like that. But I don't believe him.

Not really.

She stops and gives me a look. "*Me*? Oh, no. That boy had better go kick rocks. He is so not my type."

I shake my head. "You are such a liar."

She guffaws, swats me with a hand. "I am not. I'm serious. Have you seen him? That boy's goofy."

And cute.

"He's like one of my annoying brothers," she adds, half-convincingly. "That would be incestuous."

Now I'm giving her a sidelong glance, confusion painted on my face. But I don't say anything. When we finally arrive at her lockers, guess who's already here, waiting?

You guessed it!

Cameron.

Crystal raises a brow, and gives me a look. "See. What I tell you? Stalker."

"Hey, Cam," I say, dismissing her comment.

"Hey," he says back to me. Then to Crystal he says, "Good morning, Madame Ugly. Who's stalking you? The ASPCA?"

She rolls her eyes, then punches him. "You make me sick, boy!"

"Ow!" he yelps, rubbing his arm. "I see someone ate their Wheaties this morning."

Crystal sucks her teeth. "Whatever, boy."

He grabs her, then kisses her face.

"Ew!" she cries, shoving him away. "You're such a loser."

She wipes her face with her hand.

"Hey, but you love it." He grabs her by the waist, picks her up, and twirls her around. She yells for him to stop, but is laughing at the same time.

I roll my eyes. "Ugh. Get a room, already. Geesh."

He puts her down. And she pretends to be annoyed that he's messed up her hair as he always does. But she's still grinning. "I so hate you right now. I've been contaminated by this boy's lips." She wipes the side of her face again. "I wonder if I can press charges."

"Hey. You better frame that kiss," he says, laughing. "It's probably the only one you'll ever get."

"Yeah, don't you wish," she says back.

And then Cameron's on to the next thing, glancing at his watch. "What took y'all so long, anyway? The bell's about to ring in less than ten minutes."

"Well—"

"Hey, Cameron," Shelly Locksmith says, cutting me off and waving at him. She's a senior.

And campus flirt, I might add.

"Hey, Shelly," he says back. That only encourages her to stop in front of us, arching her back just so to make her boobs pop out of her low-cut blouse even more.

I eye Crystal eyeing Shelly as she sidles over to Cameron, putting a hand on his arm.

Crystal clears her throat. "Oh, how rude. So you don't see anyone else besides Cameron over here?"

She flashes a fake smile. Then she flips her lusciously long, sleek, hair over her shoulder as someone doing a shampoo commercial would. "Oh, hey, Crystal. Hey, Nia. Apologies. I get so overwhelmed every time I see this hard-bodied hunk that I forget my manners."

She giggles.

Crystal frowns.

And I have nothing but a blank stare on my face.

Cameron doesn't seem to know what to say to that.

"Umm..." He shoots a look over at me, then Crystal. "Thanks."

This is like the only time I've known Cameron to be totally caught off guard.

Shelly rubs Cameron's muscled arm again. "Do you mind walking me to my locker, then to homeroom?" she asks, pulling him by the arm before he has a chance to respond. "I need to tell you something...in *private*."

She shoots a nasty look over at Crystal.

Cameron has a confused look on his face, as I do. He shrugs. "Umm. Sure, I guess."

Crystal and I stare as she drags Cameron by the arm through the sea of students, disappearing into the crowd.

"Ohmygod. She's such a snot ball," Crystal says, rolling her eyes.

I can't say I disagree. "What the heck was that all about?" I ask, opening my locker.

Crystal shakes her head. "Your guess is as good as mine. She gave me a look of death like I'd seriously done something to her. I think I've officially become mortal enemy number one."

I wave a dismissive hand. "I wouldn't pay her any mind." I grab my books for the first three periods, then slam my locker shut. I lower my voice to barely a whisper. "They say paranoia runs in her family."

Crystal snorts. "Oh, so she's genetically crazy. Ha! That's good to know. That says it all."

14

Later in the evening, Crystal and I are hanging out at the Poetry Café. Her mom dropped us off about an hour ago—she'll pick us up around nine she said—and now we're sitting here finishing up an order of honey-glazed wings and cheese fries that we've shared.

Crystal licks her fingers. "Mmm. I love the wings here." She plucks a cheese fry from the plate and holds her head back, dropping it into her mouth.

I grimace. "Ugh. That's so not ladylike."

She rolls her eyes, chewing. She swallows, then says, "Who has time trying to be ladylike eating cheese fries and honey wings? Not me." She licks her fingers again, then smacks her lips. "They're so heavenly."

I laugh, shaking my head. "Well at least try to be—"

I'm not given a chance to finish my sentence. One of the Café's regular poets walks over to our table, smiling. "What's going on, Nia?"

"Hi," I say coolly.

Oh Lordy!

What's his name?

I don't want to sound lame and ask him, since he's *always* able to remember mine. But for the life of me, I can't recall his name. I just know he's really, really tall—like *extra* tall—and has lots of tattoos, and an eyebrow piercing.

This is so embarrassing.

Crystal elbows me, extending her hand out. "Hi. I'm Crystal. Dang, you're tall. And cute. Don't mind the sticky hands, though. Want a honey wing?"

He eyes her, amused. "Nah. Thanks. Nice meeting you, though."

"Nice meeting you, too. Are you married? Single? Any babies?"

"Ohmygod," I say, utterly embarrassed at the drool gathering in the corner of her mouth. "Don't mind my nutty friend," I say. "She's off her meds."

He chuckles. "It's all love. I haven't seen you around in a minute, Nia. Things good?"

"Yes. They're great. I've been around. Just haven't been here in a while, though."

He grins, revealing a row of straight white teeth. "Yeah. I see. You've been missed, though."

Aww, dang. Now I really feel bad for not remembering his name.

I smile back at him. "Thanks. Are you performing tonight?"

"True indeed," he says, nodding his head. "You?"

I shake my head. "No. Not tonight."

He eyes me thoughtfully. "You should. I dig how you move on the stage. I enjoy watching you."

I shift in my seat, feeling myself blush. "Thanks," I say sheepishly. "I might, if they still have room."

"They always have room for you," he says. "And if not, they'll make room. You know that."

Crystal clears her throat. "Umm, hello? Why am I being excluded from *this* conversation? Is this about to turn into some poets' meeting I'm not privy to?"

I roll my eyes and shake my head.

Crystal is a mess.

Mr. Extra Tall grins. "My bad. What would you like to talk about? Um..." He snaps his finger. "Crystal, right?"

She tosses a look my way. "See. He remembers my name."

I roll my eyes up in my head as she stands in front of his six-foot-something frame, hand on her hip, flirting with him. "Let's talk about *you*."

"What would you like to know?"

"Are you married?"

"No."

"Are you dating anyone?"

"Not at the moment."

"Are you looking for a date? Because if you are, I'm free every day except for Tuesdays and Sundays, and so you should know I never, ever, kiss with an open mouth. I'm borderline germaphobe."

He laughs, sliding his eyes over at me. "Wow. Where have you been hiding her? She's quite the comedian."

She eyes me. "Yeah, Nia. Tell him. Where have you been hiding me?"

I sigh.

When Crystal has her sights on someone, it's nonstop banter and a bunch of flirty nuances. I am relieved when the waitress comes to the table to collect our dirty dishes and to see if there's anything else we want.

Extra Tall tells the girl to put our bill on his tab.

I thank him. But then little Miss Flirty goes *waaaay* overboard.

Again.

Practically throwing herself at him.

"Ohmygod," she cries. "That's so sweet. What a gentleman. I could almost kiss you, if I wasn't afraid of catching the kissing disease. This is almost like our unofficial first date."

And your last, I think as I hold my head and cover my face in my hand, shaking my head, just as the lights dim.

Our cue.

That open mic is about to begin.

"Okay, gotta go." He winks at me. "Hope to see you up on that stage."

I smile at him. "I'll give it some thought."

"Nice meeting you, Crystal," he says, grinning. "I'm sure we'll flirt later."

"Oh, we sure will," she says coyly.

And then he's gone.

"Dang," Crystal mutters. "I didn't get his name."

Neither did I.

But that all changes the minute the host introduces the night's first act. "Everyone let's give it up for one of Long Beach's finest. At six foot eight, put your hands together for poet Six-Eight."

Crystal and I lean forward.

Our eyes follow his every step as he gallops up the stage and snatches the microphone from its stand. He recites a piece titled "Flirt," about a girl who entices guys using the art of seduction. It's sensual, as is most of his poetry. And when he finishes up his piece, Crystal hops up from her seat and whistles and claps, swearing he wrote that poem about her.

There's no convincing her otherwise.

So I leave her to her delusions.

By the time the seventh poet hits the stage, I'm feeling inspired to take the stage. I catch the eye of the host and wave her over.

"Hello. I'm Nia Daniels. Is it too late to go up?" I ask her the minute she reaches us.

She smiles. "I know who you are, darling. You haven't been here in a while. And, no, there's always room for a favorite." She tapped her tablet with a long, acrylic nail. "We'll call you up shortly."

Wow. I'm a *favorite*.

I smile back.

Touched by her kind words.

Two more poets take the stage—and end their pieces to thunderous applause—before I'm finally called up. "Okay, we're going to call up our next poet," she says, looking down at her electronic device. "Next up is Nia Daniels. It's been a while since we've seen her. Let's welcome her back to the stage."

Everyone claps. Of course, Crystal can be heard the loudest whistling and catcalling like a loon. But, hey, what can I say?

That's my bestie.

I take the microphone, and clear my throat. "This piece is called 'Let Me.' It goes out to anyone who has ever felt stuck, or trapped in people, places, or things."

"A'ight," someone says. "Go deep on 'em, li'l sis."

I smile.

I close my eyes for a few seconds, then open them.

> Let me . . .
> Reach into your locks
> uh
> not
> your
> dreadlocks
> no
> your
> dead
> locks
> and
> unchain
> your
> enslaved mind
> Let me . . .
> unleash you
> from an existence
> where
> mental stagnation

and
self-depreciation
keeps you
locked
in a box;
not
a
sandbox
but
a
locked box
trapped
in
fear
Let me...
Free your mind
Free your body
Free
you
from a
darkened
shell
No
No
A self-made
prison cell
of
flesh n bone
vacant
of
barbed wire
and
concrete walls
Let me...
liberate you

from
the burden
of judgment
of
stereotypes
of
contemplative silence;
Let me...
Release you
from the
pain
of
unspoken words
that cling
to a tongue
that fears
truth
That swallows
the rage
of a
past that
bares no semblance
to happiness
Let me...
reach up
into
your locks
and
free you
and
make you
breathe
again...
can
i

free your mind
can
i
free your soul
can
i
make
you
whole
yes
only
if you
let me...

The piece is well received by the crowd. I am smiling as I gallop down the steps and return to my seat. Crystal is still standing and clapping. "Oooh, yes! You killed it, girl." She gives me a hug. "That was deep as heck. Loved it."

I smile wider, hugging her back.

15

"Daddy, I'm home," I call out, dropping my keys onto the foyer table, removing my shoes, then walking toward the spiral staircase.

"So, he's cute right?" Crystal says as I ascend the stairs to my bedroom. We've been on the phone the whole ride home with me listening to her go on and on about the tall poet with all the tattoos.

What was his name again?

Six-Eight, I think.

Yeah, that's it.

"He's okay, I guess."

She shrieks. "You *guess*?! Girl, what is wrong with your eyes? Are you blind?"

"Nope. I simply don't see what you see."

"Yup. Blind. Say no more. That explains a lot."

I laugh. "What exactly does it explain? Do tell."

"Welllllll, for starters, it proves that you will never get a boyfriend if you don't start opening your eyes and expanding your horizons."

"I'm not looking for a boyfriend. They're too much of a headache."

"And that's what Tylenol is for. To relieve the pain."

"No thanks. I'll pass on the drama. I have my sights on bigger and better things, like college. There will be plenty of time for boyfriends after graduation."

Wow. Did I just say that?

Yup, sure did.

It's what Daddy has been saying to me since I was old enough to talk. And it's stuck.

Whereas Crystal has had at least twelve boyfriends since fifth grade, I've had none.

"Borrrrring," she says in a singsong voice. "Nia, it hurts me to say this. But you're turning into an old maid right before my eyes."

"Ohmygod!" I shriek. "I can't believe you just said that. I am not an old maid."

"Now, see there. I didn't say you were. I *said* you were on your way to becoming one. Face it. You'll be seventeen in what...?"

"Six months," I say. "And?"

"That's too old *not* to have had at least *one* boyfriend."

Well, she's wrong there. I've had a boyfriend before. Lorenzo Adams. We spent practically every day together, passing cute little love notes back and forth. We were the cutest couple ever.

But then he dumped me for Chrissy Evans.

And left me devastated.

I remind her of that.

She bursts into a fit of laughter. "*Lorenzo? Bwahahahahaha.* Ohmygod! *Hahahahaha*! Good one, Nia. But, sorry, second grade doesn't count."

"Whatever." I suppress a chuckle. "Anyway, you've had enough boyfriends for the both of us."

She laughs again. "That's true. But I can't seem to keep them for longer than a month, or two."

True.

That's because she keeps choosing the same type of boys— all the *wrong* ones.

Nice boys seem to bore her.

Crystal seems to be a magnet for boys with drama.

I never knew boys could be such drama kings.

Until Crystal started dating them.

Liars.

Cheaters.

Players.

Horndogs.

All Crystal dates are shallow boys with good looks.

"Well, that's because they don't know what a catch you are," I say earnestly.

"Awww. And that's why you're my BFF for life."

I smile. "So do you think I should perform at the Poet's Corner for Black History month?"

"Oh no, oh nooo," Crystal says dramatically. "I will not be dismissed. I am not finished talking about the boy of my dreams."

I shake my head, plopping down on my bed. "Well, I am."

"You're such a joy-kill. But answer me this, then I'll leave it alone. Did you see how he kept eyeing us? That boy is totally hot."

"I really wasn't paying attention to him," I say, pulling off my socks.

I stretch open my painted toes.

She sucks in air. "I'm flat-lining as we speak. Going, going, gone! How could you not notice him? He was to die for."

I laugh, stepping out of my jeans. "You're already dead, remember?"

Now she's laughing. "Oh, right. Stone-cold dead. So you really weren't paying him any attention?"

I shake my head as if she can see me. "Nope. The only thing I was captured by was his poetry." I pull off my shirt. "Not his looks."

In my mind's eye, I see her rolling her eyes. "Unh-huh. So all you *heard* was his poetry, but you didn't *see* him?"

"Of course I saw him. But I wasn't looking at him, not like that."

"Nia, I love you, girl. But you are some kind of strange. You do know that, right?"

I shrug. "I don't see the big deal. Just because I don't fall head over heels for a boy, doesn't make me strange."

She sucks her teeth. "No, that doesn't. But the fact that you can't even see sexiness when it's staring you right in the face does."

"He's no different from any other poet to me."

"Ohmygod," Crystal says in disbelief. "You need help. He's more than a poet. He's perfection. Let me dial nine-one-one. This is an emergency."

I laugh. "Oh, stop. I'd rather be fascinated by a boy's intellect, instead by his looks."

She grunts. "Well, you can have the intellect. Give me something good to look at. Eye candy makes the heart grow fonder."

"Since when?" I say, glancing over at the clock. It's almost eight p.m. I wonder why Daddy hasn't come upstairs to check on me yet.

Mmm. That's not like him.

He must be down in his office working.

Or maybe on a conference call.

I walk into my bathroom.

"Since seeing that chocolate Adonis," Crystal says. "He looked like he was chiseled out of the world's richest chocolate. He was so dreamy. So decadent. So—"

"Wait," I say, cutting her off. "Should I just wait for the infomercial?"

I pull my hair up, then put Crystal on speakerphone while I wash my face.

"Ohmygod, Nia, why do you always do that?"

I laugh knowingly. "Do what?"

"Put me on speakerphone. You know I hate that."

I run the water. "You'll survive. You always do. Anyway..."

"Yes. Anyway. Back to Mister Sweet Chocolate. Mister Six Nine..."

"Six-Eight," I correct, applying Noxzema to my face.

She laughs. "Oh, but you weren't paying attention, huh?"

I share a laugh with her. "Well, maybe just a little."

"Oooh, you're such a liar."

"I am not." I feign hurt feelings. I splash warm water on my face, then turn off the water. "I'm not blind. I just wasn't *seeing* him the way you were."

"Unh-huh. Save it."

I reach for a towel and pat my face dry. "Well, if you ask me, the amount of time you've spent pining over him is wasted energy. And time lost."

She huffs. "Well, thanks for that news flash. I'm hanging up now so I can I watch the clock until it's time to fall asleep so I can hurry up and dream sweet dreams of Six-Eight the Poet."

"Ugh. Sounds like a nightmare to me."

"Hahaha. Don't hate."

"Wishful thinking, silly. Good night."

"Smooches."

I smile, shaking my head as we disconnect.

I slip into a pair of Spelman sweats and a pink T-shirt, then hurry down the stairs to talk to Daddy.

I can't wait to tell him all about tonight.

16

"Daddy, wait until I tell you all about my night at the Poetry Café," I say, walking into his office.

He isn't there.

"Daddy," I call out again.

Still no answer.

I frown.

I head downstairs into the basement, thinking he might be down there.

"Daddy?"

I move through the finished basement, looking through the weight room, the game room, and even poking my head into the bathroom, even though the door is wide open.

That's strange.

For the heck of it, I pull back the shower curtain and peek behind it, fully knowing I'm being ridiculous.

Still, I do it anyway.

Of course, he isn't hiding in the shower.

I take the stairs back up to the main level of the house. Then I take the spiral staircase, two steps at a time. I knock on his bedroom door. "Daddy?" No answer.

I open the door. Look inside. Call his name. Still no Daddy. *But his car's outside.*

Maybe he went out with one of his frat brothers, I think, heading back down the stairs. Still, I look through the living room, then the dining room, before heading for the kitchen.

He probably left me a note on the fridge, I think, or on the counter.

I imagine seeing a little yellow Post-It with a happy-face on it.

But, for some reason, I call out to him anyway.

"Daddy?"

I walk over to the refrigerator.

No note.

I look over on the aisle counter.

Still, no note.

That's not like him. He always leaves a note or calls me if he isn't going to be home.

I pull my phone from my pocket and check for messages, even though I know there aren't any.

I call him.

Seconds later, I hear a ringing phone.

I blink.

Wait.

That's Daddy's ringtone.

Here.

He must have left it by accident.

I walk toward the ringing sound.

It's coming from the walk-in pantry.

What in the world is his phone doing in—

I stop in my tracks.

Noooooooo!!!

My heart drops from my chest. "Ohmygod! No, no, noooo!"

It's Daddy!

Facedown on the floor.

My phone hits the floor as I am running into the pantry.

"Daddy!" I scream out, dropping to the floor beside him. "Daddy!" I shake him. My heart is violently banging in my chest. "Wake up!" I shake him again. "Daddy! Daddy!"

I pull him, grabbing at his body.

Tears spill from my eyes.

"No, no, no, no, no, no...p-p-pleeeease!"

Everything I've learned in health class kicks in, and before I know it, I am pressing my index and middle finger to the side of his neck, searching for a pulse.

There is none.

I quickly turn him over, careful not to hurt him.

Then I'm placing my head against his chest, listening.

I can't hear anything.

Panic-stricken, I scramble across the floor for my phone, everything inside of me shaking with anguish.

My hands shake as I dial 911.

"Nine-one-one...what's your emergency?"

"I-I-I...it's m-my d-daddy. I t-t-think he's d-dead!"

I am frightened.

And crying uncontrollably.

"What's your name, sweetie?"

"It's Nia," I say impatiently.

"Okay, Nia. What's your location?"

I give her the address. "Please, you have to hurry! Daddy! Wake up!" I shake him again.

She asks me to calm down.

Calm down?

Is she serious?

How can I?

I just found Daddy facedown on the floor.

And I'm here alone.

How am I supposed to stay calm?

"Nia, help is on the way. But I need you to stay calm, okay, sweetie. Can you do that?"

Noooooo!

"Y-y-yes."

"Okay, Nia. I need you to tell me if your father has a pulse.

If he doesn't I'll help you start CPR until the paramedics arrive."

I tell her I didn't feel one when I checked his neck.

She tells me to try again.

This time I grab Daddy's arm. Try to find his pulse. "Nooooo, nooo. I don't feel one." I keep searching, feeling. Still nothing.

I try his other arm.

Keep pressing into his skin, my fingertips to his wrist.

And then...I feel it.

A pulse.

Just the slightest of a beat, but still his heart is beating.

He's still alive!

I scream into the phone. "I found it! His heart is still beating!"

"Okay, Nia. That's great. Now I need for you to see if he's still breathing."

I swallow.

She tells me to place my face up to his mouth and nose to see if I can hear and feel his breathing.

"Feel for air coming from his mouth and nose for me, sweetie."

Ohmygod!

There's a brush of air against my skin. I didn't feel it before, but...

I croak back a sob, my body shaking with emotion. "Y-yes. He's still breathing. Barely. P-p-leeeeease, you gotta send someone ASAP!"

"Okay, Nia. Help is on the way. I'm going to stay on the line with you until..."

I don't hear anything else.

I cling to Daddy, wailing at the top of my lungs.

17

Why won't they let me see him?
None of this can be any good.
It's a bad sign.
An omen.
All of this waiting.
I am alone in the hospital's waiting room.
An utter wreck.
Waiting.
Waiting.
Waiting.
Watching the clock.
Watching the doors.
Watching the phone.
Then I am up, pacing the floors.
Back and forth.
Up and down.
Pacing.
Pacing.
Pacing.
Wringing my hands.
Hoping that everything is okay with Daddy.
He never gets sick.
Rarely catches a cold.

And now he's here.

How can this be?

I just want to see him.

Just want to know that he's okay.

I can't do this alone.

But here I am.

Alone.

Waiting.

Waiting.

All of this waiting is driving me crazy.

If the waiting doesn't kill me, this dark cloud of doom hovering over me will.

It feels like these white walls are closing in on me.

I have no other family here.

Except for Crystal and her family.

I'm so glad I called her.

She and her mom are on their way to be with me.

My head is pounding.

It feels like I've been sitting here for an eternity.

Waiting for news from a doctor, or from anyone, who might be able to tell me what's going on with him.

Two fricking hours! That's how long I've been sitting and waiting.

And still *nada*.

No word.

Nothing.

The thought of something...of Daddy not—

Oh, God!

I should have come right home from school.

Should have looked for Daddy the minute I stepped across the threshold.

I should have never been on the phone with Crystal.

My conscience is burdened with "should haves."

I bite my lip.

Then I jump when my cell phone rings. I fish it out of my jacket pocket and glance at the screen. I sigh a breath of relief when Aunt Terri's name flashes across the screen. She's Daddy's older sister who lives in Georgia.

Norcross, I think.

I'm not really sure since I've never been out to visit.

Daddy has two sisters. My other aunt, Priscilla, lives in Arizona. She comes to visit once a year. But I don't have her new number.

Daddy does.

And it's in his phone.

So I called Aunt Terri. And it's only taken her almost an hour to call me back, even though I marked the call URGENT.

Still, I break down the moment I hear her voice.

She waits for me to calm, then starts firing off a series of questions. What happened? What hospital is he in? What are the doctors saying? Have I seen him yet?

"I'm still waiting," I tell her after replaying the events leading up to now.

"Well, keep me posted," she says, sounding distracted. She sighs. "I knew something like this would happen one day. God doesn't like ugly."

You knew what *would happen one day?*

Does she know something?

And what does she mean by God doesn't like ugly?

I wipe tears from my face with the bottom of my T-shirt.

"Aunt Terri, you knew s-something was wrong with him?"

There's a brief pause.

"Aunt Terri?"

"Yes, sweetheart?"

"I asked if you knew something was wrong with Daddy?"

"Oh, I'm sorry. Something on the television caught my eye." I frown. "But, no. I don't know anything. All I was saying is, karma is . . . I mean, your father should have taken better care of himself; that's all."

I swallow, thinking . . .

More should haves.

I knew this was a mistake.

Calling her.

She and Daddy have been estranged since forever.

She—from what I've overheard over the years—thinks Daddy stole all of her and Aunt Priscilla's inheritance when their mother, my granny, passed away, waaaay before I was born.

So there's tension between them.

Still...

She's Daddy's sister.

She should be more sympathetic.

Or at least *act* like she cares.

But what do I know?

I'm just a kid.

"There's really not much I can do from here," she says, slicing into my thoughts.

I blink. Umm. How about trying to be a bit more supportive?

"But call me the minute you hear something, okay, sweetheart?"

I don't know why I even bothered calling her. "I will," I say, feeling dismissed. "Can you give me Aunt Priscilla's number?"

"Oh, sweetie. I don't give out numbers. I'll have to call her and see if it's okay for you to have it."

I blink.

Really? "It's okay. If you speak with her, can you please tell her about Daddy."

"I will. Once I know more."

There's nothing more to say. She tells me she'll keep me in her thoughts. That she'll pray for Daddy. That she loves me. But even that sounds...um, questionable.

I tell her I love her, too, because it sounds like the right thing to do.

Then there's silence on the other end.

I'm not sure if she's hung up on me, or if the call dropped.

All I know is, I won't be calling her again.

18

"Hey, sweetie," Mrs. Thomas says, walking over toward me.

I stand and race over to her.

She opens her arms and I immediately fall into them.

And sob.

"There, there now, sweetheart," Mrs. Thomas says soothingly. "It's going to be all right. You'll see. Your father is as strong as an ox. He'll fight this. Whatever it is."

I nod into her shoulder and swallow. "I-I hope so."

She puts an arm around me and rubs the middle of my back as she walks me back to my seat where I'd left my book bag and cell phone.

She takes a seat beside me. "Have you eaten anything?"

I shake my head, wiping my face with tissues given to me by one of the nurses. "I'm not really hungry." I blow my nose. "I-I can't eat. All I keep thinking about is Daddy. What if h-he doesn't—?"

"Sssh," she says. "Don't say it. We're not claiming any negative thoughts. Okay? All positive energy and lots of prayer to see your father through this."

I nod. So, so thankful and relieved that she's here. "Where's Crystal?" I ask, looking around the waiting area. "I didn't see her come in with you."

"She's downstairs," Mrs. Thomas says. "She should be up shortly."

A wave of disappointment washes over me, but then quickly evaporates as soon as I see Crystal. She comes over and wraps her arms around my neck. "Aww, Nia-pooh. I'm so sorry about your dad. We're going to be right here with you, okay?"

I sniffle and nod.

A petite-framed Asian woman comes through the swinging doors, pulling her mask from her face. She introduces herself as Dr. Lee. Her face is void of any expression. My heart immediately lurches.

My breath catches. "Is m-my daddy okay?" I ask. But what I really want to ask, but can't bring myself to say the words, is, "Is Daddy still alive?"

She says he's in his room, resting. That they are still running tests.

A relieved breath escapes my lips. "Can I see him?"

She nods.

I get up, then glance back at Crystal and her mom.

"You go on, sweetheart," Mrs. Thomas says. "We'll be right here waiting for you."

I nod, then follow the doctor through the swinging doors.

"Daddy," I push out, bracing myself as I fight back tears.

I slowly walk into his hospital room, on legs I feel will collapse under me with each step I take. This is all too much for me. Seeing him like this.

Frail looking.

Bound to a bed.

Tubes running out of him.

Monitors hissing and buzzing all around him.

This is not how I want to see him.

Sick...

Sickly.

I walk closer to Daddy, and he looks over at me. His hand

peeks out from under the white sheet covering him. I want to collapse right here.

I want to fall to my knees, and scream out.

Sob.

Beg.

Ask God to be merciful.

To spare me from, from...

Oh, God, please.

I lower my gaze to the shiny white-tiled floor.

Take another step toward Daddy.

A faint smile forming on his face, he motions for me to come closer.

Ohmygod!

He looks so, so...old.

What is happening to him?

He does not look like himself.

I swallow hard and will my feet toward the bed. I feel weak. Feel helpless seeing Daddy like this.

"Hey, Butterfly," he says, his voice sounding strained. Small.

When I finally reach his bed, I throw my arms around his neck and hug him close to me.

"Oh, Daddy. Please tell me you're going to be okay. Please."

He lets out a slight chuckle. "Well, let's hope you don't smother me to death."

"Oh, I'm sorry," I say, loosening my arms from around his neck. I kiss him on the cheek.

"How long will you have to be in here?" I ask.

Daddy coughs. Then he says, "Hopefully not long. They're still running some tests."

"I know. The doctor told me. But you're going to be all right?"

Daddy doesn't say anything at first. He just looks into my eyes and tells me how much he loves me. That no matter whatever happens, he will always love me. He tells me this as if he knows something's wrong. As if he knows there'll be no happy ending.

I blink, once, twice, then again, clinging onto hope. That everything will be fine with him.

It just has to be.

I can't bear the thought of...of something—

A single tear falls from my eye, and Daddy reaches up with his hand and wipes it with the pad of his thumb.

"Everything's going to be fine, sweetheart," he tries to reassure me. But anxiety rushes through me. My pulse quickens. I have to be perfectly honest. I'm frightened. I'm scared for him, for me. I want to be strong. Want to trust that Daddy will be home in no time. But I am experiencing déjà vu.

Mom.

Nana.

They both were here.

Neither came home.

This is where they died.

And, now, five years later, I am right back at this same hospital.

And this time...

God, please don't let anything happen to Daddy.

I have to bite the inside of my lip to keep from crying out. No. This is different. Daddy wasn't in a car accident like my mom was. And he doesn't have cancer like Nana did.

No. This isn't anything like the other times.

I don't know what I'll do if...if...

"Promise me you're going to be okay, Daddy," I croak out. "Promise me you won't ever leave me."

I lean my body forward, covering my face with my hands, pushing the heels of my palms into my eyes.

Daddy pulls me into him. "Don't worry yourself, sweetheart," I hear him say as I'm trying to hold back an avalanche of emotions. But, despite Daddy's arms around me, the tears come anyway, gushing past my hands and sliding down my face. I don't even try to fight it any longer. My body starts to jerk, and I am sobbing.

He tries to console me. Rocks me as best he can. Rubbing my back. "Ssssh. It's okay, sweetheart. I'm going to be fine."

Then why am I so scared?

I look up at him, eyes pleading, flooded with tears. "P-p-promise?"

Daddy gazes back at me; a painful silence fills the room before he closes his eyes and blinks back what looks like tears. When he fixes his gaze on me again, it's as if he's weighing his words, racking his brain, trying to decide what to say to me. Then he smiles slightly and says, while taking me in his arms again, "Don't ever forget how much I love you."

I hug him tighter. "I love you, too, Daddy."

His lips slowly curve into a smile. "I know you do, Butterfly."

19

The following morning, I'm in school. Not because I want to be. But because I know it's what Daddy would want.

So here I sit.

In my AP literature class. Distracted. My mind is back at the hospital with Daddy. Not here. Not listening to Mrs. Stump prattle on about the conflict in an African-American family over an heirloom piano.

I thought the play *The Piano Lesson*, by August Wilson, was an interesting read since I play the piano. And under different circumstances I'd be heavily engaged in the discussion on the conflict around an African-American family's heirloom piano, decorated with carvings that date back to the slavery era.

Not today, however.

Today, I am stuck in thoughts of Daddy.

Deep thoughts.

Troubling thoughts.

I can't focus on anything else besides him.

I have to get back to him before something...before something bad happens.

I have to be by his side, every second. Every minute.

Whatever he's going through, I have to be there to see him through it the way he's always been there for me.

I don't know what I'd do if Daddy doesn't get better.

I know he told me he was going to be fine. And I want to believe him.

But the man I saw lying in that hospital bed last night didn't look fine to me.

His eyes were sunken.

He looked worn out. Tired.

And beneath that white hospital blanket, he'd looked like he was shrinking right before me. Withering away.

Maybe he really wasn't.

Maybe my eyes were playing tricks on me.

Maybe not.

All I know is, I can't shake the image.

The vision is implanted firmly in my memory.

Even after the bell rings, and all through fourth period French, I am still obsessing, still ruminating.

The rest of the day drags slowly by as I aimlessly wander from class to class, meandering down the halls, trying to focus on my studies and shake these feelings of dread.

When the bell finally rings to end sixth period study hall, I leap from my seat and quickly gather my things. I can't take it anymore. I have to call. I have to hear Daddy's voice.

I clutch my backpack to my chest as students hurry by in all directions trying to make their way to their next destinations.

Mine is inside the girl's room. Locked inside the last stall on the right side. I fish my phone out of my bag, then call Daddy's cell.

No answer.

I call the hospital, then have them connect me to Daddy's room.

No answer.

My heart sinks.

Blood drains from my face.

Something's wrong. I just know it is.

I call the hospital again.

This time have them connect me to the nurse's station.

I am clutching the phone, on the brink of a meltdown, waiting.

The phone rings once. Twice. Three times...

It's a bad sign.

The feeling of doom flashes brightly inside my mind.

A collage of fluorescent colors and muddled images swirls in and out of focus, one on top of the other, converging into one big mess.

The phone keeps ringing. Four times. Five times...

My mind's eye starts playing tricks on me.

Daddy is being lifted up on a stretcher.

I am chasing behind them, screaming, sobbing, yelling out Daddy's name. Begging them, the paramedics, the faceless men in white coats, to stop. To bring him back to me.

They keep going.

And I am stepping off the curb, oblivious to the oncoming traffic.

And then, and then...

There are lights flashing, sirens blaring.

I blink, my eyes watery with tears.

Another image comes into view.

Mommy and Nana are covering Daddy's body with a white sheet.

Mommy's face is no longer disfigured, her body no longer mangled. Her back is no longer broken. She is standing. Smiling. She looks just the way I remember her.

Beautiful.

She steps aside.

And there's Nana.

She's dressed in all white. Playing the piano. But...but... she's never played before. Mommy plays the piano. Nana sings. She doesn't play the piano.

Oh no no no no. Pleaaaase. God. No.

My palms are sweaty, my heart racing, my throat closing with dread.

My stomach churns.

Something isn't right. I know it. I can feel it.

Oh, God. I feel myself about to get—

"Nurses' station," someone answers.

My heart thuds against my ribs. Hard.

"Y-y-yes. This is Nia Daniels. I'm trying to get in touch with my father. Mr. Julian Daniels. Is he..." I choke back a sob. "Please tell me if my d-d-daddy's okay."

"Yes, ma'am," the nurse responds calmly. "Mr. Daniels is doing fine. He's downstairs having tests done. He should be back up in his room within the next hour or so."

Relief washes over me.

I burst into tears. "Oh, thank you, thank you! Will you tell him that his daughter called and that I love him, and I'll be there right after school? Please."

"I'll let him know. Try to enjoy the rest of your day."

I sniffle.

I can't let her hang up yet. My heart won't let me. The nagging feeling in my gut keeps gnawing at me. "Wait. Don't hang up," I say frantically.

"Yes, ma'am?" the nurse says. Her voice is calm and even. But it does nothing for my anxiety level.

I am on the verge of a nervous breakdown.

I feel it.

"Is m-m-my daddy g-g-going to be okay?"

"No need to worry, sweetheart," she offers gently. "Mr. Daniels is in good hands."

My stomach clenches.

That isn't the response I was hoping, looking, for.

But I take it because it seems like it's her best answer. No matter how scripted it sounds.

I reach for the toilet paper, yank some off its roll, then wipe my eyes, and sniff. "Okay, thank you."

Hands trembling, lips quivering, I press END.

20

When Crystal's mom finally drops me off at the hospital, I'm a frazzled mess. She tried to encourage me to stay positive, but no.

Daddy is resting.

I tiptoe into the room, hoping not to wake him. He needs his rest.

I sink into the chair beside his bed and watch him sleep. I glance up at the IV bag hanging from its stand, then bring my gaze to Daddy's hand. I stare at the IV in his hand.

My bottom lip trembles.

I can't help but wonder how much pain he must be in; yet he looks so peaceful. I find myself wondering how he can look so peaceful and be in so much pain at the same time?

Painfully peaceful, I think.

An oxymoron.

I watch Daddy sleep for almost an hour, my heart hurting.

Lurching.

My eyes stinging.

Burning.

I can't stop obsessing.

Worrying.

Can't stop the memories from flooding back.

Can't stop from slipping back into time, back into a kaleidoscope of painful recollections.

I lean my head back against the chair's headrest.

And allow myself to get lost in my own emotional time capsule.

My eyes roll into the back of my head and slowly drift closed.

I'm six again.

Mommy is in her hospital bed.

Unconscious.

Her face smashed in.

Her body mangled.

Daddy hadn't wanted me to see her like that.

But I'd begged him to let me see Mommy.

I cried so hard that he finally caved in. Took me by the hand and led me in.

And there she was.

A shell.

An empty vessel.

And there was Nana.

A saint.

Crying and praying over her.

Giving it all to God.

And there was me.

Frightened and wet-faced.

Unsure.

Yet determined.

To touch her.

To kiss her.

To tell her how much I loved her.

How much I prayed for her.

How much I needed her to come home.

That night, Daddy had lifted me up, and I leaned over and kissed her on her bandaged forehead. I didn't want to leave her. But Daddy had said she needed her rest. That I could come back in the morning.

But in the morning there was nothing but mourning.

Mommy died in the middle of the night, while I was home tucked in bed.

I didn't fully comprehend the weight of Daddy's words at the time: "Mommy isn't coming home, Butterfly."

"Why not?"

I remember the tears in his eyes when he said, "Because she's resting in Heaven now."

I didn't know what it fully meant to die, or to be *resting in Heaven*.

Mommy wasn't ever coming home.

Ever.

I'd had no other loss in my life. So I couldn't comprehend it. Couldn't conceptualize it.

That kind of loss was all new to me.

Still, I felt numb. And I cried.

Daddy groans, pulling me from the painful memory.

I stare at him.

He groans again, but doesn't open his eyes at first.

My heart skips two beats, then stops in anticipation.

"D-d-daddy," I stammer, looking at him anxiously, trying to contain my emotions. "Are you going to die?" The words come stumbling out of my mouth.

He looks at me.

His brown eyes are unusually intense. "I don't want to," he says, reaching for my hand. I take it. "T-t-there's s-something I want to tell you. I need for you to l-listen c-carefully, okay, Butterfly?"

I nod, my tears falling freely down my face.

"Your mother and I . . ." He closes his eyes as if he's trying to remember something. He swallows, then slowly opens his eyes. They are filled with tears.

The only time I've ever seen tears in Daddy's eyes is when he had to tell me Mommy had died. I brace myself for the blow, then push out, "What is it, Daddy? Y-you're scaring me."

Daddy pauses, looked away from me for a moment, then looks back at me. "I've loved you from the moment your mother brought you into my life, Butterfly. It was love at first sight..."

He closes his weary eyes. Swallows. The medications are keeping him groggy.

He's in pain. I can see it. Feel it.

And I still don't know what is wrong with him. No one will tell me anything.

He's been here for two days now, and he isn't getting any better.

He's worse.

Seeing him lying weakly in this hospital bed is killing me.

"Daddy, p-p-please don't leave me," I say, wrapping my arms around him, burrowing my face into his chest. The tears won't stop. They fall fast and heavy.

It's as if I already know the outcome before it happens.

"Shhhhh. Look at me, Butterfly."

I lift my head from his chest and look him in his sunken eyes.

"I'm always going to be with you," Daddy breathes, trying to stretch a smile across his face. "Your mother and I..." He closes his eyes again, then slowly opens them. "We...I... hoped to tell you at the right time..."

"Tell me what, Daddy?"

His eyes flutter.

"Tell me what, Daddy?" I repeat, my heart racing and breaking into tiny pieces at the same time.

He swallows. "Y-you'll always be my daughter, Butter-fly," Daddy says. "No matter what. Never forget how much I love you."

I nod. But what he says isn't making any sense because I

know I'm *his* daughter. And I know how much he loves me. It must be the drugs, I surmise.

Yeah. That has to be it.

His eyes shut.

And now I am on my knees at his bedside, clutching his hand, desperately holding on. But I can feel the air seeping out of my body.

He's still breathing. His heart is still beating.

Still I—

Daddy's eyes slowly open.

They are full of tears. Mine are full of tears. "This is the hardest thing I have to tell you."

"What is, Daddy? Please tell me."

He swallows. "I'm not..." he swallows again. "I..."

Machines beep.

Daddy's eyes flutter shut.

And then it happens.

The machine flat-lines.

"Daddy!" I scream, hysterically, shaking him. "No! No! No! Wake up! *Noooooooo!*"

My worst fear realized.

Daddy is gone.

21

Why God, why...?

For three days after the funeral, I stay locked in my room. For three days, I block out the world around me. I do not eat. Do not bathe. I stay in bed. The curtains drawn, I remain cocooned beneath the covers.

Wrapped in heartache.

Enveloped in shock and disbelief.

Grieving.

I feel so broken.

In the blink of an eye, my whole world has been turned upside down, then inside out. My happiness has been snatched from me. My whole world has unraveled. And, now, my life as I once knew it is...*over!*

And I have nothing.

Nothing left of me.

Nothing to be happy about.

Nothing to believe in.

Nothing to look forward to.

I am sixteen.

Motherless.

Fatherless.

Now orphaned.

And I am angry, so, so, very angry with God for taking Daddy from me. And I'm angry with Daddy for leaving me *here*.

Alone.

Afraid.

Sad.

My daddy's gone!

Dead!

How could he do this to me?

I feel abandoned by him.

He told me he'd always be here for me.

Told me he'd never leave me.

That he'd always take care of me.

Love me.

Protect me.

He promised me.

But now he's departed. Gone! Buried beneath dirt, his body an empty shell.

How could he not tell me he was sick? That he was dying? How could I not know? Didn't I have a right to know?

This whole thing feels so unreal. One minute, Daddy's fine. Then the next minute, he's dead. I keep pinching myself, hoping to wake up and find that I imagined it all. That it's all just one big, horrible nightmare.

But I know it's not. I know it's real. I saw it with my own eyes. And now I am hurting. My heart is aching. This piercing pain is excruciating. And there's an unexplainable tightening in my chest. My emotions are choking me, strangling the air out of me, wringing out what's left of me.

I feel like I am dying inside.

Dying.

Dying.

What's there left to live for? Everyone I've ever loved is gone. My grandmother. My mother. Now Daddy.

Oh, God! My chest hurts. I take several deep breaths. Try to will away the emotions welling up inside of me. But I am too overwhelmed with grief. And memories. And loss. My bottom lip starts quivering. Just a little at first, then it's shak-

ing and I have to bite it. Before I can stop the flood of feelings pooling inside of me, my vision shimmers.

Tears brim my eyes.

The storm is coming.

I blink back the burning sensation.

Then I close my eyes, just as someone taps on my door,
gently at first.

"Nia, honey?" It's my aunt Terri's voice, Daddy's sister
from Atlanta.

I wipe tears from my eyes. I feel a headache pushing its way
to the front of my head. I squeeze my eyes shut tighter, trying
to will it away. But the steady throb slowly starts to pound.

And pound.

And pound.

The knocking becomes more persistent.

"Nia, sweetheart?" Aunt Terri's voice sounds filled with
concern.

I start hyperventilating.

A wave of emotions washes over me.

And then...

I am slowly being pulled under.

And, now, I am drowning.

Drowning in sorrow.

Drowning in pain.

Drowning in loneliness.

Drowning, drowning, drowning.

I hear the door open. "Nia?"

I don't speak. I can't speak. I can only cry. It's a boo-hoo-
snot-flying-every-which-way sobbing that burns my chest, and
swells my eyes almost shut.

I am choking.

Gasping.

Thrashing about.

Fighting for air; fighting for breath; fighting to keep from
sinking; fighting to hold one, fighting to get through this.

Fighting, fighting, fighting—to survive.

22

Loneliness has no mercy...
I spend the next several days floating, in and out of a fog, in and out of consciousness. I mean, I am aware of what has happened—but everything around me has become one big blur.

I am dazed and confused.

It hurts to breathe.

It hurts to think.

Pain finds every part of me.

And I am not sure how much more of this I can endure before I, before I...lose my mind. I wonder how I can be so numb, and yet feel so much grief, so much heartache, so much despair all at the same time. How I can be so full of conflict, yet feel so much emptiness.

I am an oxymoron, a ball of contradictions.

A tortured soul.

A bleeding heart.

Slowly withering.

Withering.

Withering.

The things I have loved the most are now the things I try so desperately to avoid.

Playing the piano.

Journaling.

My poetry.

Things that remind me of Daddy, things too painful to enjoy knowing that he is no longer going to be here to enjoy them with.

I close my eyes.

Listen to the *thump-thump-thump* of my heavy heart as it pounds in my ears.

Thump-thump.

Thump-thump.

Thump-thump.

Like that of a beating drum; rhythmically pounding.

Slicing into the silence.

Morphing me into a wave of vibrations.

Trapped beneath skin.

I lie stone still, holding my breath.

Thump-thump.

Thump-thump.

Thump-thump.

The sound resonates through my body.

It pounds louder.

Echoes through the hollowness of my soul.

And leaves me feeling so, so empty.

And trapped.

Trapped in sadness.

Trapped in uncertainty.

The reality of my situation has me wondering what will become of me. Who will care for me now, now that Daddy's gone?

Oh, God, why? Why? Why?

I am still in . . . shock.

Daddy's gone!

Thump-thump.

Thump-thump.

I repeat this truth in my head, over the sound of the beating drums. Over and over and over again. Daddy's gone. Daddy's gone. Daddy's gone. It plays in my mind like a scratched disc. Over and over and over. And no matter how hard I try to trick my psyche into believing that he's coming back, that he's on some extended vacation, that he's going to one day soon walk back through the door and call me his little butterfly and tell me how much he loves me, I know it's a bold-faced lie. That he isn't ever coming back. And my mind won't be deceived.

The painful reality is: My daddy's gone!

And I am feeling resentful. And I'm angry, very, very angry. My troubled heart points a finger at him. It blames him for this pain I am in.

I open my eyes. Reach under my pillow and feel for my journal. I clutch it to heart. My fingers trail its edges as I pull in a deep, shaky breath...and wait.

And wait.

And wait.

For the steadying of my heartbeat, for the heaviness in my chest to lift, for silence to finally claim me; instead, my chest shakes. My body throbs. The drumming, its steady beat, re-verberates through me.

Deafening vibrations.

Thump-thump.

Thump-thump.

The pace quickens.

Thump-thump-thump-thump.

The beating grows louder.

Thump-thump-thump.

Thump-thump-thump.

Thump-thump-thump.

And louder...

And louder...

Until my head starts to spin, until my vision begins to blur, and everything around me starts to fade in and out.

I am too afraid to sleep.
Restless nights of weeping have taken its toll on me.
I'm tired, so, so very tired.
I don't want to give up.
Don't want to let go.
And, yet, I'm standing at the cliff—
Heart pounding.
Soul crying out.
Arms stretched open.
Drums beating.
Waiting, waiting, waiting...
Swaying back and forth, with bated breath, for someone, anyone, to finally push me over the edge.

23

Sleep evades me. Avoids me like the plague. I am afflicted. Cursed. Chained to this zombie state. I am listless. Yet the camera in my mind's eye won't stop clicking.

Click.

Click.

Click.

Nonstop snapshots of Daddy flash through my head. Daddy teaching me to ride my first bike; Daddy buying me my first pair of Rollerblades; Daddy nursing my fevers and runny noses; Daddy, front and center, at my piano lessons and every dance rehearsal; Daddy reading me bedtime stories; Daddy teaching me to drive...

Daddy.

Daddy.

Daddy.

Click.

Click.

Click.

Our first daddy-daughter dance in second grade, then third grade, then fourth and fifth and sixth grades come to me in a kaleidoscope of memories, bursting in vivid colors, flashing painfully bright in my mind.

I don't want to remember any of this. Not now. But I don't want to forget, either. No. I can't ever forget. But the memories are unbearable, just too painful.

Daddy's gone.

My heart is shredding, shredding, shredding.

Hot, angry emotions take over me. And then, I am wailing.

I don't know when Mrs. Thomas comes into my room, but she is at my bed, sweeping me up in her arms, holding and rocking me.

"Shh. It's okay, sweetheart," she says, over and over. But it's not okay. It'll never be okay. Never. My daddy is gone.

How am I supposed to recover from this?

I've lost hope.

Lost faith.

Lost my anchor.

I am crashing against fear, against uncertainty.

"I'm so sorry, sweetheart," I hear her say over and over and over again to me, trying to soothe me with her calming voice. She keeps rocking me until my crying eases some. Then she whispers, "You'll get through this. You're not alone..."

But I am...

And then comes the sobbing again.

"Shhh. It's okay, sweetheart. Let it out. That's right, get it all out. I'm here for you, Nia. We all are."

But my daddy isn't.

"I promise you, sweetheart." She's rubbing my back. "You'll get through this."

How?

I am gulping between sobs, trying to catch my breath, trying to fill my burning lungs with air. I try—want—to speak, but no words come out.

How can I get through this when I can't live for today? When I don't want to live for tomorrow?

I want to know, *how* can I get through this when I am barely holding on?

How can I get through this when there is literally nothing else left of me?

I look up at her. Try to blink her into focus through the tears. "How?" is all I can manage to push out. "H-h-how?"

She pulls me in closer, her arms wrapping me tighter, rocking me as one would a baby.

"One day at a time, sweetheart," she tells me. "One day at a time."

I look at her, not saying a word, breathing heavy and hiccupping. I'm sure she means well. I'm sure she believes this. That "one day at a time" is all I'll need to get through this.

But for me...

It's the emptiest promise I've heard.

In the wee hours of the night, against the clutter of my weeping heart, words finally find me. And I do something I haven't done in what feels like forever. I open my journal and write:

I am stuck in memories of you
I see your face in my dreams
Hear your voice
Feel the love you have for me
Surrounding me
Covering me
And still...
I surrender to the pain
I am haunted by loss
Daunted by loneliness
The memories of you
are not enough
They'll never be
I miss you so much
Not a day goes by
That I do not cry

That I do not mourn
It hurts.
The weight of losing you
Pierces my heart
Cripples my spirit
Has me slipping
Helplessly
Aimlessly
Out of control
And this emptiness
This void
Is slowly killing me
I can't go on living like this
In aloneness
In unhappiness
In despair
Desperately
Seeking answers
Seeking understanding
Seeking refuge
Seeking solace
Seeking you

When I am done, I close my eyes, take in a deep breath. I wait. And I wait. And I wait. Praying for strength. Praying for direction. Praying for answers. I need to know, what will happen now? Need to know what will be in store for me without Daddy.

I can't imagine life without him.

Not another minute, another second.

Can't imagine my existence stuck in this emptiness.

And, yet, here I am.

Alone.

I close my journal, clutch it against my aching heart, and cry.

24

I open my eyes. Rub sleep from then. I feel disoriented. Lost. I have to look around the room to get my bearings.

I blink the room into view. Everything looks familiar. It's my bedroom.

I glance over at the digital clock: 7:39 a.m.

For the last three days I've barely slept. Last night, I slept four hours, the most I've slept since Daddy's death.

I don't feel better, or worse.

I simply don't feel.

I just wish I could go back.

Just wish—

I don't want to think about it. No. Not right now.

I sigh, flipping the blankets off me. I sit up and hold my head in my hands.

My head hurts.

It's pounding.

My stomach tightens.

I haven't eaten much in the last several days.

God, why?

I wish I could free myself.

Grow wings.

And fly.

Wish I could reach out and touch the hands of time.

Rewind the clocks.

And start back to when life, my life, was full of happiness, full of joy, full of Daddy's love.

My bottom lip starts trembling.

My vision starts to blur.

Stop this. No tears, Nia.

I blink them back.

You have to be strong, Nia.

Isn't that what everyone's been saying to me?

"Be strong, Nia."

"You'll get through it, Nia."

"Push past the pain, Nia."

Nia.

Nia.

Nia.

Do this. Do that.

Don't do this. Don't do that.

It isn't fair. None of this is.

Daddy dying on me.

Aunt Terri—a lady I hardly know—making decisions for me.

How dare he. How dare she.

How dare God.

How dare all of them do this to me?

I'm tired.

So, so tired.

Tired of being told what I should do.

Tired of being told what's best for me.

Why can't I just be left alone?

Just let me be.

Doesn't anyone know what all this has done to me?

It's infected me.

It's left me sick.

Sick.

Sick.

And I've succumbed to it.

I wonder obsessively if I will ever be able to think of Daddy and not feel pain, if this gaping hole in my heart will ever close.

I glance over at the time again. Then I crawl my way out of bed and begrudgingly drag myself to the bathroom. My legs feel wobbly.

I stare at my reflection in the bathroom mirror and almost fall over. The tear-stained face staring back at me is unrecognizable. I am a total catastrophe. Eyes swollen and caked with crust, puffy bags hanging beneath them, hair matted. My once flawless complexion is blotchy. My full lips are ashy. There's dried spit in the corners of my mouth.

I look a horrid mess.

Run down and crazed.

But I am still too numb to care.

I blink back fresh, unexpected tears. Then I turn from the mirror.

This is what my life has become.

A sad state of disarray.

I turn on the faucet, then stare down into the sink. Just the thought of standing here and brushing my teeth overwhelms me.

I am so exhausted.

From crying.

From not sleeping.

From hurting.

I ache all over.

My head.

My eyes.

My chest.

My heart.

I honestly don't know how much more of this I can take.

I just want it all to go away. But it won't. It's etched into every part of me. There's no forgetting it. There's no way of escaping it. It's all around me.

Aunt Terri is still here, taking over everything, packing up the house, my house. My life. A constant reminder that nothing for me will ever be the same.

She says she will stay until I am finished with school.

But then...

"Other arrangements will need to be made..."

What arrangements?

What does she plan to do with me?

The thought of being shuffled around like a piece of unwanted furniture makes my stomach knot.

I am still too sick with grief to dissect the implications of what Aunt Terri said to me. Still too overwhelmed to try to decipher the meaning behind her words.

My gut tells me that no matter what she has in mind, I'm not going to be happy with the idea. But what other choice will I have?

None.

So, somehow, someway, I will have to find a way to accept my fate.

I am doomed.

I blow out a long breath.

Then I bend down to cup water into my hands and rinse my mouth out. I swirl the cool liquid around in my mouth, then spit it out. Even that drains me. Makes me want to turn around and crawl back into bed. Get lost beneath the covers.

I keep rinsing. Keep swirling. Keep spitting.

And then I am lowering my head into the sink bowl, splashing cold water on my face.

Trying to revive myself.

I look back up into the mirror. Stare at my reflection. Then with my thumb under my left eye, and my pointer finger under my right eye, I pull down on the skin under my eyes and peek inside. I'm not sure what I expect to see. But I look anyway. Stare at the pink flesh of my lower lids. Then let go.

I keep my gaze locked on my reflection.

Vacant eyes stare back at me.

Bloodshot eyes.

Sad eyes.

Lonely eyes.

I don't want to be alone.

But I am.

And I am scared.

So, so, very afraid.

Never in a million years did I think I'd one day wake up and be an orphan.

But I am.

Feeling shaky on my legs, I grab onto the sink.

I'm falling.

Falling.

Falling.

And now I can't get up.

I am on the floor.

Crumpled.

Sobbing.

25

"I can't keep tiptoeing around this," I overhear Aunt Terri saying into the phone a few days later. She's out on the patio, the glass door slid open. And I'm eavesdropping. Something I've found myself doing of late because, for the last several days, there's been all kind of hushed talk of wills and probate and executors and trusts.

And...

The child.

Me.

The child.

My name is Nia.

Nia Daniels.

Not *the child*.

Aunt Terri is the culprit.

She's been talking about me behind my back as if I don't exist.

As if my opinions, my feelings, my wants do not matter.

As if I am not important in all of this.

As if I'm not the one who is affected by all of this.

On the phone, whispering, and gossiping, and speaking freely about her dismay that she wasn't appointed as the executor to Daddy's estate. Still accusing him of stealing her inheritance.

I've overheard her saying all of this.

Talking about Daddy.

Daddy's gone. Yet she's relentlessly bashing him.

All over money.

His money.

Or whatever.

And now this...

"No. She's upstairs locked in her room, probably crying herself sick...I can't wait to get the hell out of this house. I'm trying...for her. I know she's innocent in all of this. But I'll be glad when this mess is all over with. I'm ready to get back to my life."

I lean up against the frame, out of view, curiosity getting the best of me, to hear more, know more.

"...He didn't even have the decency to appoint *me* as her guardian...He's such a *bastard*...I know, I know...Well, it'll be up to a judge now..."

I blink.

All of this is way over my head.

I decide I've had enough, but then I stay planted in place when I hear her say, "No, no. I haven't said anything. I'm trying to be sympathetic...Julian's lawyer suggested we tell her together, but I said I'd rather do it myself. Yes, I know...She deserves to know."

To know what?

My ears burn to hear more.

"...Yes, before he gets here..."

Before who *gets here?*

I know I probably shouldn't be eavesdropping on her conversation, but what is it they always say about curiosity?

Yeah. That.

So I stay put.

Curiosity slow-killing the cat.

"...He's supposed to arrive tomorrow...No, bus..." Aunt Terri laughs at something being said on the other end.

"...You heard me. He's riding Greyhound here." She grunts. "Too trifling to fly...It's a three-day road trip...No, no. I haven't spoken to him. I've never even seen him. The attorney's been in contact with him..."

The attorney's been in contact with whom?

God, the suspense is killing me.

I'm dying to know *whom* she's talking about.

"...No. All I know is, he's been in prison for the last sixteen years..."

Wait.

WHAAT?

I blink.

"...No. For guns and armed robbery..."

I blink again.

O-M-G!

My heart starts racing.

Who is she talking about?

And why the heck is some gun-toting robber coming here to see me?

It's all starting to sound too crazy now.

"...He just got released two months ago..." She pauses. "Yeah, I know. A convicted felon. One big mess. Well, we'll see how it all pans out. Yes, I know. Well, let me go. Uh-huh....I need to go check on this girl, make sure she hasn't done anything foolish..."

I frown.

"...Okay...Yes...I'll keep you posted."

She ends the call.

And I slide the screen door open, surprising her.

"*Oh*, Nia. Hey," she says nervously, craning her neck to look over her shoulder. "You startled me. I thought you were still up in your room."

I give her a look. Uh-huh. I bet you did.

"Who just got out of prison?" I ask, narrowing my eyes and cutting to the chase. "And why is *he* coming *here* to see *me*?"

Aunt Terri's eyes widen. "Oh, sweetheart, you weren't supposed to hear all of that. But we need to—"

I stop her with a hand. "No. Aunt Terri. Who's been in prison for sixteen years? Obviously it has something to do with me. So I want to know. Like you said, I *deserve* to know."

"Oh, Nia, sweetheart," she says, her eyes full of what could be regret. She motions to me with a hand. "Come have a seat, so we can talk."

I swallow. Shake my head. "Just tell me. Who is he?"

Her shoulders slump in her chair. "He's your *father* ..."

26

I can't believe what I've just heard. There is absolutely nothing wrong with my hearing, so I am certain I've heard wrong.

My eyes are now as round as dinner plates. "He's my *what*?" I shriek, still trying to process what she's said. My cocoa eyes search her face closely for understanding.

Clarity.

She repeats herself, slowly. "Nia. The man coming to see you tomorrow is," she pauses, pulling in a breath, "your father. Your *real* father."

I shake my head, still not comprehending. My real father was buried weeks ago. I saw him lying in that casket. I witnessed them closing it. Then rolling it out of the church. I saw the gloved men hoist Daddy up into the hearse. I followed behind them—and him, in the limo. I saw the ground open and ready. I'd laid the single white rose onto his casket and watched them lowering it—and *Daddy*—down into the earth.

I was there.

I know what I saw.

Has she been drinking?

Using drugs?

I swallow. "Th-that...that can't be. It's impossible."

Her eyes never leave mine. "I'm so sorry, Nia. But it's true. He—"

"It's a lie," I croak out, shaking my head. I feel like she's trying to play a nasty trick on me and at any minute, some-one's going to jump out from the bushes and yell, "You've just been punk'd!"

But there's only Aunt Terri and me out here.

And there are no cameras. And from the look on her face, I'm not being punk'd.

Still. I am standing here, staring at her in disbelief.

Daddy would have told me this, wouldn't he?

Yes, yes. Of course he would.

"That's a lie," I say, feeling my stomach clutch. "It can't be true."

"Sorry, sweetie. But it is."

I shake my head. "My father is *dead.*" My lip quivers. "Ju-lian Daniels was—*is* my father. W-why would you say some-thing like that, Aunt Terri? Why?"

"Because it's the truth, Nia," she says, almost sounding apologetic. A far cry from how she sounded when I'd been eavesdropping on her conversation moments ago.

A hand over my stomach, my insides churn. I feel myself getting sick.

"But I have the same last name as Daddy," I say warily. "His name is on *my* birth certificate. So how..."

Aunt Terri gives me a pained look. "Nia, honey..."

Suddenly, I am heaving.

Everything around me is spinning. I feel like I've been stuffed inside a vacuum, the air being quickly sucked out of me.

Clutching my stomach.

I open my mouth to cry out, but instead...

I lean forward.

And vomit.

Then it hits me. All the air rushes out of my lungs, and I crumple to my knees.

27

I was adopted.
No, no. I *am* adopted.

The following morning, Aunt Terri hands me the adoption papers given to her by Daddy's attorney, along with a letter. He said that Daddy kept them both in a safe deposit box. Daddy wanted me to have them, to know the truth—in case something were to ever happen to him *before* he had the chance to tell me himself.

I stare at the document.

Stunned.

Angry.

And, eventually, numb.

Yet I am trembling from the inside out.

My heart leaps in my chest as I grip Daddy's letter in my hand. My gaze shifts to the framed photograph of him and Mommy sitting atop my nightstand. The picture was taken during a trip to London. We're standing in front of Madame Tussaud's, the famous wax museum. Daddy and Mommy are on either side of me, holding my hands.

I am five.

It was the last trip I took with both my parents. I touch the glass. Then I bring the picture frame to my lips and kiss the glass.

I am so alone.

I miss you both so much.

But I miss Daddy more.

I'm not sure if I should feel guilty about this. I am not sure what I should feel about any of this. All I know is, both of my parents are gone.

And there is only me.

"Do you want me to stay with you?" Aunt Terri asks, sitting beside me on the bed. Setting the picture back on the night-stand, I shake my head. I tell her I want to be alone.

"Okay. I'll be downstairs if you need me."

I don't look at her when she says this. I find myself under-standing more and more why Daddy didn't like her.

I do not like her, either.

I wait for her to leave, shutting my door, before I open Daddy's letter. I slowly pull it out and breathe in the folded white sheets of paper. Pressing the crisp letter to my cheek, I close my eyes and try to imagine what it must have been like for him to write this letter to me. I imagine him painstakingly considering my feelings as he pressed the tip of his pen to these sheets of paper and started writing.

I so desperately need to believe that writing this letter to me was one of the hardest things he'd ever had to do.

I open my eyes.

My hands shake as I unfold the letter, and the tears fall before I start reading.

Saturday, November 10, 2012

My beautiful Butterfly,

I am writing this letter to you on your twelfth birthday for no other reason than preparation in case something unexpected was to ever happen to me. I want you to know, writing this letter is one of the most painful things I've had to do. If you are reading this, it means two things:

1). That you now know the truth about being adopted; and, 2): That I have left this earth long before I had the chance to tell you the truth myself. For that, I am truly sorry. I wanted to tell you so many times. But then I'd look into your beautiful, smiling face and see all the unconditional love you have for me dancing back at me in the reflection of your bright eyes, and my heart would melt. I couldn't find the words or the courage to bring myself to tell you.

But I knew one day the moment of truth would have to come, especially knowing how much your biological father, Omar Davis, wanted to one day be in your life. He wanted to parent you, but he knew he couldn't. So he selflessly gave up his parental rights to allow me to be the father you needed. It was a difficult decision, but he wanted what was best for you. I'm sure he still does. So please don't be too hard on him when you finally meet him. He did what he had to do. Out of love for you.

My attorney will have most likely already been in contact with him. You deserve to meet him—and have some type of relationship with him, IF you choose to. I know this is all shocking news to you, and you are probably hurting more now than ever. It's a lot for you to take in. But be open to the possibility, Butterfly.

Your mother and I had hoped to tell you together when you were old enough to understand. But then she was suddenly taken away from us. Suddenly, in that moment, your knowing the truth about who your real father was no longer felt important to me, because I am your father. I will always be your father, maybe not in the genetic sense, but on a physical and emotional level we are connected spirits. You are every bit a part of me as you are of your mother.

*You are my daughter. You will always be my daughter. No matter what you learn about the man who helped conceive you, I will always be your **dad**. No one, nothing, can ever take that away from you. I have loved you as if I played a part in your creation. You were less than a month old when I came into your life. And I have loved you from the moment I laid eyes on you. You stole my heart the moment I held you in my arms and breathed you in.*

I want you to know you have been my greatest blessing, Nia Symone Daniels. The day I signed those adoption papers and you were given my last name was the happiest moment of my life. You have brought so much joy into my heart—and life, Nia.

Even though I am gone, in Heaven, you will always be my beautiful, flitting butterfly. Don't ever be afraid to spread your wings and soar.

I will always love you, from now to eternity.

Love forever,
Dad

My eyes are burning and blurry from tears that I cannot stop from falling. My heart aches. I am so overwhelmed. He wrote this to me four years ago. I stare at the letter for a long moment. Then I read it a second time, then a third, then a fourth. I read it over and over and over until the words become blurred and the black ink begins to smear from my tears.

"Nia, he's here," Aunt Terri says, poking her head in the doorway.

My heart sinks.

My eyes and nose are running.

He's here?

OMG!

He's here!

I reach for the box of tissues on my nightstand, pull a few tissues out, then blow my nose with trembling hands. I pull more tissue.

"Are you ready to come down to meet him?"

Now?

Is she kidding?

Am I ready?

Heck no.

Never.

I shake my head, sniffling. "Give me a moment," I say in almost a whisper, trying to find my voice.

She walks out, leaving me to my moment. I lie back on my bed. I do not wipe my tears. I allow them to stream down my temples, an agonizing groan escaping my lips.

I feel like I am floating in a sea of pain.

The kind of pain I am in ebbs and flows.

The throbbing in my chest now matches the wave of pain building in my head.

I close my eyes, willing myself to be gone from here.

Daddy's face swims behind my lids. He is smiling at me. Then he says, *"I love you, Butterfly. Always have, always will."*

I hear his voice clear as day.

Holding my breath, I slowly open my eyes.

I exhale.

Sadly, I am still here.

And Daddy is gone.

After ten excruciating minutes, I finally make my way down the stairs and into the living room. Aunt Terri eyes me as he stands up. "Damn," he mutters. And then, without words or warning, he is grabbing me and pulling me into an embrace. "I've waited sixteen years to do this. To finally hold you in my arms."

I am engulfed in his muscular, tattoo-covered arms. Tightly pressed against him. He clutches me so close I think he will squeeze the breath out of me.

I feel his heartbeat.

And struggle within his arms, fighting against awkwardness, and the shock of being hugged by a man whom I never knew existed.

Until one day ago.

My so-called father.

Omar.

When he finally pulls back from me, he stares at me.

His eyes are wet.

I avert my gaze.

I am not sure what I was expecting.

But this, *he*, isn't it.

"Damn, yo. You're a real beauty. I can't believe how much you look like your moms, word is bond..."

I blink.

Shift uncomfortably from one foot to the other.

Who is this man?

He...he...looks and sounds like a...*thug*.

His gaze sweeps around the living room, then lands on a crystal-framed black-and-white photo of my mom, positioned under a lamp on one of the marble-and-glass end tables. He walks over in its direction. In the picture my mom is young and beautiful, smiling, holding a baby in her arms, looking down lovingly at her bundle of joy.

Me.

I eye him as he picks up the framed photo and stares at it.

"Damn, yo. I can't believe this..."

I see something flicker in his eyes.

Memories, I think. Maybe mistakes.

Perhaps a mixture of the two.

"On everything, I wish I woulda did right by your moms."

He sets the photo down, careful to place it back where he'd

taken it. He stares down at the picture. "Ya moms was my heart; my everything."

I tilt my head and stare at him.

I swallow.

Try to find my voice.

Then what happened?

I open my mouth to ask the question, but the words refuse to follow. They somehow get stuck in the back of my throat.

Memories of my mother come rushing back to me.

The pain of losing her resurfaces, the scabs slowly open.

And, now, I feel myself bleeding out.

The room starts to spin.

I feel myself swooning.

She's gone.

Daddy's gone.

And all that is left is anguish.

Never-ending.

Agonizing.

Haunting.

Pain.

And now...

This man, this stranger, with the sagging pants and three teardrops inked in his face.

He catches me before my legs give out and I hit the floor.

28

"Ya moms was my heart; my everything."

"I want a paternity test," I say to Omar three days later. He's sitting in the family room talking to Aunt Terri when I barge in and blurt it out. There are no hellos. There's no need for pleasantries. I have nothing to be cordial about.

I've thought it over.

And my mind is made up. I don't care what the adoption papers say, or what was written in Daddy's letter.

I want—no, *need*—more proof.

I want a blood test done.

For the last several days since his arrival, all he and Aunt Terri have been talking about is me going back to New Jersey with *him*. "Just for a while," Aunt Terri had had the audacity to say, trying to convince me that going would be good for me. "You need to get away from all of this."

Yeah. Okay.

But my question is this: Why was that man invited here as if to recover a long-lost prize?

I am not his to claim.

Or reclaim.

"I've waited sixteen years to do this."

"He's not my father," I insist. I shake my head. "He can't

be. I don't care what those stupid adoption papers say. Or what Daddy's letter says. That man is nothing to me."

Aunt Terri gasps, giving me a shocked look. "Nia, you know that's not how you address adults. You were taught better than that. Where are your manners?"

Buried with Daddy.

I don't say this, though.

But I do dismiss the question and say, "Not to be rude, but the two of you don't get to plan my life without me. I have some say, too. And I'm not going anywhere unless—"

"You're still a child," Aunt Terri says. "And provisions need to be made *until* your ... *my* ... brother's estate is resolved."

I blink. "Daddy might have been your brother. But he's *my* father. He'll always be my *father*." I shoot an icy glare over at Omar. "Not"—I point a finger—"*him*. He doesn't get to waltz into my life and start playing the concerned parent role. Sorry."

"Nia!" Aunt Terri scolds. "You watch your tone, young lady. I know you weren't raised to be disrespectful. I know you're grieving, so you'll get a pass. *This* time."

I give her a half-hearted apology, then shift my eyes, glancing down at the floor.

"Nah, it's cool," Omar says. "Yo, check it. I ain't tryna take ya pop's place, feel me?"

I cringe. "No. Sorry. I don't feel you," I say, ignoring Aunt Terri's burning glare. "And I'm *not* feeling this situation. It's so not fair!"

"Yo, I respect that. I know ish is crazy for you, li'l mama..."

Li'l mama?

I frown. "Please don't call me that. My name is Nia."

He puts his hands up in mock surrender. "My bad, Nia. I'm not lookin' to complicate ya life. I'm only here after all these years of wanting to be in ya life 'cause ya pop's lawyer hit me up."

But *why*?

He tells me two weeks before he was released from prison he'd received a certified letter from the attorney's office advising him to contact their office. He'd waited until he was released to call. And then he broke down and cried when he'd heard the news. Not of Daddy's death. But of the fact that he'd get what he'd been praying for over the last sixteen years. A chance to finally be in my life.

"I wanna be in ya life. Not take over it," he says. I can see the tears swelling up in his eyes as he seemingly struggles to keep any from falling.

Aunt Terri has the audacity to say, "Look at it on the bright side, Nia. You've had sixteen wonderful years with your adoptive father..."

I cringe. Adoptive father. It sounds so dirty the way she says it.

I feel like a reject.

Daddy's gone from *Daddy* to "your adoptive father."

Tears flood my eyes.

"Now it's your chance to get to know your biological father," she continues. "This is something you need, sweetheart."

"But why can't I stay here, in California? And he get to know me *here*?"

She tells me the house is being *sealed up*—my words, not hers—until things are resolved in court. Daddy's attorney has been appointed as custodian over me; whatever that means. Aunt Terri isn't happy about it, she says. She claims she is fighting to obtain a legal order to be able to have custody of me.

"But for now, we all agree this is for the best, Nia. You need to get to know your...*father*."

He isn't my father!

He will never be.

I scowl at Aunt Terri.

She has no idea what *I* need.

I need the man who raised me. The man who tucked me into bed and read me bedtime stories, every night until I was too old to be tucked in, and too old for his bedtime stories.

I need the man who loved me unconditionally. The man who shaped and molded me. And loved me unconditionally.

I need my Daddy.

"It's only for two weeks, Nia. Just for me to get everything in order."

"And I repeat," I say, enunciating each word, "I want a DNA test. I don't care what those adoption papers say. They still don't prove that *he's* my father. I *need* proof. I'm not going *any*where without a blood test."

Aunt Terri sighs. "Fine, Nia. And when it proves that he is . . . ?"

I take a deep, pained breath.

Choking back tears, I say, "Then I guess I'll have to go."

29

Two torturous weeks later...
The pilot makes an announcement over the speaker. "Good afternoon, ladies and gentlemen. This is your captain speaking. I'd like to welcome you aboard Virgin America flight one-sixty-two's nonstop service from Los Angeles to Newark Liberty International Airport. Once we get airborne today, our flight time will be five hours and thirty minutes..."

Omar Davis is *the* father.

My biological father.

I'm still shocked by the news. And the test results. It's just so much to take in.

Honestly, I prayed that it wasn't true. That someone was playing some sick, twisted joke. But it's as real as it can be, ninety-nine-point-nine-nine percent real.

It took a week of crying after the DNA test results confirmed paternity, then another week of me crying as Daddy's attorney met with me and discussed the news. Legally, he has no rights to me, but I am still a minor so someone needs to care for me until I am legally able to take care of myself, which is where Daddy's attorney comes in.

Aunt Terri said I'd be able to live with her once she settles whatever it is she needs to settle. And the attorney is in agreement with that. So the plan is this: I go to New Jersey

with, uh, um…Omar for three weeks while Aunt Terri takes
care of whatever it is she has to do with the court and Daddy's
will and whatever else. Then I'll be flying out to Georgia to live
with her.

"Just for a few weeks," Aunt Terri had said as she helped
me pack. But there was something in the way she shifted her
eyes from mine that had me question her true intentions. I
have to trust that she'll keep her word. That this is only *tem-
porary*.

Boarding this plane was one of the most difficult things
I've done. Daddy dying was hard. But leaving him, his grave,
behind is—

Omar grunts.

Out of the corner of my eye, I see him shifting in his seat,
clutching the armrest.

He seems anxious.

No.

He *is* anxious.

He's scared to death of flying. Although he said he'd never
been on a plane before, just the idea of being up so high in
sky makes him nervous. He thought I was going to be okay
with traveling thousands of miles across country by Greyhound.

No, no, no. Not!

And I wasn't riding on Amtrak, either.

So here we are.

I glance over at him. "It won't be that bad," I offer sympathetically. It's the least I can do.

He forces out a chuckle. "Yeah, a'ight. If you say so."

"I guess you're not used to flying." It's a statement.

He shakes his head. "Nah. Not my thing. I ain't even gonna
front, yo. I'm mad nervous."

I look at him.

Surprised to hear that this thick-muscled man with the
multiple tattoos is afraid of flying. "Well, why are you flying
now if you're afraid of planes?"

"It's all for you."

Oh.

I turn my head toward the window and stare out.

I touch the butterfly around my neck, then press it up to my lips.

Thoughts of Daddy resurface.

Oh, how I wish I could be one of those big, white, puffy clouds.

Floating.

It doesn't take long before my emotions get the best of me.

A tear slips from the corner of my eye, and I quickly swipe it with a finger before it can run down my face. All I can think about is Daddy. And how I can't let him go. How I have to hold on, to keep his memory alive. Not just inside of me, but all around me.

I sniffle and wipe away more tears.

I can't believe this is really happening to me.

I can feel Omar's eyes on me.

"You good?" he wants to know, touching my arm.

I cringe inwardly. "Yeah."

"You sure e'erything a'ight?"

I just said *yeah,* dang. Let it go.

But he doesn't.

"You can tell me whatever's on ya mind, a'ight?"

I give him a confused look.

What does he want me to say?

That I'm happy being uprooted from my life?

That I'm looking forward to whatever might lie ahead in New Jersey, surrounded by a bunch of strangers?

That I'm excited about being around a man that I don't know?

That I'm eager to build a relationship with him, the ex-con?

No, everything isn't fricking all right!

It's horrible!

I don't know what to expect.

All I know is my life in Long Beach.

Not on a plane with *him*.

I nod. Then I turn to look at him, not really wanting to, but needing to. Needing him to see the contradiction in my words. "I'm fine."

He looks deep into my eyes, and for a split second I think he sees it.

That I am really not okay.

That I'm horrified.

That I am hurting.

And lost.

But he simply grins, all crooked, and says, "Cool, cool." Then he widens his grin and shakes his head. "Damn. I swear, yo. You look so much like ya moms, for real for real. It's crazy. I know I keep sayin' it, but...damn. It's got me buggin'."

And now I'm dying to know—no. I *need* to know—how the two of them met. I need to know what it was about him that made her gravitate to him. I need to know what kind of girl she was to get wrapped up in a guy like him, to have his baby.

Why didn't she get rid of me?

Maybe she should have.

My mother's not here to ask. So I have to, however I can, sift through every piece of this sordid puzzle, and try to fit each piece into its proper place until I have a full picture. I need to understand this craziness, because from where I'm sitting, I simply do not see any logic in any of this. It just doesn't make any sense to me.

I study him for a second, then ask, "How did you and my mother meet?" I shift in my seat, then stretch my legs.

He rubs his chin. Pulls at his goatee. Then he says, "I peeped her at the mall. Menlo Park." He smiled. "She had on this li'l short yellow sundress that showed her pretty legs, walkin' up outta Macy's. She was bad as *fu*...she was mad sexy. Word is bond. I stepped up 'n' tried to holla at 'er real quick, but she looked me up 'n' down, then turned her head,

like she wasn't beat." He chuckles. "But I was a cool muhf…
I looked good 'n' had mad swag, so baggin' chicks was never
a problem for me. And the fact that she dissed me had me
wantin' to bag 'er."

He grins. "I followed ya moms 'round the whole mall. I
was determined to break her down 'til she gave in. Whatever
store she went in, I went in. When she went into the bathroom, I waited outside for 'er. When she grabbed somethin'
to eat at the food court, I stepped up 'n' paid for it."

He shakes his head, smiling. "She finally gave in 'n' let me
holla at 'er. I asked for the digits 'n' just when I thought I was
all in, her moms came from outta nowhere 'n' shut it down…"

Go Nana!

"She was not havin' it." He chuckles. "She snatched ya
moms up 'n' dragged her away from me. I was like, *damn*.
My boys clowned me for weeks after that 'cause they peeped
the whole thing."

"So then how'd you end up hooking up with her?" I ask,
twisting my whole body in my chair so I can face him.

"At the rink."

The rink?

He must notice the quizzical look on my face.

"The skatin' rink. She 'n' two of her girls was at this party
some cat from around the way was havin'."

"Oh."

He laughs. Then he tells me how he walked over and tried
to have a conversation with her, but she skated off with her
friends in tow, giggling. A few minutes later, she skated her
way back over and told him if he wanted to talk to her, he'd
better put on a pair of skates.

So he did.

"I bust my azz mad times, tryna impress her." He laughs,
shaking his head. "I knew then. She was the one. It took me
almost three months to finally bag her."

Bag her?

I frown in confusion.

"My bad. I mean before she finally gave me the time of day."

"And my grandparents *let* her date *you*?" I say, shocked.

He shakes his head. "Nah. We had to sneak; feel me? They hated me."

Hmm. You don't say.

The conversation finally shifts to his family. He tells me he has one sister and a niece and his mom. But his mother is in Florida for the summer, visiting her three sisters. She goes every year from May to September.

"But she's hoping to see you when she gets back," he says.

"Oh. That's nice," I say, forcing myself to sound interested. I ask him her name.

"Pearline. But e'eryone calls her Pearlie-May."

I smile with my lips closed, but my smile doesn't reach my eyes. I am only smiling out of courtesy because I have nothing else to say to that.

After a few excruciating moments of silence between us, I finally say, "You never really said where I'd be staying. Do you have your own place?"

He rubs his chin, slowly shaking his head. "Nah, not yet. I'm still tryna get on my feet, feel me?"

Okay, so he's homeless, too...

Now what?

"I'm crashin' at my moms' crib while she's gone. But it's all good. She has a three-bedroom. You gonna share a room wit' ya cousin, Sha'Quita..."

Sha what?

I bite my lip and then look down at my hands.

I'm instantly haunted by an image of a loudmouthed girl with a gold tooth and multicolored braids swinging down to her butt, popping chewing gum and twirling a razor between her heavily jeweled fingers, sneering at me.

"But we call her Quita," he rattles on, saving me from the

rest of the imagery. "She's a li'l knucklehead sometimes, but
she's a'ight; feel me...?"

I cut my eye at him.

No, I don't feel you.

Right now, all I want to do is stare out the window. No,
no. I want to climb out of the window and jump. Get lost in
the puffy white clouds beneath us. And if I'm lucky enough,
Daddy might catch me in his arms.

"Hopefully the two of you will click," he continues, snatching any hope of an escape away from me. "But, uh, anyway,
you'll crash in the room wit' her."

My stomach quakes.

I don't like this business of sharing a room with some girl
I don't know. Oh, no. I've never had to share a room with
anyone, not even a bathroom.

So how is this going to work, even if for only a short
while?

It's not.

I swallow. But I say nothing. What's there to say? He seems
to already have it all figured out.

"It'll be tight for a minute, know what I'm sayin'..."

No, I don't know what *you're saying.*

But I know what I'm hearing.

And I do not like any of it one bit.

I swallow. I'm almost afraid to ask, but I have to know.
"Does she have a house?"

He chuckles. "Nah, nah. We live in the projects."

My stomach drops.

When the plane finally lands at Newark International Airport, everything inside of me starts to shake. I feel as if I'm
about to throw up. I'm having second thoughts.

No, I never stopped having second thoughts.

This is really happening.

I'm really here, in New Jersey.

Omar pulls out his phone and powers it on before the seat belt warning sign stops illuminating.

He speaks into his phone. "Yo, what's good, man? I need you to come scoop me. Nah, nah...I just touched down. You got me? Oh, word? Damn. A'ight. It's all love, bruh. Yeah, yeah, baby girl wit' me..."

I cringe.

"No doubt. A'ight. Later."

He tells me we're catching the AirTrain to Penn Station, then catching another train to some town, and then a taxi to our final destination. He says the name of the town, but I am not listening.

When the taxi finally pulls up to our destination, the cab driver pulls over to the curb, then waits for Omar to pay him. He fishes out a handful of money from out his front pocket, then hands the driver a hundred-dollar bill. He tells the driver to keep the change, then opens the door and climbs out.

He reaches a hand in and helps me out next. The cab driver pops the trunk. Omar pulls my bags out, then slams the trunk shut. I glance up at the apartments and almost faint. My mouth drops open. I can't believe my eyes. It's a run-down looking building. The building next door to his apartment building looks dirtier and more torn down than this one. Dilapidated. Some of the windows are boarded up.

Please, God, help me!

30

Omar slings one of my bags over his shoulder and grips the other in his hand as we trek up eight flights of stairs. He curses under his breath because neither of the two elevators is working. It's hot and musty in the stairwell.

When we get to the eighth floor, I follow him down a long hall; there's lots of loud music blasting and loud talking from behind red-colored doors. Yelling and screaming pours out of one of the apartments as we make our way down the piss-stained hallway. Finally, he stops and I'm standing behind him. He sets one of my bags down—as I cringe—on the nasty floor, then pulls out a set of keys.

He slides his key, then turns the knob. The door to apartment 8E pushes open.

And we step in.

The door shuts behind us.

"C'mon," he says, heading down a hallway. "I'ma take you to ya room."

I try to take in everything as I follow behind him. But the thing that sticks out the most is the carpet.

It's filthy. It's not pissy-smelling like the floor out in the hall, it just has a stench.

"Yo, Sha'Quita," Omar says, half knocking while turning the doorknob to her bedroom. Music blasts from the other side of the door. I don't know the name of the female artist singing, but the guy's hook is asking if she loves the way he loves her body, or something like that.

Omar swings open the door, and we are greeted by an odor that almost takes my breath away.

The room reeks of...smoke and hot, musty funk.

My stomach flips.

"Yo, what the *fu*—"

I gasp.

The room is filthy.

Clothes are strewn everywhere.

There are candy wrappers and empty potato chip bags and empty pizza boxes and empty soda cans covering an already stained beige carpet.

I've never seen such nastiness.

There are dirty dishes and half-empty glasses left up on the dresser.

And—and—and...one window has a—what I assume used to be white—bed sheet nailed over it, while beige dirty blinds hang from the other window.

Oh. My. God!

The walls are covered in chipped powder blue paint and posters of Tamar Braxton and Keyshia Cole and K. Michelle.

I wince.

But that's not what has me standing here, looking around in disbelief, my eyes practically popping out of their sockets.

No.

There's a naked girl on her knees between some long-legged boy's thighs, her head bobbing up and down in his lap. He's stretched out on the queen-size mattress that's on the floor under one of the windows, the one with the nasty bed sheet hanging from it.

Mouth slightly parted, eyes closed, the guy seems to be enjoying himself.

Omar drops my bags and charges toward them.

The boy's eyes flutter open. "Oh, *sheeeeeeit*!" he snaps,

trying to push the girl off of him. But he's not fast enough. Omar is on her, snatching her up off her knees by the back of her neck.

"Yo, Quita! What the hell you think you doin', yo?!" Omar snaps. He tosses her across the room. "You wildin' for real, yo!"

She doesn't even seem bothered by me standing here. "I'm doin' me," she says, crossing her arms over her large breasts. My eyes bounce from her to Omar to her naked friend to the walls to the windows, then down at the floor.

"Yo, shut ya dumb-azz up," Omar snaps. "Yeah, you doin' you all right. Playin' ya'self like a real bird, for real for real."

The naked boy hops up from the floored mattress, trying to cover himself. Omar scowls at him. "Yo, Money, git yo' clothes on 'n' step 'fore I crack ya jaw." Omar snatches up the boy's clothes and throws them at him. He scurries and catches them, quickly slipping into his underwear. I try not to look. Try not to notice his deflated excitement. But it's hard *not* to see it.

I stare over at a Tamar poster.

But out of the corner of my eye, I still see him. He's stuffing himself into his jeans, before rushing out the room, brushing by me.

Omar glares at the Sha'Quita girl. "Yo, I thought I tol' you to have this effen room cleaned, yo. You knew I was comin' back today."

She sucks her teeth, pulling a white T-shirt on. "Well, I *forgot*," she says nastily. She shoots me a dirty look. "What the hell you lookin' at? And who are you, anyway?"

"I'm—"

"She's ya cousin," Omar answers for me. "Nia."

"*Mmph*. Good for her."

I swallow.

She snatches open a dresser drawer, then pulls out a teeny pair of jean shorts and shimmies them up over her wide naked hips. "I ain't invite her here."

"Well, I did. She's *my* seed..."

Seed?

"And she's *your* family."

She frowns. "She ain't none of my family. She looks like an Oreo. Ole Wonder Bread lookin' azz. And she prolly ain't even ya daughter, anyway. Who pops up after all these years tryna claim someone as they daddy?"

Blank stare.

I can't believe she is standing here saying all this as if I'm here to claim some long-lost fortune. I keep from rolling my eyes at the absurdity of what I'm hearing.

"You just gettin' outta prison," she continues, "an' all of sudden you somebody's daddy. *Mmph.* Yeah, okay. Let me know how it all works out for you."

"Yo, Quita, I'm warnin' you, yo. Watch ya'self."

"I'm just sayin'. Where they doin' that at?"

I blink.

Omar grits his teeth. "Word is bond, Quita. Ya mouth too slick, yo. Don't have me yoke you up."

She flicks him a dismissive wave. "Boy, bye. Put ya hands on me if you want 'n' I'ma call ya parole officer."

"Yo, you sound stupid as hell, li'l girl. I ain't on parole."

"Oh. Well, then don't shoot the messenger. I'm just sayin'."

I eye Omar.

His nose flares.

He shakes his head. "I'm tellin' you, yo. Keep talkin' slick, a'ight."

"It's my mouth," she argues. "I can say whatever I want. It's called freedom of speech."

Omar sighs. He sees there's no winning with her. "Whatever, man. Just don't let me find out you comin' at my daughter crazy, or I'ma bust yo head open, you know what I'm sayin'."

"Yeah, whatever. Just make sure"—she gives me an evil eye—"your *so-called* daughter stays the hell outta my stuff."

And this is how hell begins...

Me, standing in the middle of a filthy, funky room, staring into the snarling face of a girl named *Sha'Quita.*

31

"Umm, Quita, where—"

"*Bish*," she snaps nastily, after Omar leaves us alone. And all I keep wondering is why he closed the door, leaving me up in here with her and this rancid stench. "Don't call me *that*. It's *Shaaaa'Quiiiita* to you. And I don't care who Omar says you are. You ain't *sheeeiiit* to me."

I blink.

"Oh, apologies," I say meekly. "I meant no harm."

Lips twisted slightly, she stares me down. "Well, I do. So let's get a few things straight, right now. You stay"—she points over at the twin bed—"over there on ya side of *my* room. I ain't ya friend. And I ain't tryna be ya friend. Stay outta my things. Don't touch my stereo. And don't speak unless I speak to you first."

My mouth opens, but no words form to come out.

This girl acts like *I* invited myself here.

Like being here was on my bucket list of things to do, places to see.

"Okay," I say softly. I swallow. "But I'm not looking for any problems."

"Well, don't start any 'n' there won't be none."

"Fair enough," I say, exasperated. "Anything else."

She narrows her eyes at me. "Yeah, when my boo comes

around, don't even think about tryna be up in his face. He ain't gonna be checkin' for you like that. So don't play ya'self. 'Cause if you even bat a lash wrong, I'ma beat ya face in."

I recoil.

My mind quickly starts to tick off a list of adjectives to describe her.

Rude.

Aggressive.

Obnoxious.

Miserable.

Hateful.

Bully . . .

"No worries," I assure her. "I'm not here for boys."

She snorts. "*Mmph*. Whatever. Secondly, my boo ain't no *boy*, girl. He's a grown-azz man. Get it right, Cali Girl."

"My name is Nia. Not Cali Girl," I correct, keeping my voice even.

If looks could kill, I'd be dead.

In my mind's eye, I see her pulling out a knife and pressing it up to my neck, nicking the skin, drawing blood.

I swallow the knot forming in the back of my throat.

"*Mmph*. Girl, bye."

She starts snatching open dresser drawers as if she's looking for something, then slamming them shut. I feel myself getting woozy from the smell and the heat. Yet she's fluttering around here like she's in heaven.

She shoots me a nasty scowl. "So you just gonna stand there, holdin' ya bags like you scared to put them down?"

Um. Yes. That's exactly what's going on here. "No. I was trying to ask you what I should do with them."

She frowns. "Do I look like a dang bellhop to *you*? Geesh. You're dumber than you look."

I cringe.

This fight is not yours, Nia, I hear in my head.

"I'm not sure where to put them." Where the roaches won't get into them.

"Girl, bye. You holdin' them bags like somebody gonna jack you for ya junk. Ain't nobody gonna steal that late mess you got up in them bags." She looks me up and down. "You don't have nothin' I want, boo-boo. So you might as well toss them bags down on the bed, or put 'em on the side of—"

"Ooooh, heeeeeeey," someone says, bursting into the room. The first thing (no, no: the first *two* things) I notice when she steps into the room is that she's braless under her red tank top. And that she reeks of something strong, almost like a skunk smell. I try to keep from frowning.

The Quita girl sucks her teeth. "Dang, Kee-Kee! Why can't you knock? You so effen rude!"

They must be sisters, I think.

They both have the same mahogany-colored skin tone and round brown eyes with long, fake lashes.

She scowls. "Quita, you better watch ya mouf 'fore I put my fist in it. You don't pay no bills up in here."

The Quita girl rolls her eyes hard. "And neither do *you*, boo-boo."

"Well, my EBT keeps you fed; doesn't it? And I don't hear you complainin' when I'm lettin' you cash in so you can get ya knotty, bald-headed-azz head did, do I? So as long as I'm feedin' 'n' financin' you"—she stomps her foot—"don't do me, ho."

The two of them go back and forth, calling each other all types of filthy names, and I'm standing here watching it unfold—shocked, frightened, and almost amazed at the level of disrespect, my eyes bouncing back and forth like two tennis balls.

I ease back some.

Quita—I mean, Sha'Quita—opens her mouth to say something else, but the words never make it past her lips before the Kee-Kee lady leaps into the air—well, that's what it looks like from here—and smacks Quita, uh, Sha'Quita down to the floor, then stands over her and punches her.

In the head.

In the face.

Ohmygod. She's practically foaming out the mouth as she fights Sha'Quita.

I almost feel bad for her.

Almost.

"I keep tellin' you 'bout ya slick mouth. You like it when I bust you in it, don't you, Quita, huh, *bish*?"

Whap!

Whap!

Sha'Quita yells and screams for her to get off of her. Everything is happening so fast, my head is almost spinning from it all.

"Yo, what *dafuq*?!" Omar yells, racing into the room. "Kee-Kee, what the hell, yo?" He tries to pull her off of the Sha'Quita girl, but she refuses to let go. She has her by the hair, wildly punching her. Sha'Quita is kicking and screaming.

I don't know if I should call the police or run for my life.

It's like watching a horrible train wreck.

I stay planted, watching the brawl.

Omar is finally able to pry her hands out of Sha'Quita's hair, snatching her up in the air. "No, get off me, *Oh*. I'ma kill her disrespectful azz!"

"Chill, Kee, damn, yo."

Sha'Quita is still down on the floor, holding her head and face, crying. Clumps of weave are all over the floor. "I hate you!"

"Well, I hate you, too! So, go 'head, boo! Keep runnin' ya mouth 'n' I'ma snatch out the resta ya scalp!"

Omar looks over at me and shakes his head. "Yo, so I guess you've met ya aunt Kee-Kee."

32

I'm exhausted.
I couldn't sleep last night.
I spent most of the night up.
Scared to close my eyes.
See. I, um...
Last night I experienced the most horrific sighting. In the middle of the night I climbed out of bed, thirsty. So I tiptoed down the darkened hallway, my eyes adjusting to the pitch-blackness, and felt along the kitchen wall for a light switch.
I cut the kitchen light on.
And *shrieked* in horror.
There were *hundreds* and *hundreds* of different size bugs covering the walls, scattering all over the place. They were all over the floor, the cabinets; covered the stovetop, and crawled all over the stack of dirty dishes piling out of the sink. They even scurried out of the overflowing trash can.
They were everywhere.
The whole kitchen was under attack.
Invaded by nasty bugs.
I back-stepped out of the kitchen, then backed into some-one standing in back of me.
I jumped.

It was Omar.

"My bad. I heard somethin'." He scratched himself.

I was too distraught to even care. "W-what are *all* those bugs? They're *every*where."

Omar looked at me, bemusement dancing in his eyes. "You really don't know?"

My skin itched, and I struggled not to scratch. "No. I don't."

He shook his head, giving me a sympathetic look. "They're roaches," he said.

My eyes widened. Oh, God. "Roaches as in *cock*roaches?"

For a second, I thought I saw a mixture of sympathy and amusement swimming in his pupils. He stifled a chuckle. "Yeah."

I shook my head, trying to absorb all of this. "H-how does anyone live like this?"

His brow rose. And I immediately kicked myself for how the question came out, and I found myself scrambling with an apology, trying to clean it up.

He rubbed his eyes, then yawned. "You good. Sometimes you gotta do what you can to adapt; eventually, you get used to it, feel me?"

I didn't. I stood there unable to wrap my mind around ever adapting to what I'd seen. It was horrifying. The rest of the night I sat up in bed, terrified of falling asleep.

When I finally did doze off—after fighting it for a long as I could—it was nearly daybreak.

However, I was rudely awakened, deliriously, to the sound of pots and pans clanking, and cabinet doors slamming.

Someone was in that nasty kitchen, making lots of ruckus.

I rubbed my eyes, sweeping my gaze around the room to catch my bearings.

Sadly, I was still not home.

I was still here, in this nastiness.

I pulled out my cell phone, and glanced at the time.

It was seven a.m.

So, basically, I'd slept for only two hours.

And now it's a little after eleven in the morning.

I'm finally in the shower.

But I couldn't actually get in it until after I scrubbed and bleached down the walls and the inside of the tub.

I've never seen such filthiness before.

Until now.

So here I am.

With my Speedo water shoes on, standing under the spigot, warm water spraying down on me, scrubbing my skin with my loofah sponge and crying.

The running water muffles my sobs.

It seems like the only place in this cramped apartment where I might be able to have a moment and cry in peace. It's the only place where it seems I don't have to worry about prying eyes or ridicule or judgment. So it's where I've allowed myself to get lost under the heavy stream of water, releasing a river of tears.

I don't know how long I've been crying, but when I am done shedding my last tear, my skin is practically shriveled.

I shut off the water.

Reach to pull back the shower curtain.

Then stop.

There's a noise.

Panicked, I hold my breath.

Listen.

I'm too afraid to peek out to see.

Then there's a grunt.

My eyes widen.

Ohmygod!

What is that?

There's another grunt.

And then the bathroom fills with a pungent stench that almost knocks me over.

Someone else is in here.

I cough and gag, then ask, "Who's in here?" And how did you get in here?

I'm almost afraid to know.

Please, God, don't let it be Omar.

"Who do you think it is," the voice on other side of the shower curtain says nastily.

Ohmygod!

No!

Sha'Quita.

"W-what are you doing in here? Don't you see I'm in here using the shower?" I cover myself with my arms as if she can see me through the curtain.

"Bisssh, *and?*"

Then as if to punctuate her point, she passes gas.

The sound echoes in the ceramic bowl.

Loud and obnoxious, like her.

Ugh!

Oh, God!

She smells awful.

"You think I'm 'posed to hold this ish in? Girl, bye. You was takin' mad long. And I had'a go." She grunts again. "I knocked twice"—another grunt—"and you ain't open ya mouth, so I pried open the door."

She belligerently passes more gas.

And I swoon from the fumes.

She smells rancid.

And now I'm trapped inside this tiny makeshift gas chamber.

Waiting to die a slow death by inhalation.

I cover my nose with my washcloth, gagging.

"Ohmygod!"

"*Trick*, shut ya meat hole. You act like you ain't ever fart before. Or take a dump." She grunts again, then laughs. "Oh, wait. I forgot. You uppity, bougie hoes don't fart. You *poot*. You don't shit. You go number *two*. *Bisssh*, boo."

"This is so freaking gross, Sha'Quita!" I exclaim, struggling to hold my breath.

"Then get out," she snaps.

I can't. "Well, can you at least hand me my towel?" I asked, relieved that I'd packed my own bath towels and facecloths.

She sucks her teeth. "Uh, no. If you want it, get it yaself. My name ain't Hazel. And I ain't ya maid."

The small space fills with the stench of fresh poop.

"Can you at least courtesy flush? *Please*?" The request comes out muffled.

"Courtesy flush?" She grunts again. "Uh. Where they doin' that? We ain't doin' no double-flushin' up in here. You don't like the smell, hold ya breath."

She passes more gas.

And my knees buckle.

Two days later, Omar had this lady Miss Peaches—um, well, he introduced her as his *friend*, but she kept acting like she was his girlfriend or something—take us to Walmart and CVS.

I'd never set foot inside a Walmart my entire life until then.

What an experience.

That's all I can say.

Anyway, I decided if I had to stay in this apartment for however long, then I needed some things to make my stay halfway bearable.

If bearable is even remotely possible.

But, oh well. I digress.

At CVS, I bought rubber gloves and a box of surgical masks. Then, at Walmart I picked out a portable air conditioner for the window and six cans of roach spray, along with two flashlights—one for under my pillow at night, and the other for my book bag—and three boxes of Combat Gel Baits and Bait Strips.

Oh, and a vacuum cleaner.

Sweeping rugs with a broom is so not it.

But vacuuming up roaches is.

Thank goodness for Google.

I had to search online the best way to kill those nasty little critters.

Miss Peaches kind of looked at me with amusement, while Omar pulled out his money and paid for my supplies. Not that I needed him to. I have my own money. Still, it was generous of him to do so.

I think he might have felt bad for me.

Maybe even a little embarrassed.

But, um, obviously, not enough to put me up in a hotel.

Miss Peaches chuckled, and said, "Good luck, sweetie. Them stubborn-ass roaches ain't goin' nowhere."

I shrugged it off.

I know I can't kill them all. But my mind is—*and* was—set on decreasing as many as I possibly can for the time I'm here. Once I'm gone, they can breed and multiply and eat through the walls if they want.

What do I care?

But right now, I'm on a mission.

So, here I am—with Omar, be clear—in Sha'Quita's depressingly dirty bedroom, with gloves on and a face mask strapped to my face, armed with a can of Raid, spraying like a wild banshee, while Omar is pulling out her furniture and vacuuming up dust and dead roaches.

I guess this is our bonding time.

Anyway.

I'm frantically spraying all around the baseboards, near my bed in particular. Behind and around Sha'Quita's bed—although, I confess, I thought to leave her side untouched since she seems to have some sort of allegiance to insects and bugs.

All I keep wondering is, is this apartment, this bedroom the definition of a trap house?

"Damn, she's nasty, yo," Omar says, yelling over the roar and crunch of the vacuum cleaner.

I keep spraying. Never opening my mouth, but I'm wondering why he's pretending to be surprised at how filthy she is.

Oh, wait.

He's been locked up forever.

Whatever. It's in that girl's genes—nastiness, obviously.

Heck, everyone here seems comfortable living in squalor, but I'm not.

All I keep thinking is, Sha'Quita is going to lose her mind when she walks in and sees that I've killed off most of her pets.

I almost want to laugh.

I cut my eyes over at Omar. He's wiping sweat from his face with a washcloth he carries in his back pocket. I go back to the task of spraying while he pulls out the long dresser.

"Aye, yo, what *dafawwk*, man!" he snaps.

I look over and he's holding up two pair of dirty panties Sha'Quita had in back of the dresser. "This don't make no goddamn sense for a female to be this effen nasty, yo."

I shrug, reminding myself that this is not my problem.

Then I pray for God to deliver me from this hell.

33

Welllll...
I'm still in hell.

And I'm *still* petrified.

And God *still* has yet to answer any of my prayers.

The most important of them all—for *right* now: getting me the heck out of here!

ASAP!

I've been here less than a week. And I'm wishing on every twinkling star to make like Dorothy in *The Wizard of Oz*, and find my way back home.

Somewhere over these nasty brick buildings and polluted skies.

I want to go home.

Now.

This was all a mistake. I should have never let Aunt Terri or Omar to convince me to come out here.

I could have refused.

I should have refused.

But I didn't.

And now I feel like I've been locked in a closet with narrow walls and the smell of mothballs—not that I've ever been locked in one, but I imagine this is what it might be like—and I'm watching my entire life unfold through a tiny keyhole.

I feel boxed in.

And I'm scared.

That I'll never make it out of here, out of this apartment, this city, this state, in one piece. I pull out my cell and call Aunt Terri. The phone rings, and she answers on the third ring.

"Hello?"

"Hi, Aunt Terri. It's me. Nia."

"Oh, hey, Nia. How's New Jersey?"

"Horrible," I whisper into the phone. "They have these nasty bugs that seem to come out late at night and take over the whole apartment; especially the kitchen." I catch my breath, and swallow. "And I have to share a room with this really nasty girl. All she does is snarl and stare at me. No matter how nice I try to be to her, she just insists on being the opposite. Aunt Terri..." I pause, fighting back tears. "You have to get me out of here. Now. I can't do this. I—"

I stop midsentence, realizing that Aunt Terri hasn't said. Not. One. Word.

"Hello? Aunt Terri?"

There's a long silence on the other end.

Finally she speaks. "Well, Nia. What's the problem...?"

I shake my head in disbelief, staring at the screen.

Oh, the problem is you haven't heard a word I've said.

My lips quiver. I am on the verge of tears. "Aunt T-terri," I mutter. "I don't like it here."

"You just got there, Nia. You haven't even given it a chance."

"I don't want to. I want to go home."

"Nia. You don't have a home," she says curtly.

Her words stab me in the chest, and I feel myself slowly bleeding out.

A sob gets stuck in the back of my throat. "I-I-I meant I want to come to you. In Georgia, Aunt Terri."

"And you will, Nia; just not now. You agreed to go out there for a few weeks to get to know your biological father and his family..."

"Your biological father..."

I cringe.

"...and I expect you to hold up to your end of the deal until this matter with your father's estate is cleared up."

Tears flood my eyes. "I just want to go home, Aunt Terri. I don't care where; just not here." I burst into tears. "I miss my daddy. And I'm so alone here. *These* people are crazy," I say into the phone, sobbing. "They curse and smoke, and fight each other. I can't stay here. *Please,* Aunt Terri. I beg of you..."

"Listen, Nia," she says sternly. "You need to pull yourself together. I know you miss your father, and you're still grieving. But all that crying isn't going to do anything but make you sick. Not one shed tear is ever going to bring him back. So..."

Basically. Get over it.

"...you need to toughen up, Nia. Stop focusing on all the negatives, and figure out a way to make it work. God's given you a new family. And a second chance."

"B-b-but I don't want a *new* family or a *second* chance. I want to get out of here. Why are you tossing me away like this? What did I ever do to you, Aunt Terri, huh?"

"Nia. Stop this. You haven't done anything. Like I already explained. There are some things that need to be handled *first*, before you can come here."

"W-w-w-will you send for me in t-t-three w-w-weeks like y-you p-p-promised?"

She sighs heavily into the phone. "We'll see. Right now, everything is up in the air."

Uh?

Everything like what?

"P-please, Aunt Terri. *P-please,*" I beg, my body shaking uncontrollably.

"I have to go, Nia," she says brusquely. "I'll call you in a few days. Okay?"

I sniffle. Then I reach for a wad of tissue and blow my nose. "Ohh. K-kay."

"Now pull yourself together, before you make yourself sick," she says.

"B-b-but I'm already s-sick," I mutter just as she disconnects the call.

I hang up with Aunt Terri, knowing for certain—now more than ever—my dubious fate.

I'm no longer trapped in a closet.

I'm trapped in a box.

Being pushed out to sea.

And a rogue wave washes over me.

34

*I never knew the true meaning of
"That Ho Over There"
aka
THOT
Until the day I met...*

"Ooh, don't even try it," I hear someone say. "I know you hear me talkin' to you."

Pen poised over the page, my eyes flutter up from my journal.

It's Quita.

Excuse me, Sha'Quita.

Standing here, neck tilted, hand on hip.

She hasn't spoken to me in three days. Now all of a sudden she wants to speak.

A big pink bubble swells out from between her glossed lips.

"Hunh?"

She rolls her eyes.

Pops her bubble.

"I *saaaaaid*, why you sittin' out here on the steps like you lost?"

Because I am.

She snaps her gum between her teeth.

Click-clack.

I take her in.

Allow my gaze to soak in as much of her as I can stand.

Clad in a pink halter top with the words Boss B*TCH stretched across her breasts in glittery silver lettering, with a pair of white skimpy short-shorts, her hips stretching the material to maximum capacity—and a pair of strappy sandals.

Her hair, I mean weave, is dyed pink. Hot pink. And it sweeps down past her waist.

She slings it over her shoulder.

Forgive me for saying this, but she looks circus ready.

No, no, like she's about to audition for a low-budget rap/porn video.

What a sight.

I blink away the image of her wearing a big pink nose juggling four bowling pins, while booty-popping to a Lil Boosie rap song.

"I'm writing," I say, shielding my eyes from the blaring sun with a hand.

"*Mmph.* Don't you have anything better to do?"

Um, apparently not. "I like writing."

She twists her lips. "Seems like a waste, but whatever, boo-boo. Do you."

I force a smile.

Blink my eyes several times, hoping she'd disappear; that I am hallucinating.

"What you be writin' about in that thing, anyway?"

Oh, well. So much for wishful thinking.

I shrug. "Stuff."

She smacks her lips together. "Stuff like *what*? 'Cause I know you ain't writin' no juicy tales up in that diary-thing, anyway."

Click-clack.

Click-clack.

"It's a journal," I correct, closing it.

She blows another bubble, lets it pop against her shiny lips when she blows it too big, then sucks the gum back into her mouth.

She narrows her eyes and grunts. "*Mmph.* Same difference."

I think to say something more, but decide against it. I don't have the energy, or the desire, to explain to her the difference. Because, contrary to popular belief, there is a difference. But I don't think she'd get it even if I explained it a hundred different ways, in several languages, that diary writing and journaling are very different. Period.

"Actually, it's not," I offer clumsily, clutching it to my chest.

She snorts. "Oh, so you a Miss Know-it-all now, huh?"

Click-clack.

Click-clack.

No. You are. "Not at all. I was simply stating a fact."

"No, hon, what you doin' is tryna come for me, when I didn't call for you. But I'ma let it slide."

I force a tight-lipped smile.

But, as I'm looking at her, I'm slowly starting to think— no, believe—that she might have been dropped on her head as a baby.

Forgive me.

I know that's not nice.

Still...

I wish she'd go away.

I blink a few more times.

No such luck.

She's still standing here.

I take a deep breath, then glance down the street. There's a group of young girls who look much younger than me, despite their overdeveloped bodies, jumping rope.

And at this very second, I wish I could run over and join in.

It is hot out.

Ninety-four degrees.

And the humidity makes it worse.

It's almost stifling.

But those girls are jumping rope and laughing and having fun, as if there's a summer breeze blowing, keeping them cool, without a care in the world.

And here I am.

Full of trepidation.

Full of worry.

Staring at this Sha'Quita girl who is so full of—

"So, you just gonna sit out here *alllllll* day, Cali Girl?"

I swallow.

Well, it beats sitting up in that nasty apartment alllllll day. I look at her. "Please don't call me that. My name is Nia." I give her a look that says, *Should I spell it for you?*

Her eyes pop open all dramatic and whatnot. "Bye, Felicia. I'll call you what I want."

Felicia?

My name is Nia!

"It's Nia. My name. Is. Nia. How would you like it if someone started calling you Shaniqua?"

She gives me a blank look.

And pops her bubblegum, hard.

Click-clack.

Click-clack.

Clickety-click-clack.

"Sweetie, I don't care what some basic broad calls me. I'm *still* that *bish*."

I cringe inwardly.

I don't know why girls think it's cute or cool to refer to themselves or each other as the *B*-word. I'll never understand the logic in it.

Of course you won't.

It's coming from a bunch of wayward girls with illogical thinking.

"Well, I do care," I say unapologetically.

She blows another bubble, then pops it. "Well, I guess you'll have to get over it, boo-boo."

There's simply no winning with this girl.

Ignorance is at an all-time high.

It's so sad.

I give her a pitiful stare. There are no words for her.

Click-clack.

Click-clack.

Clickety-click-clack.

Her jaws chomp a mile a minute on that poor piece of gum.

I reopen my journal and glance down at the page where I'd left off, then look up at Sha'Quita before finishing the line in my entry.

this ho here
that ho over there.
No.
This ho right here...

As I hold my pen over the page to write another line, Sha'Quita grunts. "*Mmph*. Annnnyway. Are you gonna tell me what you be writin' about or *nah*?"

Right now about you, but that's really none of your business. "Mostly poems," I say, deciding to be cordial, placing the cap on my pen and closing the book again. It's obvious she doesn't plan on going anywhere anytime soon.

I take a deep breath.

"*Poems?*"

"Yeah."

She laughs. "Ooh, let me find out you tryna be the next Harriet Tubman, tryna free ya'self from ya demons."

Blank stare.

"Or the next Erykah Badu."

Say what?

I give her a confused look.

She sucks her teeth. "Ohmygod, Cali Girl! Please don't tell me *you* don't even know who Eryka Badu is. She's the poet who sings all of her poetry, like Floetry does. You do *know* who they are, right?" She raises a brow and waits for my response.

Um. Okay.

Keep waiting.

Doesn't she know Erykah Badu is a songwriter and neo-soul singer, *not* a poet?

Well, apparently not.

Heck, she probably doesn't even know who Harriet Tubman is.

I leave her stuck in her ignorance.

"*Mmph*. No wonder you stay draggin' 'round that raggedy backpack. You one of them Bohemian wannabes. You probably got a hairy bush, too."

I frown.

How vulgar.

I clutch my journal to my chest, wondering if she even knows how to spell *Bohemian*. I think to ask, but there's no way to without it escalating.

I don't need the added drama.

Sweat rolls down the center of my back. And all I can think about it is how badly I want to be in my backyard under a palm tree, sipping one of my favorite lattes.

"So what are your plans for the rest of the day?" I decide to ask; not that I care.

Click-clack.

Click-clack.

She pats the top of her head, her jaws working overtime, chomping away. "Who knows, the day is still young. Me 'n' my girls might go out to the park 'n' smoke a li'l later. Why, you tryna hang?"

Wait.

Did she just *ask* me if *I* want to go somewhere with her?

It must be bad dope—or whatever it is she smokes—that has her asking *me* to go anywhere with *her.*

I shift my body on the step, thankful I'm sitting on one of Daddy's UCLA sweatshirts.

"No. That's okay."

"*Mmph*. Fine with me. I ain't really want you to come, anyway."

Like I care.

I shrug, looking back up the street at the girls jumping rope. They're still going at it. There are now a few boys on bikes intently watching each girl alternate jumping in and out of the rope. I imagine their eyeballs bouncing up and down like mini basketballs as they eye each girl's bouncy boobs and jiggling butts.

One of the boys hops off his bike and walks over toward a fire hydrant, holding something in his hand. From here, it looks like some kind of tool. But I can't be sure.

He calls another one of the boys over, and—

"So why you be actin' all uppity?"

I blink. "Excuse me? *Uppity?*"

"Yeah, like you better than somebody."

I'm offended.

But I know she's entitled to her opinion.

Still, being called *uppity* feels like a slap in the face.

"I'm not uppity. And I definitely don't think I'm better than anyone."

"*Mmph*. I can't tell. You walk 'round here wit' ya head all up in the air, like you some Queen of Sheba..."

I almost want to laugh at her absurdity. She says that as if being referred to as the Queen of Sheba is supposed to be an insult. Sheba was the seeker of truth and wisdom, something we all should strive for. And she was a woman of great beauty, wealth, and power.

I sigh, wondering if she knows exactly who the Queen of Sheba really was.

I reckon not.

Click-clack.

Clickety-click-click.

She grunts. "*Mmph*. Heifers like you kill me. Kee-Kee told me to let it ride, but I ain't the one for bein' phony; I'm real wit' mine."

Now I feel the need to defend myself. "Well, I'm sorry you feel that way. But that's not who I am. I accept people for who they are." I just don't have to deal with them.

"Girl, bye. Lies. You stay wit' ya nose all twisted up, like we beneath you. Don't think I don't peep it. Just like when you saw those few little roaches 'n' started actin' all scary 'n' ish, runnin' out 'n' buyin' roach spray like they were tryna attack you. Girl, bye. Them roaches weren't even thinkin' about you."

Sweat starts to line the edges of my forehead. I wipe my forehead with the back of my hand.

It's hot out here.

"I apologize if I made you feel some kind of way," I say sincerely. "I was caught off guard, that's all. And..."

They freaked me out.

"And you a stuck-up *bish*. But that's beside the point. So what if we got a few roaches here 'n' there. They ain't gonna kill you."

Here and there?

Is she kidding me?

That apartment is infested with them.

She rolls her eyes, popping her gum. "You be actin' like you ain't ever see a damn roach before."

Well, I hadn't.

Not until I came here.

I keep that to myself, though.

I glance down the street again. Those boys have turned

the fire hydrant on. And now water is shooting out all over the place, flooding the street. One of the boys grabs one of the girls and scoops her up in his arms as he runs over toward the gushing water with her kicking and screaming and laughing as he gets her soaked.

Everyone starts laughing.

"Dumb hoes," I hear Sha'Quita mutter. "Who got time gettin' they weaves wet. I wish a *nucca* would."

Click-clack.

Click-clack.

Clickety-click-clack.

I stare at her.

Thinking, I wish he would, too.

35

A few days later, I'm riding in the backseat of an Acura with Omar. He's in the front passenger seat. I'm sitting directly behind him. And his friend with the long braids, Born Allah Understanding, or Born Understanding-something-or-another (I don't know, it's all confusing to me. Grown men calling themselves God. But okay!) is driving, his seat practically lying into the backseat.

I wonder how he can even see the road behind the steering wheel when he looks like he's ready for bed.

But okay. Not my business.

Still, I'm praying for safe delivery to wherever we might be going. My right hand grips the seat belt strapped over my chest, and I squeeze for dear life as he drives like a maniac. Every so often I lean slightly over to eye the speedometer.

He's going ninety!

Isn't this considered reckless endangerment?

Doesn't he know he's carrying precious cargo?

Me!

Um. Apparently not!

And Omar doesn't seem the least bit concerned by this Born guy's aggressive driving. The only thing Omar's been good about is not letting him smoke.

"Nah, God. Not wit' my seed in the whip," I overheard Omar saying when he'd put a blunt-thingy to his darkened lips and was getting ready to light it.

The car's stereo is blasting so loud that I can actually feel my eardrums vibrating from the treble. I fear they'll burst open by the time we get to wherever it is we're going, and I'll end up deaf. The bass of the music has my body literally shaking. I'm waiting to start convulsing any second now.

I bite into the side of my lip, preparing myself for a full-blown seizure.

Every so often, this Born guy eases up in his seat and I catch him stealing glances at me through his rearview mirror. At one point, I think he winks at me.

But I look away. I can't be for certain.

Heck, I'm not sure of much of anything these days.

Everything still feels so surreal.

One minute I am in California with Daddy.

The next minute he's being buried.

Then I'm in New Jersey—or *Jerzee*, as they call it—staying with a man trying to be *my* dad.

I am still so very sick from it all.

I stare out the window watching the world fly by as we zip by all the other cars on the freeway—at least that's what I think we're on. A freeway.

I lean up in my seat and tap Omar on the shoulder. He cranes his neck to look back at me. "Yo, what's good, baby girl?" he says over the music.

I yell over the music. "What's the name of this highway we're driving on?"

"The Turnpike," he says.

Oh.

I settle back in my seat, then catch this Born man gazing at me through his rearview mirror. I frown, shifting my eyes back out the window again. Suddenly, we come to a stop and wait, and then inch forward at a snail's pace. There's an accident over on the other side of the divider, in the opposite direction on the turnpike. A tractor-trailer has flipped over and caught fire. And there's lots of traffic and thick, dark smoke. And flames.

"Oh, *sheeeeit*, God," the Born man says, turning the volume down on the stereo and tapping Omar on the arm. "Check this out." He points in the direction of the accident.

"Oh, *sheeeeeit*," Omar exclaims, sitting up in his seat and letting his window down. He sticks his phone out of the window and starts taking pictures. "Yo, this some wild ish," he says. "I'ma toss this up on the Gram."

I roll my eyes up in the back of my head as the volume on the stereo raises back to an unbearable level to the sound of some gangster rap song.

My ears bleed.

My head aches.

Omar and his *God* friend bob their heads to the indecipherable gibberish.

And all I want to do is scream.

Twenty minutes and six-god-awful songs later, we finally arrive at our destination.

A park.

Mr. Born-something parks his car. As soon as we open our doors and spill out of the car, the mouthwatering smell hits me.

It's a barbecue.

With lots and lots of cars, and shirtless-bodied men and half-dressed women with tattoos and piercings wearing lots of jewelry. And lots and lots of weaves.

There are clouds of smoke everywhere.

And not just from the grills.

Seems like everyone's smoking something.

Drinking something.

Or smoking *and* drinking something.

Most of the females here—young and old—look like they're

vying for a spot on a rap video, or some sleazy amateur porn shoot.

Why in the heck would Omar bring me here?

"You a'ight?" he wants to know, looping an arm over my shoulder.

I feel myself shrinking in his embrace, nodding. "I'm okay." But I'm not.

"Cool, cool. I wanna show you off to all my peoples," he says, smiling.

Oh, happy day!

But I don't tell him of my dismay. I simply force a smile. It's the best I can offer him.

"We gonna chill here wit' some'a my peeps for a minute, then roll out. But if any of these mofos come at you crazy, you let me know; a'ight?"

My eyes widen. *Crazy* how?

My anxiety-meter quickly rises.

I am so out of my element, and here he is telling me to let him know if anyone comes at me *crazy*.

Why would he bring me around a bunch of potential crazies?

Because he's half crazy himself!

"Yo, peace to the Gods," Omar calls out, arms spread out in the air, to a group of guys—young and old, standing in a circle passing one of those nasty smelling blunt-thingies around—as we walk up to them.

For some reason, I'm suddenly panic-stricken.

"Oh, *sheeeeiiiit*," they say in unison.

"When you get home, *nucca*?" they want to know.

"Yo, I see you still got that big-azz boulder head," someone says.

Laughter.

And then there's lots of one-armed hugging and back-slapping and hand-dapping.

I step back, feeling so out of place.

"Yo, baby, what's good? You like snakes?"

Huh?

I look up into the eyes of a tall, brown-skinned guy with a head full of thick wavy hair.

He's grinning at me, and I'm looking at him wondering why he's asking me if I like snakes?

Is he about to pull one out?

My stomach drops down to my feet as I rapidly shake my head. "No. Snakes scare me."

A short, stocky guy with a thick neck snickers.

And I don't see what's so funny about my fear of snakes.

Thick Waves takes a sip of his bottled beer, then says, "Baby, you ain't gotta be scared. My anaconda won't bite. Let me 'n' my mans take you into the woods 'n' show you a great time enjoyin' ya body with it."

I blink.

Ohmygod!

He's talking about *that* kind of snake.

I crease my eyebrows and politely say, "Um. No, thank you."

"Nah, baby. I'm only effen with you. Who you here with?"

Before I can open my mouth, Omar is at my side and says, "Yo, fam. What's good? That's my seed you tryna holla at. And she's too young for you, *bra*."

Thick Waves holds his hands up in mock surrender. "Oh, my bad, fam. I ain't know."

Omar grits his teeth, eyeing him. "Well, now you do. So step."

"It's all love," Thick Waves says before he walk-staggers over to his next victim, with his muscled-neck shadow in tow.

"Yo, word is bond. I already see I'ma have ta take some-body's face off out here," Omar says, putting his thick arm over my shoulder. He introduces me to everyone in the circle.

"Yo, this is ya seed, fam? Word?"

"True indeed," Omar says proudly.

I am expressionless. But inside I am frowning at all of this *seed* talk.

Anyway, they all look at me smiling and head nodding, then looking over at Omar. Trying to figure out *how* and from *where*, I'm sure.

"Say word?" someone says. "When ya ugly-azz have to time to plant a seed?"

More laughter.

"Yeah, word is bond, fam. She mine."

I brace myself for what's to come next.

Who's her mother?

But Omar keeps it generic. And, despite the questioning eyes, I'm relieved.

"Damn, yo. She fine as *fu*—"

"Yo, fall back, my Gee," Omar warns sternly. "She's off limits."

"How old is she, fam?" someone else in the now semicircle wants to know. I'm not sure which one of these faceless guys asks this since I'm just here physically.

Mentally, I'm sort of checking out from it all, so their faces start becoming blurs to me.

"Not old enough for you, *muhfuggah*," Omar says.

The rest of the group laughs.

Omar doesn't.

"Yo, God," some guy says. "I'm just effen wit' you. You know I ain't no cradle robber. But, uh, check it. As soon as she hit eighteen, I'ma be checkin' for 'er."

"And I'ma be breakin' ya jaw," Omar says. And although he's laughing with him, the look in his eye tells me he's very, very serious.

"I'll holla at you cats later," Omar says. And then his attention is on me. "You hungry?"

Then, as if on cue my stomach growls, and I nod. "Yes."

"A'ight. Let's go see what's poppin' over on the grill."

Someone with really big arms covered in tattoos walks up

and greets Omar, embracing him in a big hug, then steps back.

"Yo, who dis pretty young thing?" he says, practically leering at me with his tongue wagging out of his mouth.

"Nah, *nucca*, fall back," Omar says protectively, pushing the guy backward in the chest. "She's my seed, yo."

"Oh, damn, big homie," he says, seemingly shocked. He looks at me. Narrows his stare, his eyes glinting recognition of some sort. He looks back at Omar. Then points over at me. "Wait. She looks like..." He shakes his head. "Nah. Hol' up." He points at me, then at Omar. "Monica's ya BM?"

BM?

What in the world is a BM?

I don't have time to decipher the acronym since my heart jumps at the sound of hearing my mom's name.

He knows my mother?

"Word is bond," Omar says. "She me 'n' Monica's."

"Girl, c'mere 'n' give me a hug," he says, wrapping his big arms around me. "Ya moms was my heart. Word is bond. I was tryna bag that, but this ugly mofo is all she had eyes for."

Omar laughs. "Yo, don't hate, nucca."

Big Arms frees me from his embrace and eyes me, smiling. "Damn, Monica spit you out lookin' just like her."

I smile nervously. "Thanks."

"Man, I'll get up," Omar says, giving the guy another brotherly handshake and one-armed hug before ushering me off by the elbow.

"How does he know my mom?" I ask as we walk toward the long rows of tables where the food is.

"He was my mans back in the day. He was wit' me the day I met ya moms."

Oh.

"How old was she again?"

"Fourteen," he says. "But she had a body like an eighteen-year-old. E'ery cat from around the way was tryna get at her; word is bond."

"For real? Why?"

"'Cause she wasn't a hood chick," he says, stepping in back of the line. "Ya moms was mad classy."

I take him in.

White tank top. True Religion jeans. White Jordans. Neck draped in gold. A body covered in tattoos.

And still...she fell for a boy/man like *him*.

36

"Heeeeeeeey, boooooo," Sha'Quita says in her annoying singsong voice.

I glance over to see whom she's talking about.

It's a boy.

Figures.

He's tall, real tall.

Maybe like six-four or more.

Lean.

Muscled.

Smooth, dark chocolate skin.

Dreads.

Half-sleeve tattoos on both arms.

He walks up and scoops her in his arms. He's wearing designer jeans, designer T-shirt, designer sneakers, and a NY Nets fitted cap pulled down over his eyes. "Yo, what's good, babe? How you?" He glances over at me and stares. Then he grins crookedly.

I shift in my seat on the hard step.

In the same spot I always sit.

At the bottom of the stairs.

I shift my gaze from his.

The heat index all of sudden seems to rise.

Hotter.

"Ooooh, I'm good now, boo," Sha'Quita coos, brushing up on him. "And I'll be even better when you stop playin' 'n' let me get a taste of that meat juice."

I frown.

He laughs. "Yo, Quita, you wild as *fawwk*, yo."

"Uh-huh. But I'm real, boo."

He steps back, still looking over at me. "Yeah, a'ight, man. You stay talkin' that ish. Yo, who's the li'l cutie over there?"

Sha'Quita sucks her teeth. "Boy, bye. That ain't nobody."

I blink.

How dare she dismiss me, like I'm insignificant!

"Oh, word?" Dark Chocolate says, scanning me with his eyes. "Well, she looks like a whole lotta *something* to me. Yo, what's good, cutie?"

I swallow. "Hi," I say softly, giving him a half wave.

"Yo, you ain't gotta be shy, ma. I don't bite." He grins. "Unless you tryna get bitten."

Sweat starts rolling down the center of my back. I shift my eyes from his. Take in his white Gucci belt, the waistband of his Ralph Lauren underwear; the intricate design of his tattoos; anything except his blazing gaze on me.

What is going on here?

Stop, Nia! Stop!

This is so not like you.

"No, she ain't tryna get bitten, boy," Sha'Quita huffs, grabbing him by the arm, stopping him from walking over toward the steps.

And, unbeknownst to her, freeing me from further uneasiness.

"She ain't even ya flava, boo. She ain't 'bout that life."

What *flavor* is that?

And what life am I *not* supposed to be about, I wonder, eyeing Sha'Quita.

But she's too busy ogling Dark Chocolate to see that I'm staring her down.

I struggle to keep from rolling my eyes at her.

I take a deep breath instead, catching the eyes of Dark Chocolate.

He grins at me. "I can't tell," he says, licking his lips. "Word is bond, yo. From here she lookin' real right. I don't know what *you* talkin' about, man. But give me a day wit' cutie 'n' I'll make her all 'bout this life, straight like that, real talk."

He'll *make* me about what life?

"Boy, bye. Since when you start checkin' for cornball hoes?" I frown. "Cali Girl, ain't ready."

"Oh, you from Cali, huh, cutie?"

My mouth goes instantly dry.

I forcefully swallow back the sawdust that has somehow formed and gathered in the back of my throat.

"Yes."

"Oh, word? What part?"

"Long Beach," I tell him.

Sha'Quita laughs. "Yeah, wit' them uppity white-actin' blacks. Can't you tell she an Oreo?"

I raise a brow. Open my mouth to say something but—

"You wildin' for real, yo," he says. "E'erybody ain't gotta act all hood to be black. You ignorant as hell for lettin' that come outta ya mouth, yo."

"*Nucca*, don't even try'n play me. I ain't ig'nant 'bout nothin'. And I ain't *actin'* hood, boo."

"Nah, yo, you *are* hood."

"*Exaaaaactly.*"

She says this as if being *hood* is something to celebrate and be proud of. Well, um. Then again, I guess it is if you don't have anything else going for yourself.

I sigh, deciding not to entertain her ridiculousness. I'm learning she is always looking for a reason to attack me, so I'm not giving her the satisfaction.

Not today.

And not in front of her *boo*.

Or whoever he is to her.

"*Annnnny*waaaay," she says, swinging her hair. "Where you been at, bae? You been MIA mad long. Oooh, I missed you, boo."

He laughs. "Yo, that's wassup. Yeah, I was ghost for a minute. Mom dukes dragged me down to Georgia for a family reunion."

Georgia?

Did he say *Georgia*?

Yes.

He did.

My ears perk up. Aunt Terri comes to mind, and it dawns on me that she still hasn't gotten back to me. I let it go—for now. I reach into my bag, pulling out my cell, and checking my phone. There's still nothing from her. No missed call. No text message. Nothing.

I drop my phone back in my bag.

Still, I want to jump up and ask him what part of Georgia, but my nerves won't let me.

So I keep my mouth shut.

"Ooh, you were out there wit' them ashy-lipped, dusty-foot, biscuit-heel bumpkins," Sha'Quita says, laughing.

Dark Chocolate shakes his head, laughing. "You stoopid, yo. But yeah, some of 'em were mad dusty; word is bond. But it was all good. We had that loud on deck. So I stayed smoked out the whole time, feel me?"

"Oooh, I know that's right," Sha'Quita says, giving him a high-five. "Put ya lighters up, yasss, yasssss!"

"No doubt. You already know."

"Yasss, boo, yassss. And them Fireballs on ice."

He laughs.

I'm lost as to what it is they're talking about.

Loud?

Fireballs?
I am clueless.
I open my journal and write.

I am in this world, but not of it.
It is foreign to me.
The slang.
The vernacular.
The attitude.
It represents everything I am not.
I am an alien.
Alienated.
Detached.
Thousands of miles away
from my own world, my own life.

"Yo, what's good cutie? What you over there writin'?"
I look up from my journal. Dark Chocolate is staring at me.
"You write songs?"
I shake my head. "No. I—"
"Boy, bye. Cali Girl ain't writin' no songs."
She lets out an annoying cackle, sounding like a
wounded hen.
I don't see the joke.
But she can *hahaha* all she wants.
"Cali Girl over there drawin' imaginary friends." She keeps
laughing.
My frown deepens.
I'm so sick of her.
I take another deep breath.
Remind myself that this girl is . . .
Trifling.
Troublesome.
And I would go on if—

"Man, you dead wrong, yo," her friend says. "That's that dumbness, for real for real."

Sha'Quita punches him. "Boy, I know you ain't even tryna call me dumb."

He just did.

Didn't he?

"You are dumb, yo," he says, plucking her in the head. "Wit' ya bald-headed azz."

"Owww, boy! You play too much. Don't even try it wit' ya pumpkin-head. I know you ain't even tryna come for me wit' that oversized globe up on ya shoulders."

He laughs. "Yo, I know you ain't even talkin' about no-body's head wit' them Nefertiti edges you got. You mad ugly tryna slick them shits down. What you usin', Crisco outta the can?"

I chuckle to myself.

She is always in the mirror with that dirty toothbrush, try-ing to brush down those edges and slicking them down with gel, like she has baby hair.

"Oh, I know you ain't even tryna call my hair nappy, boo-boo."

He laughs. "I just did. Straight-up steel wool, yo. Word is bond, fam. You look like you stepped off the set of *Roots*, lookin' like Kunta in drag."

Oh, noo! Not *Roots*!

Not *Kunta*!

Daddy made me watch *Roots* with him on DVD two sum-mers ago.

And I fell in love with that seventies miniseries.

Even if it is old, I think everyone should watch it, espe-cially kids my age. It was so, so good.

Sha'Quita sucks her teeth. "Ooh, you tried it, boo-boo. Wit' ya ugly-azz moms."

I look at her and hear Shug Avery's voice from *The Color Purple* as she says, "You sho' is ugly..."

Oh, how I love that movie.

Daddy took me to see the play, too.

But the book is *soooo* much better.

It was one of my selected readings in my AP English class last year.

And that part is still one of the funniest lines to me.

I have to bite my tongue to keep from falling out in laughter.

At Sha'Quita.

"Aye, yo. Fall back on the moms jokes, yo. You know you don't want it, man."

"No," she snaps, "you don't want it! You know how I do, boo-boo. It's whatever."

Dark Chocolate laughs. "Oh, so you really wanna play the moms game, huh? A'ight, I got you, yo. Least my moms ain't runnin' 'round lookin' like one of the Hobbits."

"Oh no. Try again, boo-boo. At least my moms doesn't look like a gorilla. Tell her to get up off her knees 'n' stop takin' back shots in alleyways."

"Womp, womp, womp. You mad corny for that, yo. But, uh, when's the last time ya moms changed her drawz, yo? Or brushed that one wooden tooth?"

"'Round the same time yours changed hers," Sha'Quita snaps.

"You a lie. Ya moms smells like spoiled clam juice, yo. She a walkin' fish market. She got flies and gnats all up in that funk-box. That booty rotten, yo. She straight garbage truck trash."

"Oooooh, I hate you!" Sha'Quita screams, laughing. "I wanna fight you, punk!" She tries to hit him, but he blocks her.

I watch the exchange between them, wondering if this is the *boo* she's *warned* me to not look at.

He keeps laughing. "Ya mouth's real slick, yo."

"And it stays wet, too, boo." She licks her lips. "Pound these tonsils 'n' let me show you."

Ohmygod!

Is she implying what I think she is?

Of course she is. It's Sha'Quita.

My frown deepens.

He shakes his head. "Yeah, a'ight. I'll take ya word for it, yo."

"Oh, don't be *scurred* now, boo. This neck work will make you drop to ya knees."

Stuffing my journal in my bag, I stand.

Brush the back of my shorts.

I decide I've heard enough.

"Yo, you rollin' out, cutie?"

I nod. "Yeah."

"Oh, a'ight. Keep it sexy, ma."

Ohmygod!

Did he just call me *sexy*?

No, silly. He said keep it *sexy.*

Same difference, isn't it?

No.

I swallow. "I will. Thanks."

He grins. "No doubt, ma. You need to come down to the courts 'n' chill one day. Tell 'er, Quita."

Sha'Quita grunts. *"Not."*

He gives her a look, shaking his head. "Yo, Quita; word is bond, yo. Stop frontin'. Bring her down to the courts wit' you."

She smacks her lips. "Boy, bye. Don't be tryna plan my life. You know I travel light."

I keep from rolling my eyes.

Well, travel light, then. I don't want to go anywhere with you, anyway. BoomQuita!

I open my mouth to speak, then close it.

It's so not worth it.

I climb the steps up to the apartment building, swinging open the door.

The last thing I hear before the glass door shuts behind me is, "I can't stand that corny *ho*."

37

Let it go, Nia...
I can't let it go.

I won't let it go.

Ho?

She called *me* a *ho*!

I've never in my life been called *that*.

Does that girl not know what a *ho* is?

Clearly not!

I'll show you what a *ho* is.

It's her!

She is the walking definition of it. I'm not the one dressing all skanky-like, and practically advertising for a good time.

She is.

She's a billboard for an easy lay; yet she has the audacity to call me some fricking *ho*. In my head, I hear Daddy telling me to just ignore her. That I shouldn't care what she thinks or says about me.

And I don't.

It's the principle.

I'm not a *ho*.

And I don't wish to be called one, or be referred to as one.

Period.

I'm so dang annoyed.

Very.

And then she tried to humiliate me in front of her, her... *friend*.

What if I would have told him just how nasty she is, and embarrassed her the way she tried to embarrass me?

How she just steps out of her panties and leaves them in the middle of the floor, most times, *stained*.

How she likes sleeping and living in filth.

I bet she wouldn't like it one bit.

Ugh.

Then, again...trashy girls like her don't care.

He probably knows how nasty she is.

And likes it anyway.

I walk over to the window and peer out, narrowing my gaze.

Mmph.

I don't see *her*.

Or him.

She's probably somewhere on the side of a building or in some raggedy bush with her *boo* doing what nasty girls like her do.

Nastiness.

Having had enough of her nasty attitude and her giving me her stinking butt to kiss, I step away from the window, determined to have it out with her the minute I see her, in private, of course.

Daddy always taught me if I have a problem with someone to address him or her on it in private; not to let it fester or escalate. He always said it was best to find a resolution, but if the problem couldn't be fixed, then both parties should figure out a way to coexist with the least amount of stress.

Well, guess what?

Sha'Quita is the problem. This I know.

And there's no fixing her. This I know as well.

Still, I can't keep letting her think it's okay to be mean and nasty to me.

I just can't.

I sit on the edge of my—and I say this *loosely*—bed with my arms folded tight against my chest, staring over at Sha'Quita's nasty side of the room.

Clothes everywhere.

Bed unmade.

Three opened Red Bull cans on her nightstand.

I tear my eyes away from her clutter, leaning my head back on my shoulders and staring up at the ceiling.

Why, Daddy, why?

I find myself counting the cracks in the ceiling, then staring up at the cobweb that's dangling from the broken ceiling fan.

"This is crazy," I huff, pulling my cell from out of my bag.

I call Aunt Terri.

The call goes directly to voice mail.

I call again.

It rings four times, then rolls over to voice mail.

I leave a message. "Hi, Aunt Terri. This is Nia. Hope everything is okay. Can you *please* call me? *Please.* I've left you three messages and several texts but I still haven't heard from you. Please call me back. It's urgent."

I get up from the bed and pace the room with my cell clutched in my fist, willing it to ring. But it doesn't.

I call Aunt Terri again. Then check my voice mail, knowing dang well I haven't missed any calls. But, just in case, I check anyway.

Nothing.

Through my teary-eyed haze, I spot a roach crawling on the carpet. I angrily stomp on it. Stomping and stomping and stomping until I've squashed it so far down into the carpet fibers that it looks like a small dark spot.

I plop back down on the edge of the bed, and wait...

38

I don't see Sha'Quita until almost nine p.m., talking on her cell obnoxiously loud. "Girrrrrl, he was puttin' that work in like he was 'bout to do a bid. Uh-huh. I know, right…"

She opens her closet door, then kicks her heels off into the closet, then shuts the door. She shoots me a look.

"You know I can't really talk like I wanna 'cause Miss Nosy is all up in mine…uh-huh. I don't know when she's leavin' up outta here. Girl, no. It better not be for the whole summer. I already tol' Omar she gotta bounce."

I blink.

"But anyway. I tol' Supreme wit' his fine self that I'm in need of some good-good." She giggles. "Boo, you know I did. You know how I get down, boo. Yassss, bisssh, yassss! I let him know what time it is. Beat this throat up. Oooh, ha-hahahaha. Right, right…you know I take it like a champ. I was built for it…"

I bite the inside of my lip.

She's on the phone a few minutes more before finally ending her call. And when she does, I'm up and ready for her. "Um. Sha'Quita?" I start calmly, since I'm not as pissed as I was earlier. Still, I need to address her. Daddy always told me if you have a problem with someone, address it with him and try to, hopefully, resolve it.

So this is what I'm going to do.

Address it.

"Can I have a word with you?"

"Um, no, you may not," she says, drawing in a sharp breath. "I'm about to watch my show 'n' I'm not 'bout to have you irkin' my soul wit' ya dumbness."

Her soul?

She's joking, right?

This girl's soulless.

I have to bite the inside of my bottom lip to keep from laughing at her.

If I weren't so agitated, I probably *would* laugh in her face. The absurdity alone is hilarious. Instead, I settle for saying, "I won't take up much of your time." I make sure to keep my tone even. Non-combative. "I just want to have a few words with you. It'll only take a couple of minutes."

She twists her lips and gives me a funny look. She stares at me long and hard.

My stare is fixed on hers.

She's not backing down.

And this time, neither am I.

We can play this stare-down game all night. I'm not the one trying to rush off to watch some brainless reality show.

She narrows her eyes, then makes a show of checking her watch, tapping a finger over the face. "You've got two minutes fifty-seven seconds," she says tersely. "And not a second more."

Daddy has always said there's no arguing with stupidity or ignorance.

Sha'Quita is both, so I'm basically damned if I do, damned if I don't.

I decide to take my chances. "Without getting defensive and turning this into a big production," I say, calmly, "I want to know why you feel it's okay for you to talk to me disrespectfully?"

She scoffs. "Girl, bye! If I *disrespected* you, you'd know it.

hon. Okay? What, would you like me to stand here 'n' bleed for you? Trust. I'm real wit' mine."

Real?

Umm. Definition, please.

I take a breath to calm my rattling nerves. "Okay. Let's be *real* then," I say, mindful to keep my tone light. "You don't like me, do you?"

She stares at me. "No."

"Why?"

She tilts her head. "Does it matter?"

No, it doesn't. You add no value to my life. I shake my head. "Not really."

"*Mmph*. Then why you ask?"

"Because I want you to know that I'm okay with you *not* liking me. But what I'm *not* okay with is you trying to bully me. And embarrass me any time you get around one of your friends."

She frowns. "Girl, bye. You effen crazy."

I sigh. It's clear nothing will get resolved.

As Daddy has always said, "Nothing changes if nothing changes."

"I didn't ask to come here, Sha'Quita. And I didn't ask to come disrupt your life."

Hand on hip, she's preparing for confrontation. "And why exactly are you here again? 'Cause the last I heard nobody else wanted you 'n' you had no other place to go."

I choke back a cry.

This girl is heartless!

Unshed tears burn the back of my eyes and make my forehead ache.

"I'm h-here because *my* father died." A lump catches in my throat.

She shrugs. "Well, I don't have one of them, so can't relate."

I blink.

She tilts her head, eyeing me. "What, what you want? A hug? A biscuit?"

I feel my face growing hot. I take a deep breath, willing my tears back. "No, Sha'Quita. I don't want anything from you."

She huffs. "Well, good. 'Cause I ain't got nothin' for you." She steps out of her teenie-weenie shorts. Then removes her shirt. Then unsnaps her bra. "All you are is a sympathy case, boo-boo," she says as she's walking over to the air conditioner, shutting it off. She turns to me. "So if you lookin' for a Hallmark card, don't. I ain't handin' out no pity."

"I'm not looking for your *pity*, Sha'Quita. And I'm not *asking* you to feel sorry for me. I'm doing a good job of that on my own. But what I am asking *you* for is some respect. Not once have I called you names, or been condescending or threatening to you. But you—"

"*Threatening* you? Girl, bye! I ain't ever threaten you. Trust. If I did, you would know it."

I pin her with a hard stare. "Well, I've *felt* threatened."

She huffs. "Well, that's too bad. I don't care what you've *felt*. That's on you. My name ain't Willy Wonka, boo-boo. I don't sugarcoat nothin'."

I frown. "Are you jealous of me?" The question comes out before I have a chance to process it.

She laughs sinisterly, standing in all of her nakedness. "Jealous? Ha. Of *you*? Girl, puh-leeze! I ain't ever been jelly of no basic *bissh*. Look at you 'n' look at me. I'm e'erything you wish you could be."

I blink once.

Twice.

Three times.

Trying to see in *her* what it is I'm supposed to want to be.

Fake hair. Fake nails. Fake lashes. Fake eyes.

Yeah, she's as real as it gets.

And everything I aspire to be.

Ha.

This girl is more than delusional than I ever imagined.

39

"*Ooh, you do me right, boo…yess…*"
And then I hear grunting.
Over the hum of the AC.
Then the sound of, of…
Something squeaking.
Wait.
Am I dreaming?
Hallucinating?
"*Mmm, yes, right there…ooh, get it, get it…*"
No, no, no. I must be hearing things.
I still my breathing.
Listen.
More grunting.
More groaning.
Low and throaty.
I don't realize I've been holding my breath until I finally inhale.
And then I smell it.
Their excitement.
Ohmygod!
It's disgusting!
My eyes snap open.

I blink several times, my eyes slowly adjusting in the dimness of the room.

I see movement over in Sha'Quita's bed.

Two bodies.

Two silhouettes.

I can't believe this!

I'm literally mortified.

She's doing and saying all kinds of things fit for a porn star, and I refuse to be subjected to this nastiness. Yet, instead of running for the door, I reach up under my pillow and pull out my flashlight, shining it over on them.

Why, I am not sure.

"Umm, do you mind?" I say calmly.

"*Bish*," she hisses, "get that flashlight off of us."

"Nah, let her watch," the guy says, his voice low and gruff.

I frown, quickly shutting the light off.

"This ho stay disruptin' my life," Sha'Quita mutters, then grunts. "I'ma be glad when she leaves. Nosy-azz. What, *trick*, you want some, too?"

The guy grunts, too. "Let her. I got enough for her, too."

"Nucca, shut up!" she says low. "She ain't gettin' none'a this good-good."

"I'm trying to sleep, Sha'Quita."

"Then go to sleep," she snarls.

"I can't. What you're doing is so disrespectful."

"No, you tryna blow up my spot 'n' eff up my groove is disrespectful. If you don't like what you hear, or see . . .

Or smell.

". . . then get the hell outta my room."

Say no more.

I snatch off the covers and swing my sock-covered feet over the bed, then turn my flashlight back on toward the floor, sweeping the light back and forth over the rug.

When I am satisfied that there aren't any roaches camping out inside of my shoes, I slip my feet inside and glance at the time on my phone.

Two-freaking-thirty-eight in the morning!

"This is freaking ridiculous," I mumble, grabbing my book bag and storming out of the bedroom, leaving the door wide open.

Flashlight in hand, I make my way down the darkened hallway. There's a glow coming from out of the living room from the television. Someone must be up, I think. I hope.

Then how did that nasty girl sneak that boy in?

What does it matter, Nia.

He's already inside the room, and inside . . . *her.*

Ugh!

I walk into the living and frown.

The sofa is pulled out into a bed.

And Omar is stretched out in a pair of basketball shorts, snoring.

And smelling!

Ohmygod!

The room reeks of alcohol and marijuana.

Through a veil of tears, I stand in in the middle of the living room, flabbergasted.

I can't stay here. I just can't.

But where else can I go?

Nowhere.

I pick up the blanket that's been tossed on the floor and cover Omar with it.

I glance over at the flat screen.

An episode of that show *Power* is on.

I've never watched it, but Crystal has. All through season one she kept bugging me to watch it with her. But after the third episode it became clear to me that she only watches it because she likes the main character, Ghost—I think, or something like that.

She thinks he's cute.

I swallow, feeling a panging in my chest.

I miss my friends.

Angling my flashlight, I shine it on the loveseat that's catty-corner on the other side of the living room, then let out a sigh of relief when there are no creepy crawler sightings. But my relief is short-lived. I stiffen and stifle a scream when I see a small army of roaches crawling up and down the wall.

I reach into my book bag and pull out my can of Raid. Being here, I have to stay armed with a can. I've already gone through eight cans in less than a week. And who knows how many more cans I'll run through before I leave this god-awful place.

This—this...hellhole.

Holding my breath, I coat the wall with it, watching roaches drop left and right. When I am done, I take up space on the sofa, book bag clutched to my chest, the can of roach spray gripped tightly in my hand, and wait for a new day.

An hour goes by.

I'm still waiting.

Idly.

And I am getting sleepy.

I fight back a yawn. Then I look over at Omar, who is sleeping, peacefully, as if he doesn't have a care in the world. As if there are no roaches swarming all around him. As if *this*—this existence—is his very best.

I ponder on the idea.

Wonder if he thinks this is the best he can do. If he thinks this way of being is as good as it'll ever be for him.

Smoking and drinking and running the streets (if that's what he's doing) and sleeping on someone's sofa bed.

My eyes are getting heavy.

The yawn comes.

Loud and wide.

I can't fight it anymore. I am too tired.

Finally, I give in, and close my eyes.

40

I don't know how long I've had my eyes closed, but I awaken—scared to death, heart pounding in my chest, hopping up off the sofa.

Not from a bad dream.

No.

To something crawling on me.

"Aaah!"

I leap from the sofa and hop up and down as if I'm doing some type of tribal rain dance.

"Yo *whatda...*" Omar's head pops up from his pillow. "Yo, who that?"

I swallow. "It's m-m-me, Nia," I stage whisper. "S-sorry if I woke you."

He sits up, rubbing his eyes. "Yo, what's wrong?"

"A roach or something was crawling on me."

He chuckles. "That's it? Yo, them roaches ain't thinkin' 'bout you; just swat 'em 'n' you good. They just a pain in the ass, that's all."

I blink back tears.

He says this as a matter of fact. Says it as if he's talking about a dog hopping up in bed with you and licking your face.

These are roaches!

Not pets!

No, no, no. I'll never be good.

He scratches the side of his head. "Yo, why you out here?"

I swallow. Think to tell him about her bed guest. But think twice about it.

I don't need the headache.

I swallow. "I-I can't sleep in there."

I feel his eyes staring at me. "Is Quita home?"

Oh, she sure is. "Yes." *Back there doing the nasty.*

"She in there snoring again?"

No, mewling like some nasty wildcat. "Something like that," is all I say.

He sighs. "You want the sofa."

I vigorously shake my head. "No. That's okay. I'm fine." Oh, but I'm really not. I am so creeped out right now. My skin is still crawling with nerves. "C-can you take me back to get more spray tomorrow?" And Bait strips?

Omar yawns. "I got you, baby girl." He yawns again, lying back down. "Try'n get some sleep; a'ight?"

Is he serious?

Sleep?

I don't respond.

And, within seconds, he is snoring again.

I fish my iPod out from my bag, sticking an earbud in each ear, hoping to drown out the screaming inside my head.

The sound of Nina Simone's "Wild Is the Wind" slowly calms me. But it fills me up with so many emotions. It reminds me of Nana. It's one of her favorite songs.

Every time I listen to this piece, it speaks to my soul.

I can hear Nana singing it. Can see her sitting at the piano, playing it.

My eyes close for a brief moment.

Then they open again.

And t-t-then...

Something catches my eye.

Movement.

I rapidly blink. Then squint.

Ohmygod!

Is that—?

It doesn't take long for it to register in my mind what I see.

I quickly jump up on the sofa, more afraid now than ever before.

I shine the flashlight, feeling my knees shake.

Right here.

In the middle of the floor.

Two sets of beady little eyes are looking back at me.

Two mice.

41

Mid-dream
My eyes snap open
I stare through the darkness
my vision blurred by the memory
wings beat up inside me
until I am rising
until I am rising
until I am rising

Sha'Quita bursts through the bedroom door. She's wearing zebra-print leggings and a black tank top with wedge heels. I haven't spoken to her in three days, ever since that day out on the steps.

No. Wait.

I haven't spoken to her ever since the night she had that boy in her bed.

"So you still all in ya feelin's, huh, boo-boo?"

I ignore her.

Don't even give her the decency of a glance.

She's so not worth it.

She's pitiful.

And she's clearly desperate for attention.

Most bullies are.
I continue writing.

Rising above the sorrow
Rising above the pain
Rising, rising, rising…
Above the despair

She boldly stands directly in front of me.
Challenging me.
Taunting me.
Trying to intimidate me.
My pen freezes over my journal page.
"Pick and choose your battles, Butterfly…"
I sigh inwardly.
"But, Daddy," I hear myself whining in my head, *"I don't know how much more of her I can take…"*
I don't want problems with this nutty girl.
I just want to do my time and get out of here with the least amount of complications.
With very little aggravation.
But this girl likes confusion.
"Oh, so you gonna just act like you don't see, or *hear*, me standin' here, right?"
Right.
I am purpose driven.
Not emotionally driven.
Intellect over emotion.
Think before you speak.
Think before you act.
Think about how your behavior will affect someone else.
Think about the consequences of your actions.
Think, think, think!
Those are the principles Daddy instilled in me.
Those are the rules that I have lived by.

Up until now I've been fine with them.
They worked for me.
Well, guess what?
I'm tired of thinking.
My black felt pen glides across the page of my journal.

Like a moth to a flame,
Heat sticks to my skin
Until my flesh burns
Until my bones melt
Until I am turning to ash

I bite my bottom lip.
The tension between this Sha'Quita girl and me is thick.
So thick that I am fighting to breathe.
Fighting to concentrate.
I'm feeling lightheaded.
She stomps over toward the window with the AC unit and yanks out the cord. "Don't speak then, *trick*. But I bet you won't be sittin' up in here suckin' up none'a this cool air."
Ohmygod.
She's so petty.
She wouldn't even have an air conditioner if it weren't for *me*.
She'd still be up in this hotbox with that raggedy ceiling fan swirling around hot air and dust and cobwebs. But okay. It's not that serious. She can unplug it. Heck. She can push it out the window for all I care.
First chance I get, I'm out of here anyway.
I place the cap on my pen, then shut my journal.
"I don't want to fight with you, Sha'Quita. But it seems like that's all you want to do. Pick fights with me. Why?"
" 'Seems like *thaaat's* all you wanna do, Sha'Quita,' " she mocks. " 'Pick fights wit' me. Why.' Boo-hoo. Boo-hoo. Cry-baby, bye. If I wanted to fight *you*, I woulda been beat the skin off you." She punches a fist into the palm of her hand to

accentuate her point. "I keep tellin' you, you don't want it wit' these hands."

"Then why are you always trying to start mess with me?"

"Start mess? Girl, bye. I'm far from messy. I was only effen wit' ya sensitive butt, but since you wanna get all up in ya stank feelin's, eff you."

"Whatever," I mumble.

Screw you, too.

"*What?*" she barks. "I know you ain't even talkin' slick under ya breath."

She steps closer in my space.

My heart races.

Beads of sweat start to line my forehead.

I don't look directly at her, but I watch her, her moving hands, in my peripheral vision.

Don't flinch.

"You had better ask them hoes in the streets about me. You don't know me."

I've had enough of her mouth. "And *you* don't know *me,*" I snap, finally looking at her.

She jerks her neck to one side. Her face is hard, her eyes narrowing into slits. "*What*, am I supposed to be scared? Am I supposed to cry? Hold on, boo-boo." She holds a finger up. "Let's wait for the tears." She tilts her head. Then snaps a finger in my face. "*Not.*"

I give her an impassive stare.

Try to keep my cool.

But inside I'm screaming, *GET OUT OF MY FACE!!*

There go those hands again. Moving inches from my face. "Girl, I don't know why you sittin' there lookin' all stupid, starin' me down. I will take it to ya face."

Be my guest.

I dare you.

I don't want this girl putting her hands on me.

I swear I don't.

But, still . . .

I double-dare her.

Because if she thinks I'll just sit here and let her hit me, she has—

Daddy's voice slices into the room.

"Don't ever let a bully think you're scared of them..."

"You lucky I'm not tryna eff up my nails today, otherwise I'd smack ya lights out." Pointing a finger at me, she leans in and grits her teeth, trying to intimidate me. "But keep it up 'n' you gonna feel my wrath."

This girl is exhausting.

This time I'm determined to keep my stare locked on hers, my expression a mixture of disgust and disbelief.

But then something catches my eye.

Movement.

There's a roach crawling up her leg.

And she is seemingly unfazed by it.

Or maybe unaware.

Her phone rings.

And, just like that, our stare down comes to a screeching halt.

She rolls her eyes. "You lucky, boo-boo."

Oh. Okay.

"Heeeeey, boo," she says all jolly-like. "Whaaaat? Say, word, *bish*! Yasss, yassss! When? Ooh, you know I am feenin' for a taste of that dark chocolate. Oooh, yasss, yasssss...I wanna ride him like a roller coaster..." She laughs. "You know that's my boo..."

Who isn't?

"Bye, trick. I'm comin' through right now. Tell him I said don't leave." She grabs her lip gloss from off her dresser, then shoots a nasty glare over at me before shaking her hips toward the door.

I think to tell her she has a roach crawling up her legging. But I decide to let her go on about her business with her travel companion in tow.

Nasty girl.

42

"Aunt Terri," I whisper into the phone, two days later. It's taken me that long to finally reach her. "Please. You have to get me out of here."

"Well, what's the problem *now*, Nia?" she asks, sounding the least bit concerned.

"The same stuff. These people are..."

"Your *blood* family, Nia," she says matter-of-factly.

"But I don't relate to them, Aunt Terri. They are—"

"Sweetie," she says, interrupting me. "We've already had this discussion. I need at least a month or two to get things situated."

Wait.

A month or two?

Am I hearing things?

Where is this *or two* coming from?

I begrudgingly agreed to *one* month, *after* she convinced me to come here for two weeks. Now she's saying *or two*. When did things change, *again*? And why am I just hearing about it? I feel myself starting to get choked up.

"Aunt Terri, I agreed to two weeks. Then you said you needed another few weeks. And I unhappily said okay. Now this."

How can she do this to me?

"Well, there's some issues with your father's estate that need to be cleared up first."

Ohmygod.

I massage my left temple, trying like heck to fight back the beginnings of a headache. "What do you mean?"

"This has nothing to do with you, Nia. So don't worry yourself. Everything will work itself out one way or another."

I frown.

What the heck does she mean this has nothing to do with me?

This whole ordeal has *every*thing to do with *ME*!!

"Please, Aunt Terri. I'm not going to make it here for a *whole* month, or *two*. That's my whole summer! What about school?"

She sighs into the phone. "We'll cross that bridge when it's time," she says nonchalantly.

But the bridge has already been crossed. And I'm ready to jump off!!

"Just try to enjoy your time getting to know your family."

I bite into the side of my bottom lip to keep from screaming, but inside I feel myself about to lose it. Being fresh and disrespectful to any adult isn't how Daddy raised me. So I keep biting, until I draw blood.

"Can I have the number for Daddy's lawyer?" I ask, sniffling.

"Why?"

"So I can talk to him about me staying somewhere else until I can come to Georgia."

"I don't have his number on me," she quickly says. "Anyway, like I said, Nia. You need to get to know them, especially your father."

"Aunt Terri, I'm not trying to be disrespectful, but why are you trying to push me off on these people, huh? Do you hate me that much?"

"Nonsense, Nia. I don't hate you."

Umm. I can't tell. "Then why are you doing this to me?"

She sighs in my ear again. "I'm doing what's best for you, Nia. I know it's hard for you to understand right now. But you'll thank me later."

I'll never thank you. Never. "Aunt Terri, what I need is to be with the family I *know*. Not with…" I pause, heaving a sigh. "These people are *crazy*. They're a bunch of alcoholics and drug addicts."

"Well, are they mistreating you?" she asks dismissively.

I blink. "Yes. Well, no. I mean, I guess."

"Well, which is it? Are they or aren't they?"

I swallow. "Not really. I mean this girl keeps trying to start stuff with me…"

"And do you not *know* how to fight?"

"Yes, but—"

"Then whip her tail."

"But I don't want to fight her. I want to come home."

"You have no home, Nia. How many times do I have to remind you of that?"

With those words, I suddenly lose my composure, bursting into tears and sobbing into the phone.

Her words, her truth, slice into my heart.

"Nia, you need to pull it together. Crying over spilled milk isn't going to bring your father back. He's gone, but…"

Through breathless gasps, I think I hear her telling me that I need to count my *blessings*.

What blessings?

I would often overhear Daddy saying Aunt Terri was crazy.

Now I see why.

She *is* crazy!

Crazy to think pawning me off on a bunch of strangers is a *blessing*!

"Daddy always said all you ever cared about is money," I blurt out. "And now you've said it yourself. You don't want me around because you can't get your hands on Daddy's money."

"Nia, you watch your tone with me, young lady. I've said

no such thing. I don't want what he left for you. So don't you dare go putting words in my mouth! All I care about is getting what's rightfully mine—my portion of *my* mother's inheritance that *my* brother stole from me. That has nothing to do with *you*."

"B-b-but you said I would come live with you."

"I know what I said, Nia," she says sharply. "But that was then. And this is now. And up until now, everything has been handed to you on a silver platter. You've been spoiled rotten, little girl. And right now, it's time for *you* to get a taste of how life is on the other side."

Ohmygod! What is she talking about? "But this place is s-so n-n-nasty," I whine, wiping tears from my face. "And these roaches..."

"That's too bad, Nia. You're going to have to figure out a way to deal with it. Now I'm done with having this conversation. You'll come here when I'm ready for you to come here. Until then, get over it. I'll call you in a few weeks to check in."

"B-b-but, Aunt Ter—"

Blooop.

The line's gone dead.

43

"Hey, Cali Girl," Sha'Quita calls out, bursting into the bedroom, swinging open the door, "you wanna roll to the park wit' me 'n' my girl Chardonnay? It's nice out so I figured I'd be nice to you today."

I look up from my journal.

Take her in.

Maybe for a few seconds longer than I should, but I let my gaze linger anyway.

She cut her weave out. Well, all of it except the one long piece she has stitched in on her right side, which she has curled around her jawline. But her hair is dyed platinum blond.

I force a smile.

But I am cringing on the inside.

This girl has some nerve!

As if she's doing me some favor by asking *me* to hang out with her and her pimply-faced friend.

I'm sooo not interested.

"No, thanks," I say nicely.

She stares at me, then dramatically bats her lashes. "What, you think you too good to hang in the park wit' us?"

I shake my head. "No, not at all. I just don't want to go. Besides, I thought you said you like traveling *light*."

She bats her lashes and scoffs. "Yeah, I do travel light. *And*?"

I shrug. "Just checking. But thanks anyway."

She rolls her eyes. "You mad shady."

"I'm not *shady*. Why would you say that?"

"'Cause you are."

"Why, because I don't want to go to the park with you?"

She sucks her teeth. "Girl, you retarded. So you rather stay cooped up in this stank room instead of bein' around a buncha cuties in basketball shorts?"

Well, the room wouldn't be stank *if you stopped keeping dirty clothes piled up over there in the corner*, I think, closing my journal.

She huffs. "You messy as hell, girl. I'm tryna get me that Michael Kors bag I saw in Marshalls last night 'n' you blockin' my flow."

I give her a dumbfounded look.

"You heard what I said. I need that bag. But Omar ain't even 'bout to drop no paper on it unless you start gettin' wit' the program 'n' bring ya stank-azz out."

I frown. "Wait." I shake my head, trying to wrap my mind around what I've just heard. "So you're saying that Omar promised to buy *you* a new pocketbook if you drag me along with you?"

She tilts her head. "Ain't that what I said?"

No.

"Oh," is all I say.

"So...?"

"Is Omar here?"

She grits her teeth. "Do I look like his keeper to you, huh? Where you think he is? He's where he's been for the last three days. Not here."

I swallow. "I only asked a question. Because he texted me and said he was on his way back."

"And I gave you an answer. So you comin', or nah?"

I shake my head. "I'll pass."

She swings her bang from out of her face. "*Psst*. Girl, bye."

"Okay, bye," I say, eyeing her as she heads for the door. "Have fun."

She stops in her tracks, craning her neck, hand on her hip. "Don't get cute. Remember, I'm being nice."

Yeah. For a new pocketbook, so please don't think you're doing me some favor.

I tilt my head. "I'm not getting *cute*."

"Oh, I know you not, sweetie. You'll need a whole new makeover to be *that*. Still, I think you tried it."

This girl really gets under my skin.

"I wasn't trying anything. I simply said have fun. How's that *trying* to be cute?"

She throws a hand up. "Girl, talk to the hand. Like I said, you tried it."

"And I said, have fun."

She sneers, stomping out the room, slamming the door behind her.

I shake my head, opening my journal again. I write.

Is this life just?
or
just
us
clinging onto
misguided hope
for
justice?
Are we deceived
by misdeeds?
Or
sadly guided
by
missed
deeds?

I sigh, closing my journal. Then I get up and walk over to the window facing the street and peek out through the curtains. There's a group of young girls in the middle of the street jumping rope. They're laughing and having a good time. They look to be no older than twelve, or thirteen. But nowadays, it's so hard to tell. Most of the young girls I see look *and* act so grown, especially around here.

I start to wonder what life is like for them behind closed doors. Are they really as happy and carefree as they appear to be now? Or are they stifled by oppressive living conditions? I can't help but wonder what will become of them. Will they become products of their environment? Will they become eaten alive by the streets? Will they become the next generation of Sha'Quitas in the world?

Or—

Ohmygod!

One of the girls twirling the rope snatches it from the girl on the other end of it and starts hitting another girl with it. Then the two of them start fighting before two other girls jump in, while onlookers pull out their cell phones and capture it, live and direct.

Disgusted, I step away from the window.

So much for wondering...

44

"You know my baby, Quita, stay tryna take you under her wing," Kee-Kee says, eyeing me as I walk by to go back into the bedroom from the kitchen.

Oh.

Is that the lie she's telling her?

Okay.

I stop, glancing over into the living room. Keyonna's sitting on the sofa in a white sports bra and a pair of cutoff jean shorts with her legs spread open.

I raise my eyebrows, confused. "Uh?"

"I *saaaaaid*, Quita been tryna get you outta this apartment." She blows cigarette smoke up at the ceiling. "But you just ain't tryna act right."

She eyes me hard. "What, ya uppity butt think you too good for my baby?"

I swallow. "No. I don't think that."

"*Mmmph*. I can't tell. You walk around here like you gotta long *di*—stick—up in your tail. You stay struttin' around here wit' ya head all up the clouds like you somebody special."

I am special.

"I don't think I am," I say apologetically. "That's not my intention."

She takes a pull from her cigarette. Newport, I think. "Uh-huh." She curls her lips and lets the smoke swirl out between them. "Well, you need to get ya siddity self up outta this house. Go out 'n' get some fresh air. It's too damn nice out for you to be sittin' up in here. I'm sick of lookin' at you all the damn time, anyway. Omar brought you up in here, but he ain't never here to be wit' you. *Mmph*. He's a savage for that. I already gotta daughter. I ain't tryna look after his, too."

I feel the palms of my hands starting to sweat.

"I don't mean to be an inconvenience," I say nervously.

She narrows her eyes. "Well, you ain't *really* no inconvenience, per se. I just want you up outta here so I can do me; that's all. I'm tryna get my back blown out as much as I can while Momma's down in Florida, but I ain't bringin' my man up in here while you here. I don't want him getting no ideas that you on the menu, too."

On the menu?

I keep from frowning.

Ugh.

She takes a long drag from her cigarette, then blows out a big, angry cloud of smoke. "Quita done already hipped me to how you are. Now, I ain't seen it for myself. But she says you sneaky. She told me how you tried to sneak some boy up in here the other night."

My stomach lurches.

What a liar!

"That wasn't me," I insist. "I've never snuck a boy in anywhere. I don't even *know* any boys here."

She twists her lips. "Mmph. So what you sayin'? It was Quita?"

All of a sudden, I hear Sha'Quita's menacing voice.

"Keep ya mouth shut. Snitches get stitches up in here…"

I swallow. Look down at my hands, then my feet, then over at the television. Then stare at the two sweaty bottles of

Heineken sitting on the table. I try to look everywhere except at her.

"No. That's not what I'm saying. I'm saying it wasn't me."

"Girl, you better look at me when you speak. I ain't one of them hoes from the streets. I'm ya auntie. Don't get it twisted. You better show me some respect. Don't have me show you how we do it up here in the hood, boo-boo."

She pulls a switchblade out from behind one of the sofa pillows, then sets it down on the coffee table.

I blink.

"See, I ain't gonna put my hands on you 'cause you supposedly my niece. I'ma just cut you. Slice you right across that pretty face."

She says this real calm-like. Doesn't even bat a lash.

I gulp in air.

My heart starts racing.

So you won't hit me because I'm supposedly *your niece, but you'll cut my face? What kind of sense does that make?*

I look at her, starting to feel unsafe. I scan the room for an emergency exit, just in case.

"I already know Quita's fast," she says before I can respond, "but I ain't even 'bout to put up wit' it from somebody else's child. You ain't getting pregnant up in here. You on the pill?"

I shake my head. "No."

She frowns. "The shot?"

I shake my head.

She narrows her eyes. "Well, you getting on something if you gonna be layin' up in here. Like I tol' Quita, you can let these boys bounce you down into the springs if you want, but you ain't bringin' no babies up in here. You like getting freaky wit' it, huh? Give me the tea, boo."

Tea?

"Um, there's no *tea*—whatever that means," I say, glancing down at the carpet. There's a roach crawling toward my foot.

I blink.

"It *means* give me the gossip, boo. You ain't ever gotta lie to me. That's what I tell Quita. But that li'l heifer loves to lie, anyway. I think that girl loves it when I gotta smack up her face. So who you twerkin' that thang up on?"

I frown. "I'm not that kind of girl."

"Well, you like sex, *don't* you?"

I shake my head. "I'm not having sex. Not until I'm married, anyway."

She makes a face. "Not until you married? Girl, you need to stop it." She stares me up and down. "*Mmmph.* Oh, you livin' in fantasyland, huh? Well, news flash, boo-boo: Ain't no *real* man gonna wife you unless you givin' him a li'l taste. Just don't be stupid about it. Be selective who you give the cookie to. Nucca gotta at least buy you six-pack 'n' some hot wings, first."

I blink.

"Um. I'm not interested in hot wings from a boy," I say. "Because I'm not looking to have sex."

She scoffs. "Girl, bye. I know you ain't dumb enough to believe he's not gonna wanna taste the milk before he buy the cow? Girl, you need to stop tryna follow behind them white people. Even the Bachelorette screwin' up in the fantasy suite."

I cringe at what she says. I disagree with her. I don't believe a girl has to have sex to be with a boy. And all boys aren't going to pressure a girl to have sex with him, even if he does want it, thinks about it, or whatever else. All I know is, if he really cares for her, and wants to be with her, then he'll wait for her. And any boy who wants to be with *me* is going to have to wait. Period.

I tell her this.

And she laughs in my face.

So I'm a laughingstock for having a moral compass different from hers?

She stops laughing long enough to say, "Yeah, he'll wait all right. For somebody who's gonna back that thang up 'n' ride 'im like a roller coaster."

I shrug. "Then I guess he wasn't ever meant for me."

I must admit, this whole conversation is dizzying.

"Girl, I don't know what fantasy world you livin' in, but you need to bring yo' azz back down to earth, boo-boo. Whoever raised you done got you brainwashed. If you think some boy is gonna be waitin' for you, you crazy."

"It's what I believe," I explain. "And I won't compromise that for anyone."

"Well, good luck wit' that," she says, looking at me, shaking her head. "But I know you givin' out head service, right?"

I give her a blank look. "What's that?"

She sees the expression on my face, then bursts out laughing. "Girl, let me stop messin' wit' ya Goody Two-Shoes butt," she says, slapping her thigh. "You should see ya face. Poor baby. You look like you 'bout to piss ya drawz."

I really can't believe what I'm hearing.

And this is coming from an adult.

A mother.

Thankfully, not mine.

Keyonna takes another puff from her cigarette, then mashes it out in an ashtray. "Quita tell you how me 'n' her jumped that li'l ho down the block?"

I shake my head. "No."

"We beat that girl down. She thought she was gonna bring it to Quita, but she shoulda knew she was gonna have to bring it to me, too. That's how we do it 'round here. You fight her, you gotta fight me, and vice versa. I go hard for mines." She balls her hand into a fist. "These hands are nice. And they hit hard."

I blink.

"Do you know how to go wit' the hands?"

I give her a confused look.

She huffs. "Damn, girl. You slow as hell. Can you fist up? You know, *fight*?"

"Oh. Kind of. I mean, if I have to. I'd rather not, though."

She looks me over. "Oh, you one of them cotton candy 'let's talk it out' kinda girls, huh?"

I shrug. "I guess."

She scoffs. "What you mean, you *guess*? Girl, there ain't no time for bein' no punk 'round here. These hoes 'round here ain't tryna hear a buncha yip-yap. And they ain't lookin' for no peace negotiations. They 'bout takin' it upside ya head, you know what I'm sayin'."

Umm, was that supposed to be a question?

She doesn't give me a chance to speak, before she is giving me the rest of her survival crash course on life in the streets.

"You gotta be ready to knuckle up," she says, becoming animated as she talks, "'n' brawl just in case some ish pops off." She punches a fist into the palm of her hand for emphasis. "Don't let no ho punk you."

And does that piece of advice include Sha'Quita?

She waves me over to her. "Girl, come over here 'n' let me see them hands."

I reluctantly walk over and hold my hands out to her.

She grabs them with hers, turning them over as if she's inspecting them. Then grunts. "*Mmmph.* Yeah, you ain't no fighter. Ya hands too damn soft. They cute, though; but *you* definitely ain't putting in no hand work. You carrying mace in that book bag you always carrying around?"

I shake my head. "No."

She twists her lips. "Well, you probably should."

"No, that's okay. I try to avoid problems," I offer, stepping back from her.

Daddy always told me to pick and choose my battles; that every dispute doesn't have to become a war.

And I believe that.

Keyonna smirks. "Good luck wit' that." She reaches for

her beer. "You want some'a this"—she holds the bottle up—"before I take it to the head?"

I tell her I don't drink.

"You smoke?"

I shake my head. Tell her *no*. Never have. Never will.

She grunts, furrowing her brows together. "*Mmph*. You don't drink. You don't smoke. You ain't drankin' watermelon. You ain't even havin' sex. What do you do then?"

I shift uncomfortably from one foot to the other. "Write. Play the piano."

She gives me a blank stare.

Yawns.

Then digs down into her sports bra, scratches underneath her breasts. "Girl, you 'bout ready to put me to sleep." She pulls out a credit card, stretching an arm out to hand it to me. "Take this EBT card 'n' go get me two cans of Red Bull 'n' a pack of Dutches. I need me a blunt."

45

I'd never seen an EBT card until now...
"Damn, girl, you fine," someone says as I'm walking by.
This is the first time I've been forced to venture off the steps
alone. I'm not going to lie, I'm nervous. Even if it is only to
walk up two blocks to the store on the corner.

Still.

This is uncharted territory for me.

Even though I know my way back to the apartment, I still
feel lost.

Real lost.

"Yo, shorty," someone else calls out. "Let me holla at you."

I keep walking.

Don't even look in the direction of the voice.

"Yo, I know you not iggin' me. Stuck-up *bish*. What, you
deaf or sumthin'?"

I swallow.

Think maybe Keyonna's right.

I need a can of mace, probably sooner than later.

"Yo, shorty, let me get a ride on that wagon you draggin'..."

Wagon?

What is he talking about?

I'm not dragging a—

Oh, oh, *ohhhhh*.

That wagon.

I'd never heard a girl's butt called a *wagon*. Until now.

I pick up my pace; not too fast, though, because I don't want my *wagon* drawing more attention than it already is.

Sweet peach.

That's what I think I hear someone say as I continue to my walk.

"Yo, ma, can I get a taste? I bet you sweet 'n' juicy like a peach..."

Ohmygod! That's *exactly* what I heard.

I frown, shaking my head.

I keep walking.

I hear them laughing behind me.

"Damn, she got a *phatty*, though...Aye, yo, ma. Let me get dem digits..."

I can feel their eyes on me as I walk by, practically undressing me.

And I am becoming increasingly uncomfortable. I'm in a pair of white shorts and a pink short-sleeved tee, but I'm wishing that I had worn a pair of sweats and a turtleneck, even though it's ninety-two degrees out.

Sweat rolls down the center of my back.

Back home guys never call out to me like I'm some call girl. The boys I know in my neighborhood—well, the ones I associate with—are respectful of girls.

Of me.

Maybe because—

"Yo, what's good, ma?" a thin, brown-skinned guy says, stepping in front of me, blocking my path. He's wearing a white tank top and torn jeans, and a red Polo hat pulled down low over his eyes.

"Huh?"

He grins. "I said, what's good?"

"Oh. Nothing."

"Yo, where you from, ma?"

"California," I say nervously.

"Oh, word. That's wassup. What you doin' out this way?"

Good question.

"Um, visiting."

"Oh, a'ight. That's wassup. Where you stayin'?"

I raise my brows.

He grins wider. "I ain't gonna kick in the door 'n' kidnap you, ma. I'm just askin'. I might wanna scoop you up 'n' chill."

"Oh. No thanks. I don't *chill*."

He laughs. "Oh, word? You one of them types."

I frown. "What type is that?"

"One of them good girls."

I shrug. "I guess."

"Yeah, I need one of those in my life. Word up. These broads 'round here burnt out."

"Oh," is all I say.

His cell starts ringing. He lets it go into voice mail. But then it starts ringing again. And I'm relieved when he snatches it from his waist and barks into the phone.

"Yo, what? Damn. I'm on my way." He looks at me. "Yo, ma, I'ma holla..."

"Okay," I say, walking off as he starts cursing someone out on the other end.

A girl, I believe, since he calls the person all kinds of stupid B's.

That couldn't be me.

I wipe sweat from my forehead with my hand.

The sun beats down on me, hot and relentless.

I see the store.

Almost there! But not close enough.

One more block, Nia. Focus.

This heat is torturous.

Brutal.

Stifling.

I feel like I'm in the middle of a concrete desert.

Surrounded by abandoned houses and graffiti.

I wish I could blink my eyes and be back home, in my backyard, under a palm tree.

"Oh, damn, that's wifey right there," I hear someone call out. I look over and there's a light-skinned boy with light green eyes and locks, blowing a kiss at me. "What's good, baby?"

He looks young. Real young.

But, obviously, too grown for his years.

I give him a half wave, the soles of my sandals still hitting the pavement with one purpose in mind: to get to the store and back in one piece.

I get to the corner, the store in reach, waiting for the light to change.

I shift my book bag from one shoulder to the other, waiting, as cars zip down the street and through the light.

A silver Mercedes truck stops at the red light, a thick cloud of smoke whirling out the opened windows with it.

"Damn, ma. You got pretty on fleek," a dark-skinned guy wearing cornrows says from the backseat, leaning out the window.

Pretty on fleek?

Me?

Who would have thought it?

Daddy always told me how beautiful I was. And the boys at my school thought I was *cute*. But no one has ever told me I had pretty...on *fleek*.

That's a new one.

I crane my neck and look over at him. He has a trimmed goatee, and looks to be at least in his twenties. *Waaaay* too old to be talking to *me*.

Still, I smile. Say thanks. Then look straight ahead, counting the seconds in my head for the light to change. *Hurry up and change*.

"Can I get ya digits, baby?"

I blink. Shake my head.

"Mofo," someone yells, "shut yo' thirsty azz up. Leave shorty alone. Can't you see she mad young?"

"Man, eff that. You see that phatty on her..."

Ohmygod.

The light changes.

And I hurriedly cross the street.

Speed up my walk.

Hope not to trip over my feet.

The truck zooms by with Mr. Twenty-Something yelling out, "Let me be ya baby daddy, sexy?"

Yuck.

Some pickup line.

This has truly been the longest two blocks of my life.

I've literally lost count at the number of boys—*annnd* men (yuck!)—who keep trying to get my attention. I almost feel like I'm walking the infamous walk of shame, even though I know I haven't done anything to be ashamed of.

There's a posse of guys hanging out in front of the store.

Great.

Just what I need.

As soon as they spot me, they start eyeballing me.

I brace myself.

My heart thumps.

Louder.

Harder.

Faster.

And then comes a chorus of "What's good, ma? What's good, baby?"

They're all nice enough to step back and let me through.

That is...

Until someone grabs my butt.

46

My whole left butt cheek captured in the palm of some boy's filthy hand!

I'm flustered, to say the least.

No boy has ever grabbed my butt.

Ever.

Then the rest of those ignorant boys thought what he'd done was entertaining, and laughed.

Savages.

Where the heck do they get off thinking that grabbing a girl's butt—or *any*thing else on her body—is acceptable? Or funny?

And they have the nerve to *still* be hanging outside, waiting...

For their next victim, perhaps.

Or maybe for me.

Like predators.

I don't know which one of the six or seven boys who are hanging outside violated me, but I'm too shaken to walk back out that door to find out.

I tap my foot, shouldering my bag, imagining myself becoming loud and belligerently cursing them all out—and, maybe, even fighting them, if I had it in me, if I were more like Sha'Quita.

I suppose it's a blessing that I'm not loud and obnoxious like her, but in this instance, I wish I had a switch I could turn on to blast them real quick, then turn off.

If I weren't so pissed, I'd laugh at the thought of Sha'Quita going all *Love & Hip Hop* on those trifling fools. I've never watched that show. But I've heard lots of things about it. And not all of it is good.

I grab the back of my neck, then roll my neck side to side.

I'm tense.

I take several breaths.

Breathe in.

Breathe out.

As cool air from the store's AC hits my skin, I somehow manage to let out a sigh of relief—from the heat and from my arduous two-block trek.

No matter how short.

I glance toward the door, narrowing my eyes, then releasing a frustrated sigh, peeling my glare away from the door, hoping like heck that they're gone by the time I'm ready to leave the store.

I fish my cell from out of my bag, then call Aunt Terri. It rings and rings. Then I'm told that the mailbox is full. I quickly send her a text.

SOS!!! I NEED 2 GET OUT OF HERE! PLEASE AUNT TERRI. CAN U SEND 4 ME NOW?? OR CAN U GET IN TOUCH W/DADDY'S ATTY N ASK HIM TO CALL ME. PLEASE AUNT TERRI.

I send the text, then try calling her again.

Still no answer.

And no text response.

Yet.

Deflated, I drop my phone back down into my bag's side pocket. Then shift my weight from one foot to the other. There's a Chinese, no, Korean man behind a bulletproof glass waiting on an older lady wearing a multicolored head-scarf and short-short skirt as she pays for her items. I look up and watch her through the store's security mirror as she digs down into her shirt and pulls out her money.

I glance over at the cashier's booth just as he frowns at her. He says something that sets her off. She goes from zero to a hundred. Curses him. Uses racial slurs. Gives him the middle finger. Then pulls her shirt up and flashes her boobs before storming out of the store.

Wow.

I take a step forward in line.

Wait my turn.

I'm the fourth person in line.

I want to get back to the apartment (never thought I'd say that!).

But I am in no rush to go back out in that heat.

Or be harassed.

I close my eyes, just for a second, to kind of get my thoughts together, when I hear a deep voice over my shoulder say, "Yo, what's good, ma? I thought that was you."

I crane my neck and look up into a familiar face.

But I can't remember his name.

He grins. "Nia?"

I nod. "Yes. I don't remember yours, though."

"It's Shawn. Don't forget it."

"Oh, okay. I'll try not to."

He smirks. "Yeah, you do that. But, yo. I bet them clowns were sweatin' you hard, too. Cats mad thirsty out here; especially when they see a cutie wit' pretty legs 'n' a phatty."

I blink.

Nervously shift my weight from one foot to the other.

"My bad." He shrugs. "I'm keepin' it a hunnid. It is what it is."

He lets his gaze drop down to the flare of my hips. Then grins. "You real right, ma."

Oh, okay.

I really should have worn those sweats and that turtle-neck.

"Thanks, I guess," I say, shifting my gaze from his to pre-vent him from seeing that he's managed to make me blush.

I move up the line.

Three more people ahead of me.

"Where's ya peoples at?"

I give him a confused look. "My *peoples*?"

"Yeah. Quita."

Oh.

Her.

His obsessed girlfriend.

I shrug. "At the park, I guess."

"Oh, word? And you ain't wanna go?"

I shake my head. "No."

I look straight ahead.

Try to avoid the heat from his eyes staring in back of me.

Don't turn around.

Just don't do it, Nia.

I ignore the voice in my head and glance over my shoulder.

Our eyes meet.

"You pretty as *fu*—"

His cell rings.

And I'm glad.

The line moves up.

Two more people left in front of me.

"Yo," he says when he answers. I stare at the back of the head of the lady in front of me, trying not to listen to his con-versation. But it's hard not to since he's practically up on me, and all in my ear.

I step forward, trying to put some distance between us, as best I can without stepping on the heels of the lady in front of me.

"Nah, nah . . . tell them mofos I said fall back. I'ma be through

in a minute...Nah, I'm on the bike...oh, a'ight. Word...
A'ight. Bet."

I glance over at the door.

Those disrespectful idiots are still out there.

Great.

I roll my eyes and take another step forward.

Finally, I'm next.

I place the two cans of Red Bull on the counter, then ask
for a pack of Dutches. I feel funny asking for them since I
don't even smoke. I've never even purchased a pack before.
Or used an EBT card alone. Or seen what one looks like, for
that matter.

I'm shocked when the guy doesn't even ask me for ID,
even though it clearly states that anyone purchasing cigarettes must be at least nineteen.

My hands are sweaty pulling out Keyonna's EBT card. I
hand it to the cashier. I don't know if I should feel embarrassed or not, but I do. The cashier peers at me, then swipes
the card.

I am relieved when the transaction is completed, and the
cashier bags my items. But then my anxiety kicks back in the
second reality sets in.

That I have to walk out that door.

I grab the bag, and give a half wave to Shawn. "Okay, bye,"
I say, not really knowing what else to say. I'm too afraid to ask
him if he'd walk out with me. I'm not comfortable telling him
that some boy grabbed my butt and now I'm nervous to walk
down the street by myself, even if it is broad daylight.

"Nah, yo. Hol' up," he says. "I'ma walk out wit' you."

Thank you.

"Okay," I calmly say. But inside I'm so, so relieved. I could
almost hug him, and kiss him on the cheek.

Almost.

I wait and watch as he pays for his purchase: a pack of cin-

namon gum, a pack of Twizzlers, and a can of Sprite. He
grabs his bag, and grins at me. "You ready?"

I nod, following him toward the door.

He holds it open, and I step out.

The wolves start salivating.

"Here she come, yo," someone says.

I try not to look to see who is saying what. I don't want to
look at any of them.

They're repulsive.

"Damn, baby. I need to hit that, yo..." one of the guys still
hanging out in front of the store says.

I ignore him.

But Shawn doesn't. "Yo, fam. Fall back. That's my peoples, yo."

"Oh, word?" someone says. "That's *you*? My bad, Slick. I
ain't know."

"Well, now you do," Shawn says, his voice filled with au-
thority.

What does he mean by, 'That's you'?

Is "that's my peoples" synonymous to family and friends?
Or does it imply she's yours as in *your* girl?

I lower my gaze to the sidewalk. But then something inside
of me tells me to look up, to look at them. And I do. I eye them
all, taking in everything thing about them. Then I decide to
boldly ask, "Which one of you grabbed my butt as I was walking into the store?"

I tilt my head.

I have the right to know, don't I?

They all look at me like I'm crazy for asking such a thing,
as if I'm making it up.

Shawn frowns. "Say what?"

I repeat myself, feeling slightly empowered.

Bolder.

A tall and wiry brown-skinned guy is the only one who
opens his mouth to speak. "Man, ain't no one—"

"Yo, fam, I know how you cats move," Shawn says, shutting him down. He eyes them all, gritting his teeth. "Word is bond, fam. Don't let me find out who disrespected my peoples, yo. It's gonna be a problem." He looks over at me. "You sure you don't know who did it?"

I glance around the group of guys. Then I shake my head. "No. I didn't see who it was."

He shoots the posse of idiots an icy glare. "Y'all lucky. Word is bond. But let me find out who disrespected her 'n' I'ma see you. On my bruh's seed, you already know."

He leads me by the elbow toward a shiny black motorcycle. A Harley.

I blink.

Try to remember if I saw it here earlier. I can't recall.

He opens the storage compartment, drops his bag inside, then reaches for mine. "No, that's fine. I got it."

He removes his helmet from off the handlebars. "Nah. C'mon. I'ma take you back up the block." He glances back over at the group of guys. "Man, that ish got me hot, yo."

Now I'm embarrassed. "Let it go, okay. Please."

"Yeah, you right. For now. Let's roll."

I take a step back, shaking my head. "Uh-uh. I'm not getting on that."

Not with you.

"You safe wit' me, ma."

I shake my head again. "No, thanks. I'll walk."

He looks me up and down, then shakes his head. "So you really gonna have me leave my bike here and walk you up the block in this heat?"

"You don't have to," I say halfheartedly. "I can walk by myself." No, I really can't!

"Yeah, I know you can. But I ain't 'bout to let you. Not after some dumb mofo grabbed ya butt. Nah, I ain't feelin' that."

He shuts the storage compartment, then calls out to the

group of guys. "Yo, y'all ugly *muhfuggahs* watch my bike. I gotta make sure shorty gets back to the crib all right."

They tell him they'll keep an eye out on it for him.

He tucks his helmet under his arm, then ushers me by the elbow. "You lucky I kinda dig you, yo."

Relieved, I try not to smile.

But I do anyway.

47

Omar walks into the living room from the back of the apartment, wearing a white, ribbed um—what is it they call those tank tops?

Wifebeater, I think.

Yeah, that's it.

He's wearing one of those, and it clings to his muscled chest, showing off his numerous tattoos.

"Yo, baby girl. You eat yet?"

Baby girl.

Ugh.

I wish he'd stop calling me that. "I'm not really hungry."

"No, she ain't eat," Keyonna answers for me. "She's too busy layin' 'round here, waitin' for someone to feed her behind like she royalty or some mess. Ain't nobody over here playin' *Master Chef.*"

Omar frowns at her. "Well, maybe if you tried masterin' the kitchen, you'd have a man 'n' ya own spot."

"Really, O? That's how we doin' it? You really tryna go there, huh? Says the nucca fresh outta prison. *Mmph.* Don't do me, boo-boo."

He sucks his teeth. "Man, shut ya trap up, yo. You always runnin' ya mouf 'bout nothin'."

She grunts, snatching open the bag and pulling out the pack of cigarettes.

No, wait.

Cigars.

No, no, *blunts*.

That's what I meant.

Blunts.

Lord, help me. I know not the difference between the two. So forgive me if I call them the wrong thing around here.

Ugh.

Cigarettes, cigars, blunts: they all smell horrible, if you ask me.

Omar looks over at me. Asks what I want to eat. I tell him I'm not hungry.

Keyonna grunts. "*Mmph.* What, you on a diet now?"

No. I'm just not ever eating out of that nasty kitchen.

I shake my head. Tell her *no*.

Omar pins her with a hard stare. Then he frowns as she takes her knife and slices open a cigar.

"Yo, *whatdafuq*. I know you ain't even 'bout to do *that* now."

She huffs, stuffing it with marijuana then rolling it. "Do *what*? *Smoke*?"

"Don't play stupid, yo."

She lights the cigar.

"I ain't playin' stupid. You the one playin' dumb, askin' me some mess like that. You *know* what time it is, *nucca*." She laughs. "Don't front."

I blink.

So he smokes, too.

Keyonna takes a deep drag off her blunt, smoke curling around her head as it floats to the ceiling.

Omar gives her a hard stare.

"What, boo? You mad or *nah*? You better c'mon 'n' get you some of this good-good."

"Yo, you trippin', man."

She takes another pull from her blunt. "Boy, bye." She points her cigar at Omar and blows smoke in his direction. "You sure you don't want some?"

He grunts. "Nah. I'm good."

She shrugs. "Good. More for me." She takes another pull, then pulls it from her mouth and stares at its glowing ember as she slowly exhales and draws smoke into her nose.

I watch her with a mixture of fascination and disgust.

"Mmph. I don't even know why you tryna put on a show in front of her. We was just smokin' three nights ago. Now all of a sudden, you *good*."

I glance over at Omar.

He furrows his brows and sucks his teeth, shaking his head. "This broad," he mutters. "Yo, c'mon, baby girl. Let's go get sumthin' to eat."

"Ooh, boo," Keyonna says sweetly, "if you 'n' 'baby girl' goin' to that Caribbean spot downtown bring me back some jerk wings."

Well, we don't make it downtown to the Caribbean restaurant Keyonna was hoping for. Instead, we're at a soul food restaurant; something I'm really not that into.

Fried, fatty foods slopped with gravy and heavy sauces just don't do it for me.

But okay.

We're here.

Together.

Me.

And Omar.

Yippee.

Anyway. We caught a taxi to the train station, then rode the train into, uh, I can't remember the town.

I ask Omar where we are again. Downtown Newark, he tells me.

Not that it matters. I'm lost, no matter where we are.

But, anyway, from the train station we caught another taxi to the restaurant.

So here we sit.

Across from each other.

And I'm eyeing Omar as he sucks meat juice off the bone of an oxtail.

Yuck.

He eats fast and furious and smacks while he eats.

How insane is that?

But for some reason, I'm not the least bit embarrassed sitting here watching him eat like Conan the Barbarian.

It's almost amusing.

Still, I want to ask him why he gobbles up his food like he's rushing off to a race and it's his last meal.

But I decide against it.

Not my business.

Still, I'm curious to know.

He licks his fingers, then his lips, before taking a sip of his drink. "So, how you gettin' along wit' Quita?"

Umm. I'm not. "Okay, I guess." I pick at my small plate of garden salad.

"Cool, cool." He picks up another oxtail. And slurps on it. Then looks up at me. Grease and meat juicy coats his lips. "You 'n' her been kickin' it?"

Define kicking it? I shake my head. "Not really. But she told me you bribed her with the promise of a new pocketbook if she dragged me along with her."

He frowns, furrowing his brows. "Yo, word is bond. Quita's full of BS, yo. I ain't tell her no *shi*—mess like that. She asked me to cop that joint for her on the strength."

"It really doesn't matter. I was just surprised when she said it."

I take a sip of my cranberry juice.

"Yo, don't listen to that girl. She likes to keep a buncha mess goin', like her moms."

Yeah, I see. "Oh," I say.

He looks at me and grins. I try not to stare at the meat stuck between his two front teeth. "Yo, don't front like you ain't peeped it, too."

I shrug. "Sort of." I don't trust him to say more than that. After all, blood is thicker than water.

The ties that bind them run deep.

He may embrace me as his, um...

I swallow.

Fight to bring myself to finish the sentence.

To say the words.

But I can't.

I am not what he believes I am.

I am not what he wants me to be.

I feel no kinship to him.

He sighs. "Quita's a..." He pauses, shaking his head.

Liar.

"...piece of work; for real for real. She's got mad issues. Her moms just lets her run the streets 'n' do whatever she wants. So she's not used to dealin' wit' people. Her mouth's real slick."

No kidding.

He eyes me. "Yo, on e'erything. Don't let Quita bully you; real ish. If you gotta check 'er, then check 'er. Otherwise she's gonna stay poppin' off at the mouth; you feel me?"

I shrug one shoulder. "I guess. Fighting isn't really my thing, though," I say. Truth is, I've only had one fight my whole entire life, and I cried every day for almost a week after that. I was in seventh grade and this eight grader kept taunting me, pushing me around, until one day I'd had enough of her and punched her in the mouth.

The scary thing is, I kept punching her over and over until there was blood everywhere, and the poor girl was almost passed out.

I was suspended for a whole week. Not because I defended myself from her bullying me, but because I'd beaten her up really, really bad and her parents were all up in arms about it.

What else was I supposed to do?

I'd colored within the lines. Followed the rules. Told the teachers. Told the principal. Daddy had even come to the school and had a big meeting with the girl and her parents. And, *still*, she kept taunting me every chance she got.

"Well, sometimes you gotta go wit' the hands to show a mofo what time it is," Omar says, steamrolling over the memory, "otherwise they're gonna keep testin' you, nah'mean?"

He wipes his mouth with a napkin, then his hands.

He belches.

Loud.

Doesn't even cover his mouth.

I frown.

"Yo, my bad."

Our server comes back to refill his orange juice. I can't remember what she said her name was, so I glance at her name tag. *Alani*.

Nice name, I think.

Her pierced eyebrow rises at the sight of my barely touched salad. "Umm. Is the salad okay? Can I get you something else?"

"It's okay." I force a smile. "I'm not really that hungry." She asks if I want a refill on my cranberry juice. I shake my head. "No, thanks."

She eyes Omar, clearly interested in him, judging by the way her gaze glides over him. He grins at her. And she smiles back. Then swishes her hips a few shakes harder than she had before coming over here.

He waits until she's out of earshot, then says, "She's gonna knock a few dollars off the bill; word is bond."

I give him a puzzled look. "Why would she do that?"

His grin widens. "'Cause I still got it, baby girl."

I stare at him.

Not knowing what it is he thinks he *still* has.

I hear Aunt Terri's voice in my ear, *"Try to get to know him...give it a few weeks...I'll send for you in a couple of weeks..."*

Yeah, okay.

I glance at my watch.

Time is so not on my side right now.

Oh, how I wish I could click my heels three times and find my way home.

I'm so, so homesick.

"What you wanna do now? You wanna go check out a flick?" Omar asks, reaching for his drink.

Do we have to? I shrug. "I guess."

The waitress comes back, wanting to know if there's anything else she can get us.

"Coffee?"

"Tea?"

"Or me?"

I imagine her saying this.

"Nah, we good, pretty," Omar says, licking his lips.

She giggles like a love-struck schoolgirl. "Okay. I'll bring you your bill in just a sec."

"Cool," he says eyeing her as she walks—no, *shakes*, off, before he turns his gaze back on me. "What you into? Action flicks? Comedy?"

Poetry. "Thrillers, mostly," I say.

"Oh, word? Cool, cool. You wanna catch the new Morgan Freeman flick then?"

No. Not really. "If you want."

He smiles.

And something tugs at me.

I'm not sure what it is.

It makes me uncomfortable.

But not in a creepy, perverted kind of way.

It's strange.

That's the only way to describe it.

This feeling.

"So how you enjoyin' ya'self so far?"

I shrug, reaching for my drink. I take a slow sip. Then I wipe my mouth and take another long sip. Yes. Stalling. "It's okay. I guess. Different." No. Horrible.

He eyes me as if he's hoping for more.

I have nothing more to give him.

I hate it here.

The word *hate* is such a harsh word.

Detestation.

Abhorrence.

Loathing.

Okay, I have strong dislike.

Yeah, that's it. I strongly dislike it here.

But I despise that Sha'Quita girl even more.

Detest her.

And, yet, I still attempt to take the high road every chance I get to keep some level of peace between us.

"Just okay, huh?" Omar says, slicing into my thoughts.

I swallow. "It's nothing personal," I say diplomatically. "I'm just homesick."

"Oh, a'ight. But you think you might wanna live out here?"

I keep from frowning. Which part of *I'm homesick* didn't he understand?

The *I'm*?

Or the *homesick*?

"Heck no! Never!" I hear myself shouting. But what comes out of my mouth is, "I really don't think so."

"Oh, nah?" he says, a tinge of disappointment resonating in his voice.

I shake my head. "It's too fast here." And dirty.

"Yeah," he agrees, nodding, "it's definitely fast-paced; you gotta know how'ta keep up. But you'll get the hang of it if you stay."

I sigh, feeling a wave of melancholy rush over me. The fact that I am here and not back home saddens me.

I shudder at my reality.

Omar eyes me, catching the movement. He seems to notice everything. "I know you miss ya home, baby girl. But this can be home for you, too. If you'd let it be."

And then, just like that, I feel it coming. Tears. Hot and salty on my lower lids.

Oh, this is so not the place for a meltdown.

But my tears were threatening to spill over in any moment.

I bite into my quivering lip. Then I reach for a napkin and touch it to my eyes, hoping to cut my tears off before they pour out.

Omar stares at me, alarmed, reaching over and touching my hand. "Yo, I know this is hard for you. But you ain't gotta go through it alone; a'ight? I got you."

But I want Daddy.

Not him.

But he's all you got, I hear in my head. *Even Aunt Terri has abandoned me.*

He's all you have, Nia...

Sadly, this is good enough.

Not for me.

48

A week has gone by since the night out at the restaurant with Omar. And I haven't really seen him since. He comes in and out. Usually *in* by the time I'm already asleep. And *out* by the time I awake.

I get an occasional text asking if I'm *good*.

No, I'm not good.

I'm still here.

"So, how is it living with the convict?" Crystal wants to know. She and I are on FaceTime, playing catch-up. As close as I am to her, I feel like I'm a million miles away from her.

I roll my eyes. Scoot back on the bed I've been assigned to. Then lean back against the wall. I jerk forward, looking in back of me, up and down the wall.

No creepy crawlers.

But just in case, I lean forward, not letting my back touch the wall. "I'm *not* living with him. I'm *staying* with him for the summer." If that's what you want to call it, since he doesn't technically have his own place. And he's never here.

But, okay. The semantics aren't really all that important.

"And he's an *ex*-convict," I add.

"Ohhhh, okay, touchy, I see. So how's it going so far?"

Horrible. "It's okay, I guess. It's nothing like back in California. It's..." I sigh. "It's different."

She narrows her eyes. "Uh-huh. And how's that MoNeefa girl?"

MoNeefa? I stifle a laugh. "You mean Sha'Quita."

"Yeah, her. Is she still acting trashy?"

"*Acting?*" I giggle. "It's what she is."

She shakes her head. "Is she still bothering you?"

I sigh. "Depends on what side of the bed she rolls off of."

She grunts. "*Mmph.* She sounds like she's been raised on a cattle farm, the way you've described her."

I let out a disgusted breath, glancing over on her side of the room. "More like a pigsty."

"And," she leans into the screen, her voice lowered to almost a whisper, "how's it going with those cockroaches?"

I shudder in disgust, feeling my skin crawl. I glance back at the wall. "I go through a can of spray a day; just to keep them away."

She laughs. "Hey, that rhymes. Please don't come home writing poems about those nasty little scavengers."

I frown. "Ugh. Not even." I'll most likely write about scavengers of the human kind, or not.

"Did you know there are about four thousand species of those little nasty buggers? And they have six legs. Two antennae. And some have wings? And they can actually live for weeks without their heads. *Weeks*, Nia! You could be among some headless cockroaches right now and not even know it. Be careful, Nia-pooh."

Ohmygod! How random.

"No. I didn't know that," I say sarcastically. "Why don't you tell me all about the plight of a headless cockroach. Please and thank you."

"Well, since you insist," she says. "Wait. Are you being sarcastic right now?"

"Um, yes," I say, shaking my head. "You didn't possibly think I was serious, did you?"

"Well, yes, Nia. I did. This is not the time for sarcasm. I've been reading up on those critters. And it sounds like a pandemic is happening over there in that apartment. And did you know that they're filthy pests in the States, but are considered tasty treats in places like Cambodia."

"Ohmygod! Are you serious right now? Like are you really going to spend our FaceTime talking to *me* about roaches? Huh?"

"Yes. I am. This is serous, Nia. And if you are going to be living among those disgusting little creatures, then you need to know they carry nasty bacteria on their bodies and can wreak havoc, causing all types of diseases to spread. And they can even be transported from place to—"

"Crystal, stop it! I don't want to hear anything else about it. You're making my stomach turn with your newfound fascination with—"

She cuts me off. "I'm not fascinated, Nia. I'm concerned."

I narrow my eyes.

"Okay, okay. Maybe a little curious as to how my best friend is living among them."

I frown, wishing I'd never told her about their roach problem. Okay, maybe it's not a problem for them, since they seem okay living with them.

But it's a problem for me.

Those things give me the creeps.

And I haven't had a good night's rest since I've been here, afraid I'd wake up to them in my bed, or crawling on me in the middle of the night.

Or worse.

Making a nest in my hair.

"Anyway," she says, switching gears, "when are you moving to Georgia?"

I let out a frustrated breath. Aunt Terri still hasn't returned any of my calls. I don't know what is going on with her. I keep thinking that maybe something's happened to her.

I hope not.

But the longer I don't hear from her, the bleaker my future seems.

She's my only chance at freedom from this hell.

"I don't know," I say sorrowfully. I swallow the lump in my throat. "I haven't heard from my aunt."

Crystal gasps. "Ohmygod, Nia! Not even a text?"

I sadly shake my head. "No."

Her eyes widen. "Nia-pooh. Do you think she might be avoiding you?"

I close my eyes, willing back tears.

God, I hope that isn't the case.

"*Yes,*" I say, my voice in almost a painful whisper, before the first tear falls.

49

"Ooooooh, I wanna get pounded out real right," Sha'Quita loudly announces, seductively sucking her cherry Blow Pop into her mouth, then popping it from her lips. She flicks her tongue over it.

I frown, wondering why I let Kee-Kee—I mean, Keyonna—talk, I mean badger, me into coming out to this park with Sha'Quita and her friend. Everything in my spirit told me it was a bad idea. But did I listen?

Nooo.

Now here I am.

Bored out of mind, biting bullets and holding the shells between my teeth.

"It's been a minute since I got piped out," I hear Sha'Quita say, pulling me out of my thoughts. I blink, glancing over at her as she's sucking her Blow Pop back into her mouth.

I cringe, feeling sorry for that poor lollipop as she assaults it with her nastiness.

I'm convinced she does it for the attention, though.

There's a group of guys playing basketball, and some sprinkled about on the bleachers watching the game. And watching Sha'Quita.

The featured attraction.

She bends at the knees, then winds her hips, giving them what they want. A show.

Her friend, Chardonnay, laughs. "Tramp, you stay tryna get piped out."

"Girl, bye," Quita says dismissively. She flicks her hair over her shoulder. "Ain't nothin' wrong wit' gettin' ya back twisted every now and then."

Twisted?

This girl is ridiculously crazy.

She's disgusting.

All she ever talks about is sex.

Sex.

Sex.

Sex.

Any way she can get it.

Or give it.

She seems obsessed with it.

I've never met a girl like her. No. Correction: I've never had to *hang* around a girl like her. Honestly speaking, I'd never befriend someone like her.

Fast and easy.

Quick to give up her most prized possession.

Wasting *her*self.

Disrespecting *her*self.

Hating *her*self.

Yes. She has to *hate* herself to keep degrading herself, to keep using her body as some boy's playground.

Yes. That has to be it.

Hate.

Pure.

Unadulterated.

Self-hatred.

And, even though I know it's none of my business what she does with her body (after all, it *is* her body), I can't help but wonder how many boys she's let *gut* her out—as she so distastefully put it. How many times she's been passed around? How many of them did she not use a condom with? How many visits to the clinic has she had?

I'm thinking this, wondering...

I simply can't fathom being so recklessly carefree about sex; or being sexual, for that matter. Maybe because I'm still a virgin.

Still saving myself for the right time, with the right person, for the right reasons.

Not for love.

Not for acceptance.

Not for validation.

Not for the sake of having a boyfriend.

No.

I won't be some boy's conquest.

Or his cause.

Or his casualty.

No. I'm worth more than that.

Because I say I am.

Because I know I am.

And she should know, too.

But obviously she doesn't. I guess girls like her only know what they know by the examples they're surrounded by. Her mother is her example.

A closet drunk, I suspect. And marijuana—I mean, *weed*—head.

And she doesn't know her dad.

So I understand why...I guess.

I'm glad Daddy always told me to never let a boy or sex validate me. He told me my self-worth should never be defined by sex. I thank God he had the *talk* with me about sex and boys. Even though I knew it was probably one of the most uncomfortable things he had to do, he had it, because I was his baby girl. His butterfly.

I was eleven when we had our first talk. Then twelve. Then every birthday after that, I knew to expect *the talk*. *"It's my responsibility to prepare you for life as best I can,"* he'd said, shifting in his seat beside me. He took my hand in his and looked me in the eyes. *"I love you, Butterfly. But there are some things about life you'll have to learn on your own. I can protect you best I can. But I can't shield you from heartbreak. I wish I could. All I ask is that you don't confuse sex with love. I ask that you wait. Hold out for as long as you can. With sex comes a lot of responsibility… What feels good to you isn't always going to be good for you… Don't ever let sex be what defines you…"*

And I won't.

Ever.

Heck. I've only been kissed, and only by one boy. The last time he pried my lips open with his tongue, and I welcomed the taste of him.

Still, I am untouched.

And, yet, in the corners of my mind, I sometimes lie awake at night and try to imagine, sometimes wonder… what it'd be like to go a little further. Not that I'm ready for it, or entertaining it.

Still…

I flip open my notebook, pull off the cap to my pen, and scribble:

In a world where
~~black~~ women
fight
patriarchy
misogyny
sexism
~~seems like~~
there's a
new breed of witlessness;

a group
of
disconnected girls
whose loose tongues
spew
~~a thick~~
venom
of ignorance
and
self-hate
and
cling
to
negative connotations
that ~~they allow~~
~~to~~ validate them
A ~~rights of~~ foolish
rite of passage
to be
labeled
to be
defined
to be
stamped
to be
nailed down
by
degrading labels
Bitch
Ho
Slut
Tramp
Whore
Trick

*terms of
endearment
for
the
emotionally
inflicted…*

50

"I think I'm a nympho," I hear Quita say as I close my journal and slide it back into my bag. I screw the cap back on my ink pen and twirl it between my fingers.

She says this so matter-of-factly, as if she's talking about something as simple as a new pair of jeans, or the weather.

Chardonnay says what I'm thinking. "Oh, you *think*?" She laughs. "Tramp, you definitely a nymph. You know you stay with sex on the brain."

She waves her on. "What. Ever. Annnnwaaayz. Speaking of *brain*, Becky. I heard you let John-John touch ya tonsils last night."

I'm not sure whom she's talking about. And I don't dare ask.

Besides, I'm just not that interested in *what*, or *who*, touched her tonsils.

"You'se a damn lie," Chardonnay snaps, giving her the finger. Her shoulder-length braids swing back and forth. "That boy ain't never been in the back of my throat, boo."

Now Quita laughs. "Girl, *you* the lie. Star done already spilled the tea, boo. So don't even front. And why was he sneakin' outta ya bedroom window, then, if you ain't let him swab ya neck up?"

Chardonnay sucks her teeth. "Trick, you 'n' Star can kiss

my *phatty*. John-John ain't ever been inside my bedroom. And he definitely ain't swabbed nothin' over here."

They're both talking loudly, as if they're talking over jackhammers and blaring horns, as if they want the boys over on the court to hear how nasty they are.

I look over at some tall, lanky guy in sagging sweats snatch the ball from another player, then take off running toward the opposite end of the basketball court. Arm in the air, and the ball sails through the air. *Swish*. "Nothing but net," as Daddy would say.

I sigh inwardly, sick of hearing these two going back and forth about who's lying about who sexed who, when, and where.

I pull out my journal again.

"This broad. *Psst*." Quita sucks her teeth. "Here she goes wit' that damn corny-azz notebook again. I know you ain't even 'bout to start writin' out here... *again*."

She snaps her fingers. "Wait. I forgot, this chick thinks she's the next Erykah Badu."

Chardonnay chuckles. "Don't play, girl. I love me some Erykah Badu."

Quita grunts. "*Mmph*. Well, Erykah Badu she ain't."

This girl's really clueless.

I give her an incredulous look. "I'm not *trying* to be anyone but me."

"*Mmph*. I can't tell," she says nastily.

The question at the tip of my tongue, I contemplate asking it, knowing it might be received with attitude. But I'm tired of her. Tired of her mouth. Tired of her testing me. So I ask it anyway. "And what's wrong with me writing out here, in *my* journal? How is what I'm doing affecting *you*?"

She huffs. "Oh don't get it twisted, *bish*. I'm *not* affected by it. But you supposed to be out here chillin' with us, but you bein' mad rude, pullin' out that funky ole book. I should burn it."

I blink.

She cranks her neck from side to side. "Yeah, I said it. I should. Burn. It. And *whaaat*? Think I won't. You coulda kept ya corny butt home for that. You real whack."

Then let me be whack. How is it bothering you?

Chardonnay chuckles. "Quita, let Cali Girl do her. It ain't like we got anything in common wit' her. Let Miss Corny write. All we doin' is babysittin', anyway."

Babysitting?

Corny?

I frown.

Quita laughs. "Uh-huh. But I ain't changin' no ho's diaper, though."

I sigh.

I've never been called so many derogatory names in my entire life as I've been called in the last month being here, around this girl.

I've had enough.

"Why do you have to refer to me as a *ho*?" I say brusquely. "I'm *not* a ho. Nor will I *ever* be one."

Quita bats her lashes, then rolls her neck. "Well, you must *be* a ho if you gotta tell me you ain't one."

I match her stare. This time I'm not backing down. "I'm telling you I'm not one, because that's what it is. It's disrespectful."

She rolls her eyes. "Girl, bye. It's a figure of speech."

"I know that's right," Chardonnay chimes in. "These sensitive hoes need to stop."

Quita sucks her teeth. "*Psst*. I ain't thinkin' 'bout her. You already know how I get down. I call you whatever I wanna call you."

I pull in my bottom lip.

Think before I speak.

I know this girl isn't the most intellectual, but that doesn't stop me from telling her that I don't see it as *just* a figure of speech. I tell her I don't carry myself like a *ho* so I don't want her calling me one.

But look in the mirror and I can show you one.

She stares at me, long and hard. "*Bish*, please. I know you not even tryna check me."

Chardonnay pulls out a pack of Newport cigarettes. "*Mmph*. Looks like somebody tryna see you *turnt* up."

She gives Chardonnay a dismissive wave. "Girl, *puh*-lease. Don't even try'n instigate this chick. Put a battery pack up on her back if you want 'n' see how I turn up. I keep tellin' her she don't want it wit' me. She knows she don't wanna see these hands."

I shake my head. Decide to keep quiet.

Silence is sometimes the best remedy for ignorance.

Chardonnay taps her Newport box on the bleacher before opening the pack and thumping one out. She puts it between her bright orange lips, then pulls out a lighter and lights it.

I scoot down to the next bench so the smoke doesn't blow in my face.

"Whatever," she mumbles under her breath, but still loud enough for me to hear.

There's something so unattractive and unladylike about a girl smoking a cigarette.

But then again...

These girls aren't all that ladylike to begin with. And their attitudes make them extremely ugly.

I promise myself to never, ever, go anywhere else with these two. I wouldn't hang with these types of girls back home, and I don't want to start now. I don't have to. But, *if* I have to be a hostage over here on the east coast, then I need to find someone, *any*one, who is likeminded.

I need positive energy.

Not unnecessary drama.

The sound of a ball bouncing breaks my reverie. I glance to the left of me.

Shawn. I try to suppress the relief I feel at the sight of him.
I don't even know why I'm feeling this way. It's not like he's
said more than a few words to me whenever he's come
around. Still, it's the way he looks at me that intrigues me.

"Shaaaaaaaaaaaaaawn," Quita says in a singsong voice.
"Heeeeeey, boo."

"Yo, what's Gucci?" he says to her and Chardonnay.

"Not a damn thang," Chardonnay says, grinning.

"This neck work," Quita boldly states, sliding her lollipop
back into her mouth, then pulling the stick in and out.
"That's what's *Gucci*, ninja. Thought you knew."

Chardonnay giggles.

Shawn laughs. "Yo, Quita, you shot *dafuq* out."

She smacks her lips together. "*Mmmph*. I'm real, boo."

"Yeah, a'ight." He glances over at me. "What's good, cutie?"

"Nothing," I say, blushing.

Quita narrows her eyes to thin slits. "Ooh, let me find out,
you checkin' for my man. *Ho*, I'll claw your eyes out."

"I know that's right," Chardonnay chimes in. "Slice right
into the white meat."

I frown. But keep my mouth shut. Like always.

"Annnnnyway," Quita says, dismissively. "You smokin', boo?"

"Nah, not today, yo. Tryna cut back."

"Lies," Quita says. She laughs. "Since when?"

"Nah, real spit. Since I got hired at Walmart."

"Ooooooh, word?" she says, excitedly. "When they hire you?"

"Today."

"Oh, that's wasssup. My future baby daddy got him a j-o-b
so I can collect them future child support checks."

He cracks up laughing. "Not. I ain't havin' no babies, yo."

"Yeah, okay. Not today we not."

He ignores the comment and takes a seat next to me on
the bench, and suddenly I'm feeling nervous.

"So how you likin' Jersey so far, cutie?" he says to me.

I shrug. "It's okay, I guess."

He shifts his body and studies my face. His eyes are melted pools of deep, dark chocolate that I feel myself slowly drowning in.

I don't know why he makes me so nervous.

I shift my eyes from his stare. Glance down at my sandaled feet. But he says something else that causes me to look back at him. "You should let me show you around."

I blink him into view. And I notice he has long, thick lashes for a guy. Okay, yes. I'm checking him out.

But why?

Because he's a welcome distraction from the Chardonnay and Sha'Quita show.

"You've been to the city yet?" he wants to know.

I shake my head. "No, not—"

"What, you tryna be her tour guide now? Or nah?" Quita butts in.

"Maybe," he says, lightly tapping my leg with his long leg.

Is he flirting with me?

He winks at me. And my face heats.

Ohmygod, he is.

Nia, stop. He's only being nice to you.

"Yeah, okay," Quita says. "What. *Ev. Errr.* Annnnywaaaay. Later for the tour guide ish. When you startin' ya job, boo?"

"Next week."

"Ooooh, I know you gonna hook me up wit' ya employee discount," Chardonnay says excitedly. "You know I stopped boostin', right? So I'ma need them discounts."

Before I can stop myself, I make the mistake of asking—no one in particular—what *boostin'* is.

Quita and Chardonnay both look at me as if I have three heads.

"You're jokin', *right?*" Quita says, indignation coloring her voice.

"No, I'm serious," I say innocently. "I've never heard of it."

Chardonnay laughs. "Girrrl, you told me she was slow. But I ain't know she was *that* damn slow."

"I'm *not* slow," I snap defensively. "*Slow* is thinking Erykah Badu is a poet."

Shawn chuckles, shaking his head. "Yo, ma, leave it alone. You don't wanna know."

Quita glares at me. "*Bish*, I know you not even tryna call me slow. Let me show you how slow these hands are..."

And with that, she's snatching my journal out of my hand, waving it in the air.

"Now, come again. Who's the *slow* one?"

"Please give me back my journal, Sha'Quita," I say calmly.

"Nope. You stay tryna shade me. Ole shady-azz ho. I ain't givin' you *sh*—"

"I'm not playing with you," I say calmly, masking my rising anger.

She flicks me a dismissive hand. "What. Evvvvver. I was only playin' wit' ya butt. But since you wanna turn up. Turn up. Let me see ya work, boo. And while you at it, why don't you tell us why you always cheesin' up in Shawn's face, like you tryna get at his eggplant."

I blink.

Eggplant?

I try to wrap my mind around what the heck she's talking about.

I don't even like egg—

Ohmygod!

Finally it dawns on me what she means.

Her filthy little muddled mind stays in the gutter.

Shawn laughs. "Yo, Quita, chill, chill. You shot out, yo."

She snorts. "*Chill*, hell. This little slut-bucket stays tryna get in yo' drawz on some slickness. I done already told her that you're saving yourself for me. And this undercover top gobbler still tryna give you the business on the low. She knows she wanna give you the cookie. Tramp-azz."

My face flushes.

Embarrassment floods me.

I give her a baffled look.

Where in the heck did she come up with this craziness? And what does it have to do with being called slow?

I'm convinced, now more than ever—she's bipolar.

Shawn keeps laughing. And I'm not sure what part he finds most hilarious, *him* saving himself for *her*, the look on my shocked face, or her ridiculously ludicrous notion that I'm a *top gobbler* (yuck!) or trying to *give* him—or *any*one, for that matter—my *cookies*.

"I'm not you, Quita. I'm not giving up anything to a boy."

"*Mmmph*. Maybe not them drawz, but you a top slopper, *bish*."

"Yo, you buggin', for real for real," Shawn says, shaking his head. "Relax, yo. You play too much, Quita." He glances over at me, a mixture of what looks like amusement and mischief and sympathy dancing in his eyes. "Yo, don't pay her silly butt no mind. She stays talkin' outta her neck, for real."

I shrug. "She can think what she wants. I know what I am."

"I don't *think* anything, boo. I know what you are, too. I know ya kind. Undercover tricks. And I know you tryna get pounded out like a porn star."

Shawn huffs. "Damn, Quita. Sit down 'n' relax, yo. Give shorty her book back. You effen up the vibe, for real for real."

"Oh no, *nucca*. I knooooow, *you* not even tryna play me for this corny broad."

"Yo, ain't no one takin' up for no one; I'm just sayin', yo. Chill *dafuq* out."

Quita shoots me a nasty look.

Head tilted, brow raised, I match her glare. I've had enough of her.

"You can call me names all you want," I say through gritted teeth. "But I'm not the one wearing cheap weaves and hooker heels, and walking around with a clown face on with

all that crazy makeup caked up on your face. You can call me
what you want. But I'm not the one who looks like one of
the Muppets."

Someone laughs.

"Ohhh, snap," someone else says. "She called you out."

"Oooh, she callin' you Miss Piggy, girl," Chardonnay insti-
gates. "She tried it."

Quita sucks her teeth. "*Bish*, please. She can't come for
me. Ain't no pigs over here. Try again."

My chest starts heaving.

"I'm *not* playing with you, Quita. I'm asking you *nicely* to
give. Me. Back. My. Journal."

I'm trying hard to keep it together. But I feel my temper
rising. Feel myself being pulled into the inferno.

"Or *whaaat*, Miss Corny?" she challenges, defiantly snatching open my journal and preparing to violate my private,
most inner thoughts. "Okay, let's see what kinda juicy tales
you servin'..."

My eyes flash wildly.

My temper flares.

And then I am hopping up from my seat. "No!" I scream,
spittle flying out of my mouth. "Give me back my book!"

She smirks. Amusement dances in her eyes as she begins
to back away while preparing to read one of my entries. And
this only incenses me more.

"Ooh, she—"

Slap!

Before she has a chance to say anything more, my hand
connects with her face. I smack her so hard her whole head
swings to the right, practically spinning her around.

I don't give her a chance to think.

Before she can gather herself, I am punching her upside
the head until she's stumbling backward. And my journal
flies out of her hand.

She's awakened something deep within.

And now I can't stop myself.

All I see is red.

I'm on fire.

And now she's going to get burned.

She's going to learn: Don't. Mess. With. Me.

I am smacking and punching her, then wrapping my hands up in her weave and swinging her down to the ground.

She screams and curses and tries to fight me off. But my hands are faster, my punches harder. I fight her for every disrespectful thing she's ever said to me.

I fight her for every kid she might have ever bullied.

"Ohhhhh, *sheeeeeeeeeeeiiiiit!*" I hear someone yell out.

"Ohmygod! Ohmygod! She's beatin' Quita down!"

There's hooting.

And hollering.

And cheering.

"Fight!"

"Fight!"

And then...

There's Sha'Quita screaming for someone to jump in and help her.

But no one does.

51

"This is some straight BS," Omar says, a look of disbelief on his face, as he opens the passenger-side door. He shakes his head, and waits for me to get in, then slams the door. He's come to pick me up from the police station. I can't remember much of anything after I swung Quita down to the ground and punched her in the face. I remember everything around me starting to fade in and out. I remember my heart beating hard. Remember heat flashing through me. Remember hearing screaming and, at some point, feeling hands trying to pry me off of her.

And then I am in the backseat of a patrol car. Hands cuffed. Shirt torn. Face scratched. Being taken to the station. Sitting in a tiny cell.

Waiting.

Waiting for my racing heart to slow.

Waiting for the blaze to extinguish.

Waiting for the ashes.

Waiting for Omar.

None of this would be happening if I'd never been forced to come here. If Aunt Terri hadn't lied to me, if Daddy hadn't died and left me, I would never know these people.

These derelicts.

Yeah, that's what they are. Derelicts. Degenerates.

Okay, okay...that's not nice. But, oh well. I'm not in the mood for niceties at the moment. I'm angry. Still.

Sha'Quita caused this.

She asked for this.

Not me.

I open and close my right hand, and wince. It hurts like heck.

I rub my swollen knuckles.

I wouldn't have had to beat up that troublemaking girl if she hadn't kept pressing me.

Quita.

Quita.

Quita.

I can't stand her!

She's still inside. Locked up. *Good.* She has some kind of warrant for not going to court, or something like that. So they're keeping her.

Serves her right.

She had the audacity to blame *me* for her troubles when she's the one who started this. All she had to do was give me back my journal.

Wait—

My journal?

Oh, noo!

I quickly dig through my bag.

My heart sinks. No, it stops beating.

It's not here!

My journal.

"*I should burn it...*"

I feel lightheaded.

My chest tightens.

No, no, no, no...

Not my journal!

My thoughts.

My feelings.

My entire life...

Gone.

I start rocking.

And hyperventilating.

No, no, no, no...

That journal is my whole existence.

Without it, I'm, I'm, I'm—

Dead!

Flatlined!

Do not resuscitate!

Please and thank you.

No, no, no...

"Yo, I need you to tell me..."

I hear Omar talking when he gets in the car, but I am too distraught to comprehend a word he is saying.

All I can think of is my journal.

Missing.

"Y-y-you have to take m-m-me b-b-back," I stammer, trying like heck to keep from crumbling. But it's too late. I'm cracking open, and have become a babbling mess. "M-my j-j-journal..."

"Huh? Take you back where?"

The tears fall heavy.

"B-b-b-back to the p-p-park."

"The *park*?" He gives me a look of disbelief. *"Now?"*

"Y-yes. Please. M-m-my j-j-journal. It's *losssssssst*."

And now he's looking at me as if I'm insane.

Maybe I am.

Maybe I've finally fallen—or jumped—off the proverbial cliff.

Omar starts the engine, then pulls off. "Yo, I'll buy you another book, a'ight? It can't be that serious. It's dark as hell out there by now."

I choke back a scream.

Is he kidding?

I don't care.

It is *that* serious.

Everything I am is in that journal.

I've been carrying that 192-page black leather book around with me since I was twelve. Four years of front-and-back free-thinking and self-expression has been captured on most of those pages over the years.

Gone.

Thanks to that—that heathenish girl.

I sob louder.

"A'ight, yo. C'mon. Don't cry. I'll take you back to the park."

52

It wasn't there!
My journal.

My knees buckled when I finally resigned myself to the fact that we weren't going to find it, no matter how hard we looked.

We combed through the park. Nothing.

We searched up and down, under and around the bleachers. Still nothing.

I cried so hard that it made me dizzy. Blood rushed to my head. All I could do to keep from collapsing on the ground was plop down on the bleacher and cover my face in my hands and scream.

I cried out until my throat burned.

I even cursed.

Shocking.

Yes.

Me.

Used words I'd only heard in movies and in the streets.

Formed a string of profanity that shocked, and excited, me.

I punched and pounded the bleacher.

Cursed and screamed. I think I might have even made up a few words.

I don't know. I don't remember all I said. But I know what I felt.

What I'm *still* feeling.

Omar seemed confused. Still, he tried to console me best he could. But he clearly wasn't used to seeing—or *having* to deal with—an uncontrollably sobbing teenager, spewing out obscene language, almost sounding like she's speaking in tongues.

I didn't expect him to, anyway.

He wasn't Daddy.

He could never be Daddy.

So he wouldn't understand.

He couldn't understand.

Ever.

Daddy had bought me that book.

So the sentimental value of that leather book was irreplaceable.

I'd read some of my best poems out of it.

And now, and now—

What am I going to do?

I can't recapture any of those words written.

I fought that girl—that—that scallywag, to get my journal back from her, and I *still* don't have it. It's really missing. Gone! All I can think is, it's somewhere, in someone's hands, being read. All of my personal thoughts on display for prying eyes.

I'm not crying anymore.

But I'm still angry.

And I feel sick.

"I want to go home," I say the minute Omar slides back behind the wheel and shuts the door to this raggedy piece of car he's picked me up in. The outside of the car is sparkling, with glossy black paint and red shiny rims.

But the inside is...is...a hot smelly mess.

I was too distraught when I first got in to really notice.

But now...

Now I see it for what it is.

It's an old four-door black Honda, with cloth seats—cloth

seats, for God's sake!—that reeks of marijuana and cigarette smoke.

Not that I'm an expert on marijuana smells, but I've smelled enough of it being around Quita's stank butt to know what it is.

I look up, frowning. The cloth from the roof is torn.

And hanging.

I sweep my gaze around the interior.

There's a pair of red dice dangling from the rearview mirror.

For a split second, I think, *gang*.

I eye Omar and wonder whose car we're in. But I am too agitated to care. My hands are shaking—and are itching to finish smacking up Quita's face. *That stank girl had no business snatching my journal from me! And now it's gone! Lost!*

I clasp my hands in my lap to keep from hitting the dashboard. I've never been arrested. Never been inside of a cop car. Never, ever, been in trouble a day in my life.

I've never even had a fight!

Until now!

Thanks to that, that, ghetto-girl!

"We'll be home in minute," Omar says, slicing into my thoughts as he starts the engine.

Omar pulls off. Surprisingly, it purrs like a kitten.

I hadn't noticed that, either, until now.

The ride is smooth, as the engine hums along.

And like my life, this pretty, ugly car is one big elusive illusion.

An oxymoron.

He glances over at me. "You hungry?"

Am I hungry? Is he kidding me?

My brain is pounding. I just want to grow wings and fly as far away from all of this drama as I possibly can, like three thousands miles away.

Back to palm trees, golden sunshine, and crystal blue waters.

Back to Long Beach, my home.

I shift in my seat. Lean my body up against the door. "No. I want to go *home*."

"We'll—"

I shoot him a look, cutting him off. He catches my stare, and, suddenly, realization takes root. He understands. I want. To. Go. *Home*. Back to California, back to the life I was forced to abandon.

I do not fit in here.

Do not feel comfortable here.

Do not feel wanted here.

This is not *my* life.

It's *his*.

And I want no part of it, *him*, or any of this ghetto-*ness* that I've been dragged into.

I tell him this. Well, not the ghetto part. But I tell him everything else. Tell him I don't like it here. I'm not nasty or disrespectful when I tell him this. I'm simply being direct. And he tells me that I have to give it some time. That he knows it's an adjustment for me, for the both of us.

I stare at him blankly.

Time is not my friend. There's nothing to adjust to. I want out. Now.

I take a deep breath. Open and close my hands. Make two tight fists. Then open them again. All I see is Quita's face. All I see are my fists connecting to her eye, then her nose, then her mouth.

I am mad at myself for letting that girl get to me, for taking me out of character.

For making me become someone I am not used to. Turning me into someone that I'm frightened of.

This is not who I am.

Or who I want to be.

But she asked for it.

And you beat her up real good!

Served her right!

So why do I feel so bad?

I touch the side of my face. It's bruised and swollen where she punched me.

"I don't mean no harm," I finally say. I take a deep breath and clasp my hands together in my lap, "but I'm *not* ever going to adjust to this, this...*environment*," I say for a lack of a nicer word.

He makes a left turn, then a sharp right before I feel his stare on me. I look straight ahead. Stare at the road ahead of me. And pretend I don't see him. But even in the dark cabin of the car, I see him. See him searching for...something, anything.

"I know it's not the life you're used to, but..." He pauses as if he's trying to find the right words to make me a believer. "It'll get better," he offers, trying to reassure me.

It doesn't.

I feel myself shaking from the inside out.

And then I am bursting into tears.

Angry.

No, enraged.

How dare that girl!

The car swerves over. Then it abruptly stops at a curb.

Omar tries to console me, but I push away his attempt.

I want my daddy.

Want the man who raised and loved me.

I miss him.

"Yo, c'mon, baby girl, don't cry. I ain't know shit was goin' down like this, for real for real. I ain't know."

I huff, wiping my face with the back of my hand. He hands me a napkin from some takeout place, I think. In the midst of my tearful frenzy, I am still cognizant enough to glance at it, to make sure it's clean.

I wipe my eyes, then blow my nose. It's hard. The napkin, that is. "Of course you didn't know what was going on," I say, blowing my nose again. "You're *never* there."

"Word is bond, yo..."

I struggle not to roll my eyes up in my head.

How can I be related to this man? What did my mother ever see in him? Why would she have a baby with someone like him? The mother I knew was polished and articulate. She was well spoken. She was into art shows, dance recitals, and opera houses. Not...not...riffraff. Not ruffians. Not street thugs.

Not this kind of man.

Or was she?

No. This has to be some kind of mistake, some type of sick, twisted prank. This man cannot be my father. He just can't be.

I'm still waiting for someone to walk up and say—in their Maury Povich voice—that he is *not* the father.

"The minute they release her," Omar says, cutting into my thoughts as he pulls away from the curb, then speeds up the street, "I'ma check 'er, for real for real. I promise you, on everything." He makes a sharp right turn. "She'll fall back once I get at 'er."

I say nothing. Simply turn toward the window and look out at everything, and nothing at all, staring into the darkness.

I miss you so much, Daddy.

Why'd you have to leave me?

I feel myself ready to burst into tears again.

This is all just too much for me.

I bury my face in my hands and sob.

53

"*Ohmygod!*" Crystal shrieks, looking into the phone screen, mortified. "I can't believe she scratched your face and neck up."

I remove the ice pack from my hand. The swelling is starting to go down some, but it still hurts.

It throbs.

"Yeah, but you should see her," I say, not that I'm proud of the fact that she has two black eyes, a swollen lip, and possibly a broken nose.

That's what Omar said.

"Well, if you ask me, she got what she deserved," Crystal says. "She had no business bullying you."

I purse my lips and nod slightly. "You're right. Still..." I look up at the ceiling as if I know Daddy is looking down at me shaking his head. I groan inwardly. "It doesn't make it right what I did to her."

"Nia, stop. It doesn't make it wrong, either. I know you. You don't have a mean bone in your body. But obviously she does. She should have given you your journal back when you asked for it."

I agree. "And I gave her ample time to."

"Exactly. Where is she now?"

My breath comes out in a frustrated huff. "She's still locked up, I guess."

"Oh. When is she getting out?"

I shrug. "I don't know. Hopefully never."

"Wouldn't that be nice, then you wouldn't have to ever see her again."

"Exactly."

"I still can't believe you were arrested."

I shudder at the memory. "Unfortunately."

"I can't believe you were in handcuffs. And they placed you in the back of a cop car? And read you your rights?"

"Yeah."

"Ohmygod! That's so crazy."

"I was scared out of my mind," I confess.

"I bet. I'm horrified for you. Did your, uh, . . ."

"Omar?"

"Yeah, him. Did he bail you out?"

I tell her there's no bail in New Jersey for teens. God. It's a good thing I had his number in my cell; otherwise I don't know whom I would have been able to call. I guess I would have been stuck in there.

"You're a statistic now."

I roll my eyes. "Really, Crystal? Is that your best attempt at consoling me?" I shake my head. "Some friend you are."

She laughs. "I'm sorry. I'm only playing. But did they put you in a uniform?"

"Crystal!"

"Sorry. You know my heart is aching for you. But that is sooo *Orange Is the New Black*."

I suck my teeth. "Bye, Crystal. I'm hanging up on you."

"And I'll call right back," she says, suppressing a smile. "You know I will."

"Bye."

"No, don't you dare. You're my best friend."

I can't help but smile. "I can't tell," I say teasingly. I feign a pout. "If you were really my friend, you'd help me escape this modern-day Alcatraz."

She shakes her head. "I still can't believe you lost your journal, though."

"Me either. I'm so sick over it."

"I would be, too. I can't believe that girl. What's her name, again? Rita?"

"No. Sha'Quita."

Ghetto Girl.

"Yeah, that. She's so . . ."

"Ratchet," I finish for her, pacing the cheap carpet in the bedroom.

"Well, that's not quite exactly the word I was going for. But I'll take it, for a lack of a better one."

"Well, that's what she is. I have to get out of here, Crystal." I lower my voice. "I can't stay another minute around any of these crazy people. They're a bunch of alcoholics. And weed smokers. And sex addicts. I—"

I step on something, and practically jump out of my skin.

I look down. *Ohmygod! Ewww!* I've just stepped on Sha'Quita's leopard-print panties.

I kick them across the room. Then I start pacing the floor again. "I'm afraid I'm going to lose it if I stay here another night. I am so out of my element here. I feel like a leper. I don't fit in here, Crystal. I swear I don't. I've tried but I can't do this. These last two weeks have been awful."

I feel the tears coming.

I fight them back.

"I can't believe you beat her up, though," Crystal says, clearly not hearing a word I'm saying to her. "Did you pull her weave out of her head?"

"Crystal, stop!" I hiss. "Are you listening to anything I'm saying? I just told you I have to get out of here. Do you see this place?" I hold my iPhone up and slowly turn it around the room so that she can see the bedroom in its entirety, particularly Sha'Quita's side of the room.

She gasps. "Oh no."

"Oh, *yes*. And all you can think to ask is if I pulled that girl's weave out of her scalp. As you can see from the look of this nasty room, I have more pressing issues to deal with other than that girl's weave-*less* head."

She giggles. "*Sooooo* you did pull her nasty horsehair out. Good! I hope her scalp is raw."

"Crystal!" I plead. "Focus here. *Please.* I need you to stay with me. Geez! I'm in a crisis."

"Okay, okay. I'm sorry. I feel awful for you."

"Well, you should. *I* feel awful for *me*."

"Wait. Did you say they smoke crack?"

I shake my head. "No. Marijuana." I whisper into the phone. "Lots of it, especially Sha'Quita and her mother."

"Ohmygod! They smoke it *together*?"

"Sometimes, I guess. I don't know. I only walked in on them once passing it back and forth. She even offered me some."

I don't know why I tell her this, but I do.

Crystal gasps. "Who? *Rita*?"

"No. *Sha'Quita*. And, yes, she did. Her mother did, too. Once."

Truthfully, it feels good to not keep so many secrets from Crystal. She groans as I fill her in on the goings on the last several weeks. But, for some reason, I don't tell her about the time I woke up to the sounds of Sha'Quita in bed with some boy. Or the time I overheard her on the phone, making out.

I'll save that foolery for another time.

For now, I need to get out of here.

Fast.

Before Keyonna comes home and tries to fight me, too.

"I just can't believe any of it," she says, shaking her head in disbelief. "It all seems like something from off of a horrible reality show."

"Yeah," I say, solemnly. " 'Raunch and Filth,' they'd call it."

She chuckles, then apologizes. "I don't mean to laugh. But this is all too unreal."

I push out an agonizing breath. "I know. Imagine how I feel. I'm seeing it with my own two eyes. I'm living it in *three-D*. And I still can't believe any of it. I can't believe people live like this. I mean, I know they do, but it's still unbelievable to me. To not want better. To not want to *do* better."

"Nia, you know you can't do better if you don't know better. Maybe that's the best they have in them."

I shrug, half believing that this is the best for anyone. "I guess."

"I'm not saying it's right or wrong. I'm simply saying, who are we to judge? We haven't had to walk in any of their shoes, so we don't know what their stories are. Everyone isn't as fortunate as us."

I swallow. She's right.

Still...

I'm not in the mood for a moral lesson. Nor am looking to play social worker, or social scientist, or be in a social experiment to try and figure it all out.

I'm just not that invested in knowing the cause.

The only thing on my mind is an escape.

She wants to know why I didn't tell her how miserable things really were here for me. I tell her because I wasn't ready for her to know the whole truth, only bits and pieces of it. That I hoped things might improve. But they haven't. And I can't keep it in any longer.

"I'm telling you, Crystal. I've been living in hellfire ever since I stepped off that plane and walked through these doors. These people are unreal."

"Poor thing," she says sympathetically. "What are you going to do now?"

Hurl myself over a cliff.

"I don't know. As soon as I get off the phone with you, I'm calling my aunt. She has to send for me."

Crystal gives me a look of uncertainty. "You think she will?"

"Of course. She has to. Once I tell her everything that's been going on, she'll get me the heck out of here."

"I wish you didn't have to go to Georgia."

I sigh. "Me either. But what other choice do I have? It's either here, or there."

She frowns. "That sucks. I wish there was a way you could come back here. To Long Beach."

"Yeah. Me too."

Sadness washes over me. I miss my home. My friends. My life. I miss Daddy.

"I can't stay here," I whisper into the phone, wiping tears as they fall from my eyes.

Crystal cries with me. "You don't have to. I'm going to ask my parents if you can stay here with us. I know they'll say yes."

My heart leaps. "Ohmygod, Crystal! Thank you! You think they will?"

"I know they will."

There's hope after all.

"Ohgod, thank you! I love you, girl. I owe you big time."

"I love you, too. And, as soon as they get back from vacation, I'll ask them. Okay?"

Wait—

"*Vacation?* Your parents are away?"

"Yeah," she tells me. "They're in South Beach."

"When are they coming back?"

"In two weeks," she tells me.

My heart drops.

All hope deflates.

Oh, well... so much for an immediate rescue.

"Oh, no." I sob. "I can't stay here that long, Crystal. I have to get out of here *now*."

"I know. Don't cry, Nia. I promise I'll see what I can do. Maybe you can go to your aunt's until then."

I nod. Sniffle. Wipe tears away. "Yeah, maybe."

I glance at the time. It's almost eleven. I don't want to call Aunt Terri too late. But this is an emergency. It's a life-and-death situation.

"I better go," I say, sitting on the edge of my bed, wiping my wet face with my hand. "I need to call my aunt before she goes to bed."

"Okay. But make sure you call me back right after you talk to her."

"I will," I say, right before hanging up.

Seconds later, I am scrolling through my phone in search of Aunt Terri's number. Then dialing it. It rings twice before a recording comes on. "The subscriber you've reached has a number that has been disconnected or is no longer in service..."

I blink.

Oh, no. This can't be right.

I try the number again.

"The subscriber you've reached..."

My heart stops beating.

I immediately try her house number.

Then I burst into tears, when the recording says, "The number you have reached has been disconnected..."

Defeated.

Dejected.

Distraught.

I end the call.

54

Frantically, I scramble around the room, pulling open drawers and stuffing my things inside my duffel bag. I snatch open the cramped closet and start yanking my clothes off hangers, tossing them inside my suitcase.

I have no plan.

Well, I do.

To get the heck out of here.

But with no money and no friends here, I'm at a loss.

My options are limited.

Real limited.

Stay here. Or wander the streets.

No, you can't just wander the streets. Are you crazy, girl? Those streets are dangerous at night.

What if you're kidnapped, or worse... killed?

Ohmygod, ohmygod, ohmygod, ohhhhhhhhhmygod! What am I going to do?

I start pacing from the door to the window and back.

Back and forth.

Back and forth.

I feel myself starting to lose it.

All of my life I've done what's right.

I've been a good kid.

Never broken any rules.

Gotten good grades.

Stayed out of trouble.

Never gave Daddy any problems.

Did everything asked of me.

And for what?

Just so Daddy could die on me?

So I could be bamboozled into coming to New Jersey?

For Aunt Terri to disappear on me?

It just isn't fair.

All these crazy thoughts start racing through my head. Thoughts of running away, thoughts of hitchhiking my way back across country, back to Long Beach.

Then I start imagining Sha'Quita getting out of jail and coming back to slaughter me in my sleep, or having me jumped by her crazy friends.

Stop. Get it together, Nia. Think.

I try Aunt Terri's number again. "The subscriber you've reached has a number that—"

I end the call.

Oh. God.

How could she do this to me?

How could she—

Something slams into the wall, startling me.

It's the door.

"Oh, you like sneakin' hoes, huh, *bisssssh?*"

My eyes widen in horror.

It's Keyonna.

And she looks crazed.

"I-I-I didn't sneak her." The words stumble out of my mouth as I step back.

She lunges at me. "Don't lie to me! Quita tol' me everything! You got my baby locked up. Snitchin'-azz trick!"

"I—"

Whap!

Ohmygod!

She smacks me so hard tears spring from my eyes, and I'm seeing stars.

My hand goes up to my stinging face.

And then Kee-Kee has me cornered, fist clenched into tight fists. "Sneak me, *bissssh*!"

"I-I-I didn't sneak her!" I scream, tears flooding my eyes. "I don't deserve—"

Whack!

"No, tramp! You deserve ya azz—"

"Kee-Kee, *whatdafuq*, yo?!" Omar demands, charging into the bedroom, yanking this crazy lady away from me. "Yo, I know you didn't just put ya *muthafawkin'* hands on her." He's up in her face, pointing his finger inches from her eyeballs.

Now I'm more scared than ever because he has this ice-cold look in his eyes. And every vein in his forehead is protruding. I'm afraid he's going to hit her.

Or worse.

I'm terrified.

I've never been witness to any of this type of violence.

Ever.

I'm shaking.

"Yeah, I slapped that sneaky ho," she yells in his face. I can see spittle flying from her lips as she speaks. "Quita's locked up 'cause of this trick!"

"Yo, shut ya dumb-azz. Quita's locked up 'cause of her own damn self. She stay runnin' her mouth 'n' you know it. She popped off at the wrong one 'n' got that top rocked. Period. But word is bond, yo," he warns, his tone bone chilling. "If you *ever* put ya hands on my seed again, I'ma break both ya arms, sister or not; ya heard?" He narrows his eyes at her.

She curses him, calls him every dirty street name you can possibly call someone. Tells him she hopes he ends up back in prison. Then she threatens to have him *handled* for getting up in her face.

I can't believe any of this.

"Yeah, a'ight. Tell them mofos they know where to find me!" He walks over to me. "Let me see ya face." I drop my hand. He touches the side of my face, and I wince.

His nostrils flare.

He shakes his head. Then he says, "Yo, pack ya stuff. We gettin' the *eff* outta here."

55

A week later...

"**H**ey, sweetness," Miss Peaches says, poking her head into the bedroom she's so graciously given me to stay in. "There's someone outside to see you. And honey, if I were fifteen years younger I'd hike up my skirt and show him a real good time."

I look up at her in her red halter top and short denim skirt.

Her lips are bright red and glossy.

"Did he say who he is?"

She bats her lashes. "Oh, his name is *Fine,* girlfriend. That's all you need to know. Now get up 'n' go on out there to see what he wants. He says he has something for you."

I furrow my brow, perplexed.

She playfully rolls her eyes up in her head, placing a hand up on her hip. "Well, don't keep him waiting. Get on up 'n' go claim your prize."

I groan inwardly, getting up from the bed, slipping into my sandals, then shuffling out into the living room.

My mouth drops open when I get to the screen door.

The last person I ever expected to see is standing out on the porch.

Shawn.

He's smiling.

"Ohmygod. What are you doing here? How did you know I was here?"

"Whoa, whoa. Slow down, ma." He pulls a hand out from behind his back, holding out a leather-bound book. "I thought you might be lost wit'out this."

My eyes widen.

OMG!

It's my journal.

And before I know it, I am sprinting out the front door, practically knocking him over to take it from him. "Ohmygod! Thank you! Thank you!" I say, tears springing from my eyes as I clutch it to my chest. "I thought I'd never see this again. Thank you so much. Ohmygod!"

I can't stop crying.

He has made my day.

"Yo, it's all love, ma-ma. I scooped it up when you 'n' Quita started rockin'," he tells me, easing himself down on the top step. "Yo, sit wit' me for a minute."

I swallow. Then I sit beside him. He leans over and lightly bumps my shoulder. "You a'ight, though?"

I wipe my face with the bottom of my shirt, then nod. "Yeah. I guess." Then I look down at the journal in my hand. "No. I'm better now. Thanks to you. You have no idea what you've done by bringing this here. I can't thank you enough."

He grins at me. "I'm glad I could brighten ya day, love. You too pretty to be sad."

My face heats. "Thank you."

"Yo, how's ya hand?"

I drop my gaze and open and close it. It still hurts, but not as bad. And it isn't as swollen.

I shrug. "It's okay."

He rubs his chin, nodding. "Oh a'ight; that's wassup. But, yo, ya hand game is mad nice, for real for real. Where'd you learn to rock like that?"

I shift uncomfortably. "My father." There's a panging in my heart as I say this.

"Oh, word? Damn. That's what it is. You took her whole face off, yo."

I shift uncomfortably. "I didn't want to. Can we not talk about it, though?"

"No worries, ma. She ain't really effen wit' me right now like that, anyway, 'cause I told her she was dead wrong for how she came at you."

I am surprised. *Wow.* "Really?"

He nods thoughtfully. "Yeah. She was definitely outta pocket."

I look at him. "Thanks. But you didn't have to do that."

"I know. Still, it was effed up, yo. Quita stay runnin' her mouth."

Yeah. I know. "She's home?"

He shakes his head. "Nah. She's still locked up."

Oh.

He chuckles. "The homeys' still clownin' her for how you knocked her on her back. You a real thorough chick, ma. She definitely slept on you."

I swallow. "I feel bad for that. I—"

"Nah, yo. She deserved that beat-down, for real for real."

"Maybe. Still, I'd like to apologize to her."

He gives me a perplexed look. "Why?"

I shrug. "Because that's how I am. I don't like seeing any-one hurt, and I don't like hurting anyone. She's a bully. But I still could have..." I sigh, shaking my head. "...I could have handled things differently."

"Nah, yo. Not wit' Quita, word up. She ain't as forgivin', ma. You handled her exactly the way she needed handlin'. Trust me. She won't ever eff wit' you again."

I shift uncomfortably, tucking my hair behind my ears. "Still..."

"You got heart. Hands down. And you know how ta rock. She ain't got no choice but to respect how you get down."

"I don't like bullies," I say, shaking the whole Sha'Quita ordeal from my thoughts.

"I hear you, ma. Me neither." He glances at his watch. "Yo, I gotta bounce. But I'ma come through 'n' chill wit' you in a few days, a'ight?"

I surprise myself when I say, "Okay. I'd like that."

His grin widens. "Yeah, me too." He stands, brushing off the back of his designer jeans. "Be easy, a'ight?"

I nod.

And then he's off down the steps and down the sidewalk, slipping on his helmet.

He gives me a head nod, hops on his motorcycle, then turns on the ignition. He revs the engine, then speeds off, leaving me holding my journal up against my heart.

Touched by his kindness.

56

I am
the dove that cries
the caged bird that sings
the mockingbird that hums
I am
the blackbird
trying to fly...
I am
feathers
and
wings
I am

My pen freezes over my journal entry at the sound of squealing brakes.

I look up, surprised, as a black two-door Dodge Charger pulls up in front of the house.

It's Shawn.

Again.

He grins, his arm hanging out of the window. "What's good?"

I wave. "Nothing."

"Can I chill wit' you?"

My heart thuds. *Ohmygod*.

He wants to hang out with me.

All of a sudden my palms feel sweaty.

I shrug. "Um, I don't think that's a good idea." Not after all the drama I went through with Sha'Quita.

He feigns shock. "Why not?"

The act brings a small smile to my face. "Well, um...it's better that way."

He places a hand over his heart. "I'm crushed, yo. You actin' like I'm gonna kidnap you or sumthin'. I'm not a serial rapist or killah or anything crazy, yo. I promise you. I ain't on it like that, ma. I just wanna holla at you for a minute. Keep it real light."

I raise a brow. Ohhhkay. I'm going to need him to define *light*.

On second thought, never mind.

I don't need the headache.

He must see the hesitation in my eyes. "Yo, real talk, ma. I'm tryna keep it easy breezy. Real casual; feel me? I ain't tryna take much of ya time. Just like twenty minutes of it. Then I'ma bounce."

I look him over. "Well..."

He simulates a pout, holding his palms together. "Pretty please."

That gets me to smile. I cap my pen, then shut my journal. "Okay. But"—I narrow my eyes—"twenty minutes; that's it."

He grins, shutting off the engine. "Yo, that's all I need, li'l mama."

I eye him as he opens the door, then unfolds his six-foot-something frame from out of the car. It's hard to pretend not to notice how just how *hot* he is.

He's practically on fire.

And I'm feeling the heat as he makes his way toward me.

He stuffs his hands in his pockets, his left foot resting on the bottom step.

"I knew I'd find you out here on these steps wit' that book in ya hand."

"Writing calms me," I say, clutching my journal to my chest as I try to steady my nerves.

"Oh, word? That's wassup."

I fidget with the edges of my journal.

He is making me increasingly nervous.

But why?

Then it hits me.

Because I haven't had any real, genuine social interaction with a boy since I left Long Beach. All the guys I've come in contact since being here have all been disrespectful, leering pigs.

Shawn's never been like that around me.

Still, that doesn't justify my mouth going dry, or my heart beating faster.

He's just a boy.

Okay, okay, yes—a very cute boy.

"You lookin' good," Shawn says, his eyes gliding over me as he takes a seat beside me.

I scoot over, feeling my face flush. "Thanks." I tuck my hair behind my ear.

So what's good wit' you?"

I give him a confused look. "What do you mean?"

"I'm sayin', ma. What's up wit' *you*? You gotta man back in Cali?"

I swallow, then slowly shake my head. "No." I've never even had a boyfriend, much less a *man*. But there's no need for self-disclosure of my nonexistent relationships with anyone of the male species.

"Oh, a'ight. That's wasssup."

Oh. Is it?

"So, what about you? Do *you* have a girlfriend?" The question is asked before I can reel it back in. I'm not even sure why I've asked it. It's not like anything can ever come of it if he doesn't.

He locks his gaze on mine. "Nah. Not yet."

I raise a brow. "Oh. Well, what about Sha'Quita?"

He frowns. "What about her?"

I shrug. Then shake my head, looking away. "Never mind."

"Nah. Don't do that. Say what's on ya mind."

I swallow. Then I glance back at him. "Aren't the two of you..." I pause, silently scolding myself for opening my mouth.

"Are we *what*?" he pushes. "Gettin' it in?"

I nod.

He laughs. "Hell, nah."

Oh.

I give him a confused look. "I thought you were her *boo*."

"Nah, nah. She's just my peeps; she stay talkin' mad ish, that's all. I ain't ever pipe that."

My face flushes, but I manage to give him a side-eye "yeah right."

More laughter. "Nah, nah. Don't look at me like that. I'm keepin' it dead-azz, yo. I ain't tryna kick my girl's back in, but Quita got too many miles on that thing to be my girl, yo."

Oh.

I open my mouth to say something, but no words come out. It's probably for the best.

"Quita stay doin' the most," he continues. He looks me over. "I like my girls classy..."

Oh. Not trashy.

I mentally scold myself again.

Stop it, Nia. That's not nice.

Yeah. But it's true.

She *is* trashy.

"I'ma keep it straight up. Quita's the type to meet a dude up on the Gram..."

I give him a confused look.

"...on Instagram; my bad. Or up on KIK or the Book..."

Okay, Facebook. Got it!

"...then two days later she talkin' 'bout that's her *boo* 'n' ish. And she in love. I be like 'yo, if you don't go sit ya dumb-azz down somewhere.' Then she be all up in her feelin's when she doesn't hear back from dude."

I keep my expression neutral. But inside I'm saying, "Tell me about it. I've seen her nasty ways firsthand." Instead I say, "Well, maybe she just needs someone to call her on it."

He laughs, shaking his head. "Nah, she needs to go some-where 'n' read a damn book. I keep tellin' her all she ever gonna be good for is a smash 'n' go if she doesn't fall back 'n' relax 'n' stop lettin' mofos hit it on the first *hello*."

"Oh. So you don't meet girls online to hook up with?"

He frowns. "Hell nah. I'm good on that, ma. Trollin' for booty online doesn't do ish for me. I can't build anything wit' you through keystrokes; feel me?"

I nod.

"So, no girlfriend?"

He shakes his head. "Nah. I'm searchin' for the *one*. The right one, that is. Why, you tryna put in an application?"

All of a sudden, this is not feeling so much like an easy, breezy, light conversation. Well, actually, it stopped being easy, breezy the minute he sat down beside me.

He leans back on the step and stretches out his long legs. I can't help but look at his long feet covered in a pair of Gucci sneakers.

"But anyway. That's my peeps. She wild as *fawwk*, but she good peeps when you get to know her."

I give him a shocked look.

"A'ight, a'ight. She got her moments."

"Oh, you think?" I say, half joking.

"After that hand work you put in on her, she prolly won't

ever come outta her neck at you." He glances at his watch.
"Damn. I gotta bounce."

Oh no. Already? Just when I was warming up to him, he's
already up on his feet, brushing the back of his designer
jeans. "Oh," I say, my heart sinking. I don't really want to see
him go. Not yet. It's nice to have someone to talk to around
here.

Since Omar and his friend Peaches are hardly ever here.

I'm tired of sitting here alone.

I keep my thoughts to myself, though.

He faces me and grins, tapping the face of his watch with
a finger. "See. Twenty minutes. I'ma man of my word."

I swallow back the pit swelling in the back of my throat.
"That's good to know," I say earnestly.

"No doubt." He grins. "But dig. If you act right, next time
I'll stay longer."

I try not to smile, but it's no use fighting it. I wave him on.

"Later, Beautiful."

Ohmygod! He called me *beautiful*.

Is he flirting with me again?

Stop it, Nia.

It's a compliment. Nothing more.

"Bye, Shawn."

He opens the door to his car, then climbs in.

He watches me watching him as he shuts the door then
starts the engine. He gives an impish grin. "I'ma come through
e'ery day 'til you bounce. See you tomorrow, shorty."

He speeds off, before I can respond.

I uncap my pen, and open my journal. I finish the rest of
my lines.

fluttering
upward
soaring
soaring

rounded wings
gliding in the wind
until
I am
finally
free...

57

"How's it going, Nia-Pooh," Cameron says the minute I answer my cell and his face pops up on the screen. I've only spoken to him once since I've been here. And the first time was real brief. "You miss *me*, yet?"

"Ohmygod! Where have you been?" I say, holding my phone up in front of me as we FaceTime. "You have no idea how much I've missed you."

He grins. Then he waggles his eyebrows at me. "I've missed you, too, Nia. A lot. I haven't stopped thinking about you since you've left."

"Awww," I say, smiling. "That's so sweet."

"I wasn't really going for sweet here, Nia." He looks at me seriously, something he hardly ever does. "What I'm saying here is, I *really* miss you. You know what they say: 'absence makes the heart grow fonder.' Or in my case, your absence has me going crazy. I feel like the other half of me is gone."

Huh?

He feels like—?

Wait.

Wait.

Wait.

Is he saying...?

No. He can't be.

I quickly shrug it off. "Soo, have you and Crystal been hanging out?"

He shakes his head. "Not really. We talk here and there. But it's not the same. Don't get me wrong, Crystal's the apple in the pie. But you're the whipped cream, the vanilla bean ice cream, and the cherry on top. I miss being around you, Nia."

"Aww, Cam. I miss being around you, too. You're my bestie."

"Yeah, I know. That's the problem."

Huh?

My brow furrows with confusion. And just when I'm about to probe, to push further to see what he means, he saves me from the answer. "Crystal told me you might be coming back to Long Beach."

"No. I *am* coming back."

He smiles. "When?" There's eagerness in his tone that makes me blush.

I nibble contemplatively on my forefinger. "Uh. As soon as Crystal's parents get back from their vacation."

He grimaces. "She says they won't be back for another two weeks."

I sigh. "I know." The thought alone makes my stomach lurch. They've extended their vacation.

"We'll just have to be optimistic," he says. "It'll go by quick."

"Yeah. I guess."

"And there goes the optimism. Right out the front door."

"I know, I know." I take a deep breath. "I'm just so ready to come home." Well, I don't really have a home.

"I'm ready with you. You still haven't heard from your aunt? Crystal mentioned it."

Figures.

I shake my head. "No. It's like she vanished off the face of the earth."

"You want me to get my Atlanta crew to do a drive-by?"

"No I don't want you doing a *drive-by*. She's made her choice. Now I have to live with it."

He grins. "Oh, okay. I was about to have my Atlanta crew run up on her. All you have to do is say the word."

I laugh. "Boy, what Atlanta crew? Who do you know in Georgia?"

"Uh, no one, yet. But I was about to go on Facebook to see who I can recruit."

I suck my teeth. "Boy, stop."

He laughs. "You know I'm only talking trash."

"I know. That's why I don't ever take you serious."

He gives me a look. "Well, maybe you should. Start taking me serious, I mean."

"I know what you meant," I say back.

"I know I joke a lot, Nia. But there's also a serious side to me."

I know there is. He just never likes to show it.

"Oh, brother," I say, trying to make light of it. "Please don't get all heavy on me, Cam. I can't handle anything too serious right now. Being here is heavy enough. Let's just keep it easy, breezy."

Ohmygod. Did I just say that?

Easy breezy?

I did.

He laughs a little. "Cool. I'll save the heavy stuff for when you get back. Deal?"

"Deal."

"Are you still writing?"

I nod. Tell him some. "You wanna know what I miss most?"

"Me?" He waggles his brows.

"No, silly."

He grabs his chest, feigning hurt. "Way to go, Nia. You've managed to break my heart into a million pieces. You sure know how to bruise a man's ego. I don't think I'll ever be the same now."

I playfully roll my eyes. "Boy, stop. You and your ego will be fine. You know I miss you. But I miss all of the poetry lounges more. I miss being on stage."

He smiles. "You're really good. I love watching you on stage. All you need is some baby oil and a pole."

I roll my eyes. "Ugh. That is so not cute."

"I know, I know. But you are."

I blush. Why does he seem so different?

I don't know. I can't put my finger on it. But something's definitely *different*.

Cameron leans forward into the screen, his expression intense. "You're different, Nia." He says this as if he's been snooping through my thoughts about him.

I stare back. "Losing a father, then finding out that the man you *thought* was your father really wasn't, then being dragged three thousand miles away from your life to stay with a man who really *is* your father sort of has a way of changing a person."

"I know all of that, Nia. But you weren't dragged," he says, sorrowfully. "You went willingly."

I blink. "Wait a minute. I didn't have much of a choice here. Where else was I supposed to go? What was I supposed to do, Cam, kick and scream? I thought Aunt Terri was taking me in, but you see how well that turned out. This whole thing was supposed to turn out differently. If I had known for one second my aunt wasn't being honest with me, I would have never let her convince me to come here. I would have refused."

I feel myself getting emotional. "This has been extremely hard for me, Cam. You haven't lost your parents. I have."

"I'm sorry," he says, softly. "That was insensitive of me. I'm such an ass sometimes. I know you didn't ask for any of this. It's just that..." He pauses, taking a deep breath. "I wish you never left."

"So do I."

"Nothing's been the same without you, Nia. It was really

hard saying good-bye to you, when I never really got to say hello."

I swallow, blinking a mile a minute, confusion coursing its way through me.

What the heck is he talking about?

Wait. Why does it feel like there's some hidden meaning behind his words?

"Cam, you know I—"

The rest of my sentence goes on hold, when he cuts in with an apology for not calling as much. I tell him it's okay. "No, let me finish. I'm sorry for only calling you once since you've been gone. I should have been more available to you. I've been avoiding you," he says, softly, shaking his head.

I frown. "But why?

He sighs. "Because it's hard seeing you on a screen, Nia, and hearing your voice, but not being able to really be around you."

"It's okay," I say softly.

He shakes his head. "No, it isn't, Nia. I was wrong. It's lonely here without you."

"But you have Crystal."

"But I don't have *you*."

"Awww." I smile. "You know she likes you, right?"

He gives me a blank stare. "But I like *you*, Nia. Always have. You're my best friend, Nia. But I want more."

My eyes widen. I don't know what to say to any of what he's said.

But he saves me from an awkward tongue-tying moment, and says, "Don't respond, okay? Just let it marinate. You've been through a lot, Nia, in such a short time. I admire your strength. I think that's what attracts me to you the most. You're resilient. And smart. And pretty. And funny. Oh, and did I mention how pretty you are?"

I laugh, feeling tears welling up in my eyes. He's never shown me this side of him before. Only the silly him, and I don't know what to make of this other side.

"Look," he says, before any of my tears get a chance to fall. "I have to go. Hopefully, you'll be ready to talk more about what I've said. I have a big hug waiting for you when you get back."

"And I need one," I'm able to honestly say without my tongue sticking to the roof of my mouth.

"I love you, Nia," he says. And the way he says it, the way he's looking at me, tells me he means it. I smile, and my face warms.

"Bye, Cam."

"Later, Nia-pooh."

The call ends.

I sigh.

In a matter of weeks—no, months—my world has been turned upside down, and I've been tossed around. Everything's become so complicated for me.

My whole life has become quite the horror show.

And now my best friend tells me he *loves* me.

58

"Hey, sweetness," Miss Peaches calls out the next morning, knocking and opening the door at the same time. She peeks her head into the bedroom.

"Hi," I say, looking up from my journal.

I glance at the clock. Then I take her in, as I always do, without staring too long or too hard. It's close to ten in the morning, and she's already made up and pre-ready for a night out on the town.

Today, she's wearing a low-cut T-shirt—with the words BIG GIRLS DO IT BETTER scrawled in black lettering on the front—that has her oversize breasts practically bursting out of it, with pair of white leggings and wedge heels that make her look even taller than she already is.

Amazonian.

Lumbarjack tall.

"Have you heard from Omar?" she asks, placing a manicured hand up on her curvaceous hips.

I shake my head. "No. Not really. I mean, not since yesterday." Omar had texted me the day before saying he'd be back later in the evening. But when I'd finally gone to bed at eleven o'clock, he still hadn't returned.

And Miss Peaches wasn't home, either.

Her ruby-red painted lips curl. "*Mmph*. This mess with him has got to stop."

What mess?

"All I know is, I hope he's not back out there in them streets. I'm not 'bout to have my doors kicked in, or my car shot up behind none of his foolery."

She must notice the horrified look on my face.

She waves a dismissive hand. "Well, maybe they won't kick in the doors, so don't go worrying ya'self, sweetie. I just don't wanna be on the receiving end of a bullet not meant for *me*. You know these fools out here are crazy."

Oh. Like this news is really supposed to make me feel better.

"Omar's tryna change, you know. For you."

I give her a look, but say nothing. Daddy always said a person needed to change for himself first, before he tried changing for someone else.

I really think he was talking about Omar.

"I don't want him to change for *me*," I mutter.

"This is all new for him. Having a daughter 'n' whatnot."

I give her a blank stare.

"I'm sure this is no easier on you than it is on him. But y'all two gonna have ta figure it out."

"I'm leaving, Miss Peaches," I push out.

Her eyes widen. "You are? And where is you going, boo?"

"Back home."

She considers me thoughtfully, then asks, "Does ya *fahver* know?"

"He's not my father," I say, feeling defensive. "Please don't call him that."

She steps into the room and sits on the edge of the bed. The mattress sinks low. "Now you listen to me, boo. It may be hard for you to accept, but those blood tests don't lie. Omar is ya *fahver*, hon. Now you may not want him to be, and he may not know how to be, but that's what he is to you, whether you like it or not."

She reaches over and places her hand over mine. "You can't change who you're related to, but you can change how you relate to 'em; you know what I'm sayin'?"

I bite my lip and nod, wishing I didn't.

"*Mmph*. My sperm donor ran all up in my *muhver*, then split like the no-good coward he was the minute she told him she was knocked up. Dirty bastard. He the reason I don't trust men."

She shakes her head. "Oooh, just talking about that man makes my blood boil. I need to turn up. But I don't ever like to drink before noon."

I blink.

Oh.

"Anyway, Sugah. The point I'm making is..." She sucks her teeth. "Oh, hell. I done forgot my point. Dammit." She gives me a stern look. "Just say no to drugs, Sugah. I don't care what nobody tells you, they eat up ya brain cells."

"I don't do drugs," I say earnestly.

"Well, good for you. Don't smoke, either. Weed kills the brain cells, too."

"I don't do that either."

"Ooh, that's even, better. Stay wet-free, boo."

Wet-free?

I decide it's best I not know why not getting wet is "even better."

"Oh, I know what I was about to say," Miss Peaches says. "I don't know who my *fahver* is, and I don't wanna know who he is 'cause I'd probably spit in his face, or worse." She squeezes my hand. "But you, sweetness. You now know both of your *fahvers*. That ain't nothin' but God, baby." She waves a hand up in the air. "Yes, Lord. He took one away 'n' gave you another. You know what that is, right?"

Tragic.

I shake my head. "No."

"It's a second chance."

For a split second...

She sounds like Aunt Terri. Almost.

Later in the afternoon—around three or so—my butt is parked out in my usual spot, on the porch step with my journal and pen.

I awake to another sunrise,
but I do not feel the sun on my face.
I do not see the gift in waking up to
another day.
I am still breathing,
but I do not feel alive.
I am numb to my surroundings.
There is no beauty in despair.
This pain I'm in is unforgiving.
I am still motherless.
Still fatherless.
Still homeless.
And still so very lonely.
Where is the beauty in this?
Where is the justice?
What have I done to deserve this?
Am I not loveable?
Am I not worthy of love?
Yes.
I.
Am.
Then why God...
Why do you take everyone who has ever
loved me away from me?
Why?

Feeling my emotions starting to well up inside of me, I take a deep breath, then take a few seconds to collect myself before shutting my journal. I reach into the side pocket of my book bag and pull out my cell. I try Aunt Terri's number. Again.

"The subscriber you've reached has a number that has been disconnected or is no longer in service..."

I know what I've heard, but that doesn't stop me from calling back a second and third time, as if the recording would somehow miraculously disappear and her phone would start ringing.

It doesn't.

I press END. Then toss my phone back into my bag.

I'm not sure what to make of this. I'm struggling to understand why her numbers aren't working anymore. Or why she hasn't reached out to me.

I close my eyes, then allow hot, angry tears to stream down my face, believing—*no*, knowing—in my heart that Aunt Terri's has officially turned her back on me.

59

Neither Miss Peaches or Omar is here. No surprise in that. They're never here. Well, Omar, more specifically, isn't. Miss Peaches pops in and out randomly. And when she *is* in, all she wants to do is talk about Omar. She says he's just a friend. However, she acts like she wants more from him.

All I keep thinking when I look at her is, *Good luck with that.*

He is in no position to give her anything.

Heck. He's not in any position to be anything to anyone.

I almost feel sorry for her.

Almost.

But she's a nice lady; and, seemingly, a good friend to Omar. And I can tell she really cares about him. And the fact that she's taken me in, too, means a lot.

Speaking of Omar, he sent me a text stamped at six forty-three this morning saying he had to make a run, but would be back sometime this afternoon.

Ha!

It's already close to five o'clock.

And he's still not back.

Luckily for me, I've learned quickly not to hold my breath, or I'd end up suffocating in disappointment. The last several days, Shawn has made it his mission to keep me company, like now.

Every so often words are exchanged between us. However, even in the quietness, it feels nice to not be alone, physically.

Shawn has offered me his kindness.

Shown me compassion.

Something no one else here has offered me.

Not once.

And I take it willingly, and with great appreciation.

"So you definitely outta here in another week, huh?" Shawn wants to know.

I nod. "Yes."

He stretches out his long legs again. "I feel you. You should stay, though."

I shake my head. "I don't belong here. There's nothing here for me."

He stretches out his arms. "Yo, what am I? I'm here."

Nice. But still not one of my besties. I lower my gaze, then apologize. "I didn't mean it like that. I just miss my life back in California. I want my daddy. I know he's gone. But I just need to be closer to him."

"Nah, you good, ma. I know what you meant. I'm only effen wit' you. I know ish is mad hard for you bein' way out here. So I definitely feel you. But on some real ish, yo. Until you ready to bounce, you got me, a'ight?"

I half smile. "Thanks. That's really, really sweet of you."

"It's all love. I know you gotta do you. But I'm sayin', yo. I might have ta come out 'n' check for you one of these days."

That makes me smile wider. "You should. It's really nice. You'll love the weather."

"Oh, word? Is that all I'ma love?"

I shift in my seat. A nervous energy sweeps through me again. Everything about this boy screams all kinds of trouble.

Good trouble.

Bad trouble.

Double trouble.

I'm not—um, how did Sha'Quita put it?

I'm not about this life.

No, no. *That* life.

Yeah, that's it. And I'm not.

Shawn glances at his watch. "Aww. Damn. Yo, come take a ride wit' me."

I eye him as he stands.

I blink.

Stare at his outstretched hand.

"Umm, ride?"

"Yeah, real quick."

I shake my head. "Uh-uh. I'm *not* getting on"—I point over at his shiny motorcycle—"that thing."

He laughs. "What, you don't trust me?"

"No. I don't *trust* being on that bike."

"But you can trust *me*."

"No, I can't. I don't know you."

"Oh, word? It's like that? After all we've been through to-gether in the last"—he glances at his watch—"three days, thirteen hours, and twenty-seven minutes and forty-two sec-onds. The snot 'n' tears, the laughter, the—"

I put my hand up to stop him. "Okay, okay. Point made. Still..."

He shakes his head. "You really think I'ma let sumthin' happen to you?"

I shrug. "Maybe not intentionally."

He places a hand over his heart. "I'm crushed, yo." He pokes his lips out, feigning a pout. "But it's all good, yo. I see how you move. Get all emotional, lean on my shoulder, blow snot on my sleeve—"

I laugh. "Ohmygod. Stop. That's emotional blackmail, you know."

He grins, shrugging. "Nah. It's me remindin' you of all the snot you got on me. I'm still plucking boogers off me."

Now I'm laughing through my embarrassment. "*Ill*. Gross. I did no such thing."

"Yeah, a'ight. Maybe not snot, but you coulda 'n' I woulda been cool wit' it."

He extends his hand out again. "You owe me."

I groan. "Oh, God. You're still going to hold my moment of weakness over my head, aren't you?"

He grins. "Yup." He motions his hand in a come-here motion.

Hesitantly, I acquiesce.

He takes my hand and lightly tugs to pull me up.

I stand.

I grab my bag and shoulder it, then give him a puzzled look. "Where are you taking me?"

"It's a surprise," he says, pulling me along.

I snatch my hand back. "No, thanks." I sit back on the step. "I don't like surprises."

"Trust me, ma. You'll like this one."

There goes that word, again.

Trust.

How can I trust him, when I'm not sure if I can *trust* myself being somewhere alone with him?

He glances at his watch again. "C'mon, yo. You makin' us late."

I glance back at the house, fidgeting. Fighting the urge to throw caution to the wind.

But what do I have here?

Nothing.

What reason do I have to sit around doing nothing?

None.

Omar is off doing whatever it is he does when he's gone for hours, *days*, at a time.

Miss Peaches is working her shift at the bar.

And I'm here.

Alone.

Shawn eases his helmet on over his head, then mounts his bike.

He looks so, so...rugged.

And, and...*sexy*.

What is it about this boy?

He turns the ignition, and the Harley roars to life. "You comin', or *nah*?" He extends a hand.

Yes.

"This is against my better judgment," I say over the engine's low-pitched rumbling as I nervously climb up on the back of his bike.

"Live a li'l, mama," he says, before shutting the visor of his helmet.

Instinctively, I wrap my arms around his waist. Mold myself to his back.

And hold on for dear life.

Breathe, Nia. Breathe...

60

Thirty minutes later, we're pulling up in front of a two-story redbrick building. Shawn turns off the engine, shifts the bike backward, and the kickstand engages. He waits for me to climb off.

I'm so, so...breathless.

I shudder.

That was so much fun.

I felt like I was flying.

"Ohmygod, that was..." I shake my head, shifting my bag from one shoulder to the other. "So exhilarating."

Shawn removes his helmet and grins. "You like that, huh?"

I nod.

"Stick wit' me, ma. I'll have you ridin' it like a pro."

Something about the way he says that, the double entendre lingering, causes me to blush.

"C'mon." He reaches for my hand and leads me toward the door. My hand gets lost in his, but I don't mind. "You ready for your surprise?"

I nod, allowing him to lead the way.

The minute we step over the threshold of the storied bohemian space, there's a welcoming vibe that makes me feel connected. Instrumental music greets us. Coltrane. Immediately, I melt into a zone of excitement and high anticipation, followed by nostalgia. My heart skips a beat when a Roy Ayers song starts streaming through the large speakers on either side of the stage.

I practically gasp.

"Everyone Loves the Sunshine" is one of Daddy's favorite songs.

Without thought, I sway a little and hum along, remembering how Daddy would sing this, and I'd laugh at how horrible he sounded. But that never stopped him from tearing up every note.

Shawn glances at me and grins. "Yo, what you know 'bout that?" he asks, leaning into my ear. "That joint's before ya time."

"I'm an old soul," I say sheepishly.

"Yo, me too. I grew up listenin' to this kinda music. But I'm sayin'...I know you a poet 'n' all, but do you dig open mics?"

Open mics?

My face lights up. "Ohmygod! Is this where you've brought me, to an open mic? I love open mics!"

He grins, wrapping an arm around me. "Cool, cool. I figured you needed some poetry in ya life."

That word *poetry* is like music to my ears.

Beautiful, sweet, soothing music; something I've longed for.

Something I so desperately need.

"Ohmygod, you have no idea how bad," I say as he holds my hand tighter and leads the way toward the tables. We settle in our seats to the left of the stage just as the emcee—a mocha-colored guy with oval-framed glasses wearing a white T-shirt with a huge black fist in the center of his chest and a pair of army fatigues and black Timberland boots—steps up to the mic and welcomes everyone.

Bright lights bathe the stage.

"Check. Ladies and gentlemen, welcome to the Poets' Corner. Tonight we have twenty poets who are about to grace the stage. Remember the house rules: Be respectful of time. Each poet has three minutes to do his or her thing. There's a five-dollar penalty for anyone who goes over. Got it?"

"Got it," the crowd says in unison.

"A'ight. Give it up for Sunshine, from Brooklyn, New York."

The crowd claps.

I lean forward.

She's breathtaking.

Her burnt-orange–colored hair is worn in a wild, woolly afro. Large hoop earrings adorn her ears. She's wearing a white ruffled midriff top, showing off her pierced navel, and a pair of hip-hugging low-rider jeans.

She steps up to the mic and says, "I'm eighteen and I've been through a lot..."

An astonished hush falls over the crowd.

"I've seen a lot. And I'm done licking self-inflicted wounds. I'm done settling for less than what I'm worthy and deserving of. I'm done making excuses for my own self-imposed misery, and everyone else's. I'm no longer slashing tires, or balling up my fists to take it to another chick's face. She can have him. You see, I'm taking on a new fight. Not with my fists. Not with my heart. But with my intellect. I'm letting go of people who are not worthy of me. Letting go of no-good boyfriends. Letting go of jealous friends. Letting go of family members who silently hate me..."

"Speak!" someone cries out.

"So tonight's piece," she says, swaying ever so slightly from side to side, "is a celebration of my ever-changing self. It's called 'Here I Am.' I hope you like it."

She's already captivated the audience long before she starts to read. When she finishes her piece, the room erupts into thunderous applause filled with lots of whistling.

Even I stand, clapping and stomping and finger snapping.

"Yo, she killed that ish; word is bond," Shawn says when I finally sit back down in my seat.

"Yes, she did," I say, feeling every nerve ending in my body coming alive. I'm almost feeling like myself again.

Almost.

I thank Shawn for bringing me here, for freeing me, if only for a short while, from my own painful reality.

"No doubt, ma. It's all good." He wants to know if I'm enjoying myself. I tell him I am.

"I knew you'd dig this spot," he says assuredly.

The whole time we're out, he only checks his phone once. Then he shuts it off.

I check mine as well.

But twice.

For voice messages and texts. In the hope that Aunt Terri has finally called or texted me back.

She hasn't.

And because of that, I almost allow it to drag me into a dark place. Almost. But the energy around me is too powerful to let go of, so I stay in the moment, enjoying the pieces of six other poets before a twelve-year-old girl from Jamaica, Queens—I *think* that's where the emcee says she's from— steps onto the stage carrying a set of mini conga drums and blows us all away with her piece, "Little Black Girl." The palms of her hands slap the skins of her drums in a rhythmic cadence that matches the tempo of her piece. The drum thuds repeatedly as she drones out, "I woke up...and...discovered...I do not exist. I am...a little black girl...lost in the texture of my hair...burdened by the color of my skin... I am. A little black girl..."

By the time she finishes, half the room is in tears.

And I have melted into the energy.

The emcee calls up the next act. An eighty-eight-year-old man who goes by the name Black Knight. Everyone claps for him. I smile as he hobbles up the stage. He's wearing a New York Yankees fitted hat with a white button-up shirt and a pair of dark-colored khaki pants.

Aww. He looks adorable.

He steps up to the microphone and tells us his piece is titled "Lick It and Stick It."

"Yaaassss, yaaaaasssss, granddaddy!" someone calls out.

The crowd laughs.

He opens his mouth and delivers the piece in a raw, silky voice, each line filled with lots of double-entendres that make me blush. The room is still as he begs to "lick it, stick it, and lay it all up on it" to only find out that the whole time he's really talking about licking a stamp to put on an envelope.

Shawn and I laugh.

"Yo, Pops did his thing," Shawn says. "He got me with that."

"Ohmygod. Yes. That was real good," I agree.

"Pops still nasty, though," Shawn says, laughing again. "Yo, I bet he be still gettin' it in. Lickin' it 'n' stickin' it."

"Oh, God," I groan shamefacedly. "That's an image I don't need to see. Ever."

Shawn bumps his shoulder into me. "Yo, I think you need'a do ya thing tonight."

My eyes widen. "What, perform?"

"Yeah, I wanna see how you put it down."

My pulse starts to race.

I haven't been on stage since before Daddy's death.

I'm not ready.

Am I?

I don't know. "I'm not prepared," I say, glancing around the room. This is a whole other type of world. Nothing like the laid-back ease of the west coast. It's so much more fast-paced. I don't think I'm ready for it.

Shawn raises his brow. "Whatchu mean, you ain't prepared, yo? You a poet, *right*?"

"Well, yeah. But—"

"But nothin', yo. Do what a poet does. Get up there 'n' drop some of that west coast love on us, mama."

My heart starts to beat harder. "It's too late, isn't it? All the names have already been—"

"It's never too late, shorty." A sly grin eases over his face. "Just say the word. And I can make it happen. Hol' up." He pushes back from the table and rises to his feet.

Oh no! "Wait," I say, anxiously grabbing his arm. "Where are you going?"

He grins. "Relax, ma. I got this."

And then he's off.

I cover my face in my hands and groan. Then I look up at him across the room talking to the emcee. Shawn points over toward our table, and I slowly feel myself shrinking in my seat. The emcee nods. Then the two of them are embracing in a brother hug and handshake.

Several moments later, Shawn is back in his seat, grinning. "It's on now, shorty."

"Ohmygod," I say frantically. "What did you say to him?"

His arm stretches out over the back of my chair as he leans into me. "I tol' him you were my peoples wit' that hot fire to spit..."

I blink.

Is he serious?

I don't have any *hot* fire to spit!

Heck, I don't even like to spit.

61

"Yo, word is bond," Shawn says as we're walking out of the building toward his bike. "I ain't think your skillz were like that, yo. You slaughtered that ish. Hands down, you did ya thing."

I blush. "Thanks. It was fun." And it was. It felt so good stepping up on that stage, being bathed in the heat of the spotlight and caught up in all of the energy in the room. "I really needed that."

"Word is bond. I can tell. Yo, you stepped up on the stage 'n' the minute you took the mic, you became this whole other person..."

After I'd worked through my nerves, I closed my eyes to pull my thoughts together. And when I opened them again, I was pushing out lines about the broken heart of a daddy's girl, left in the world, alone and lonely, chasing butterflies.

That girl being *me*.

Shawn takes my hand and helps me climb back onto his bike.

"Yo, ma?"

"Yes?"

"I'm not ready to take you back yet."

"Then don't," I boldly say, shocking myself as I slide my

arms around his waist and put my chin on his shoulder to catch his expression under the light of the street lamp.

He starts the bike, and we speed off.

I don't know how many miles we've traveled on the open highway before we're finally turning off on an exit. Several miles later, he's easing into a parking space, then parking his bike and helping me off.

My eyes widen.

It's a boardwalk.

A beach.

Ohmygod!

He's taken me to a beach!

"I've had you on the brain for a minute," Shawn says coolly as we walk on the beach. He reaches for my hand, slipping his fingers through mine as we saunter along the edge of wet sand.

It's a warm, breezy night out. The sky is filled with twinkling stars.

I glance up, smiling. "It's so beautiful. The sky."

"No doubt, like you," Shawn says. "I wish you weren't leavin' yo. But I understand you gotta do what you gotta do. Still, you kinda got me goin' through it." He shakes his head and grins. "Seeing you up on that stage tonight really did it for me."

I nervously smile, tucking a strand of hair behind my ear as the cool sand squishes between my toes. I don't say anything; just take in his words along with the sound of the ocean.

I glance around, surprised that there's no one else on the beach. I'm out here alone, with him.

I swallow.

"I don't know what it is about you. But you got me wantin' to be all up on you. I ain't never wanna sweat no female 'til you. From the moment I peeped you, I knew you were type special; word is bond."

My heart thumps.

Then stumbles over a beat.

He stops walking and turns to me. "You feelin' me, aren't you?"

He grins, taking his jacket off then spreading it out on the sand.

Um. No. Yes. Maybe.

Uhh. I don't know.

I open my mouth to say something, but I'm struggling to form a coherent thought. For some reason, my brain turns to mush. "Huh?"

"You heard me, yo. What, the cat got ya tongue? I said you feelin' the kid, aren't you?"

I struggle to keep from smiling. "I don't know you."

"C'mon." He gestures toward his jacket. "Sit. So, what's good? You diggin' me or nah?"

I grin. "I plead the Fifth."

"Yeah, a'ight. Plead all you want. I already know what the verdict is. But it's all good. You ain't gotta admit it. If I were you, I'd be feelin' me, too."

I playfully nudge him in the ribs with my elbow. "Ohmygod. You're so conceited."

He laughs. "Nah. Convinced. Keep it a hunnid, yo. You want me?"

I swallow. I'm not sure what I'm feeling toward him. I mean. He's nice. And, he's ... really, really cute. And he seems thoughtful.

But—

"I want you, yo. Bad."

Ohmygod, ohmygod!

Um, wait! What does he mean by this? Wanting me as in *wanting* to get to know me, or as in wanting to get me in bed?

Not that I'm admitting to liking—I mean, *feeling*—him, too. I'm just shocked that he's admitting it to *me*.

I may not be well versed in street lingo, or have a lot—no.

Scratch that, *any*—experience dating boys. But I had a father who always talked openly with me about boys, and some of the mind games they play. So I might not be from the hood, so to speak, but I'm definitely not overly naïve, either.

I know boys will say all types of things just to get what they want from a girl.

Unfortunately for Shawn, I'm not like most girls. I have nothing I'm willing to offer him, so there's not much he can *try* to get.

I'm not easily manipulated.

No matter how cute and sexy some boy is.

I look at Shawn, wondering if he's sincere, or if he has some hidden motive.

He grins. "Yo, like I said, ma. It's cool. You ain't gotta admit. I already know what it is."

I smirk. "Then why'd you ask if you already know your version of the answer?"

He laughs. "Oh, word? My version? Haha. Is that what it is?"

I shrug. "Probably."

"Yeah, a'ight. Whatever you say. But dig. You mad sexy, ma. But you already know that, though."

I cover my nervousness with a chuckle. "No, not really. But I bet you say that to all the girls."

He bunches his brows together, shaking his head. "Nah, nah. Just the ugly ones."

Oh.

So he thinks I'm *ugly*.

That stings.

Hurts my feelings.

But he's entitled to *his* feelings.

Still...

My heart sinks.

He smiles. "I'm just effen wit' you, yo."

His chocolate-brown eyes lock with mine.

I smile back at him. Then look out into the night. The

ocean is ours—Shawn's and mine—just for tonight. More waves crash, and hiss into white foam, rushing up the sand, then stopping just below out feet, which we've planted slightly beneath the sand.

He smiles again, then leans in. And, this time, when I glance over at him, my heart thuds loudly in my chest. *Ohmygod!* That smile of his. I've never been stupid over a guy before. *What is wrong with me?*

"I like you, yo," he murmurs, lightly brushing his lips against my ear. His warm breath kisses my cheek. And I shiver. He takes a finger under my chin and turns my head to him.

He leans in closer.

Ohmygod, ohmygod, ohhhhhhmygod!
I'm really about to let this boy kiss me.

I close my eyes.

Anxious.

My heart racing—no, stuttering stupidly in my chest.

Waiting.

Wanting.

Needing.

62

"How you?" Omar asks, stepping into the house. He's been gone for almost three days, sending me the occasional text to check in on me. But what does it matter?

I'm leaving in two days.

Crystal's parents have finally returned from their travels. Crystal called me all excited this morning and gave me the best news of my life. I can stay with them for as long as I want.

I don't need Omar's permission, or his blessing.

And I don't need to ever hear back from Aunt Terri.

I can simply get on the plane and go.

Back to California, where I've always belonged, where I never should have left.

"You good?"

I'm sitting cross-legged on the sofa, watching reruns of *How to Get Away with Murder* when he disrupts my marathon moment.

I glance up from the television and look at him.

"I'm fine," I say, my tone clipped.

Omar shuts the door behind him with his foot.

I narrow my eyes, scrutinizing him. He's wearing a pair of True Religion jeans and a brand-new pair of Jordans. There's more jewelry dangling from his neck. And bigger diamond studs in each earlobe.

For some reason, I'm annoyed.

I'm not sure if it's because he's back, or because he's been gone for days, obviously up to no good.

Either way, I'm irritated.

"Yo, sorry 'bout not being around much," he says, plunking down in a chair across from me. "I'm tryna handle some things."

Oh, really? I reach for the remote and mute the television. "It's fine, Omar. I'm learning to manage without you."

I shift my gaze back to the television, turning the volume up.

I can't get out of here *and* away from him soon enough.

"Ouch," he says. "You have my digits, though. You know you can hit me up anytime, right?"

Umm. That works both ways. I shrug. "I guess."

"Yo, why you say it like that?"

It doesn't even matter. "No reason."

"Listen, baby girl. I know I already said this, but I know I can't bring back ya pops. And I can't take back what I've done. Or the time lost. But I'm hoping one day, you can forgive me."

I blink back tears.

Forgive him?

What is there to forgive?

Like Daddy said in his letter to me, what Omar did was really selfless.

So why am I really mad at him?

Because Daddy's gone.

And *he* exists.

Because he's appeared out of nowhere and, and—

"You hate me, don't you? I see it in ya eyes."

No. I'm *mad* at you.

I don't want to be. But I am. I just don't know how not to be.

But is it him I'm really mad at?

Honestly?

No.

I'm still mad at Daddy.

I'm still mad at God.

And I'm mad at Aunt Terri.

Daddy didn't turn his back on me; he just died on me. And I still blame God for taking him from me.

I hold my hands over my face and smooth away the tears. "I don't hate you, Omar," I say, in between sobs. "I just want my life back."

He gets up and walks over to me, sinking into the space next to me. "And I wanna be in it," he says, softly. "In whatever capacity, feel me?"

I bite into my bottom lip to keep it from trembling. "School starts in a few weeks," I say pensively. "I'm going back to California."

"When?"

I tell him in two days. He plops back in his seat. Runs his large hand over his face. And then he's upright again. Looking, staring, at me. "Is there anything I can do to change ya mind?"

More tears.

I shake my head, allowing my tears to wet my cheeks. I choke back a sob, shifting my body in my seat so that I can let him *see* me. Hurt and broken.

"Look at *you*. Look at *me*," I say, my lips quivering. "We're both *homeless*, Omar, staying in someone else's place. What kind of life is this for either of us? You can barely take care of yourself, let alone a teenager. If things were different, maybe." I shake my head. "But they aren't. Things are a mess. I'm a mess. You're a mess. We're both two big messes, Omar."

The tears keep flowing. And I can't stop them even if I wanted to.

I don't want to.

This is the first real conversation Omar and I have since

I've been here. And I'm afraid if I don't get it all out now, there may not be another opportunity to. I catch my breath, then straighten myself. "No disrespect. But you made a baby. *Me*. But you didn't raise me. You didn't parent me. You gave up your rights to me the day you signed your name on the dotted line. Don't forget that, Omar."

He runs a hand over his face. "I can't ever forget that. It's been effen wit' me for the last sixteen years. And, now, all I gotta do is look at you 'n' see what I gave up. Sixteen years of my life, Nia. Sixteen years of not having *you* in it. I regret ever givin' up my rights. I swear, yo. I did what I had to do."

"For who, Omar? *You*?"

"Nah," he says softly. "For you. I thought I was doin' what was right for *you*. I knew I had a mad long bid to do. I ain't wanna put that kinda pressure on ya moms. She wasn't built for that life. She didn't deserve that ish. Jailin' wit' some *nig*—cat. So when she came to see me wit' you in her arms to tell me she wanted out, that she'd met someone..." His voice cracks. He looks over at the muted TV, then back at me. "I did what I had to do. What she asked me to do. I let her go, yo."

"And *me*, Omar. You let me go, too."

"Because I loved you, yo. I've never stopped lovin' you, baby girl. You a part of me; no matter what, I'm still ya father."

I wince. "No, you're not. You're a sperm donor. That's all you are. Just some man who impregnated my mother. Then wasn't man enough to stay on the streets long enough to take care of his responsibilities."

There's a flicker of shock in his eyes when I say this. And I almost feel bad for saying it. But, right or wrong, it's how I feel. And I won't apologize for that.

He gives me another pained look. "You really don't like me, huh?"

I stare at him. "I don't *know* you, Omar."

"I wanna change that. All I'm askin' for is a chance to make it up to you. I know things been kinda crazy lately. But I'm workin' on makin' things right; feel me?"

"No, Omar. I don't *feel* you. What I *feel* is abandoned. I *feel* empty. I *feel* alone. I *feel* lost. And I'm tired of feeling this way."

He winces. "On e'erything I love, yo. We can get through this."

I shake my head. "No, we can't. Sorry. I gave it all the chances I'm going to give it. I'm *still* miserable. And, right now, all I know is, you're not ready to be a grown-up, Omar."

He opens his mouth to say something, but I put a hand up, stopping him from getting his words out.

"Are you working?"

"Nah, not—"

I shake my head. "My point exactly. How do you expect to provide for me, or for yourself, huh?" He gives me a dumbfounded look. "I may not be from the hood, Omar. But I'm not stupid or slow, either. I'm smart enough to know when someone's in way over their heads."

"Yo, you gotta understand, baby girl, I been locked up for close to sixteen years. I'm just gettin' home. Shit ain't the same. I mean, the streets are the same. But e'erything else around me is different. Ain't no one tryna hire a muhfuggah like me. A cat wit' a record."

"Sounds like a bunch of excuses to me," I say, feeling emotionally exhausted.

His brows furrow. "Ain't no excuses, yo. It's fact. Mofos ain't checkin' for a cat like me. Period."

"Well, have you *tried* looking for work?"

When he doesn't respond right away, I keep going. "What you do with your life, Omar, is none of my business." I swipe away more tears with my hand. "But it's real selfish of you to want to drag me into it. You should have never brought me out here knowing your living situation was chaotic. You say you care about me, then prove it. You gave me up *once* because you couldn't be there for me, or take care of me. Well, you still can't. I don't deserve to live like this. And you have no business trying to make me."

He blinks. "On e'erything, yo. I'm sorry I wasn't in ya life, a'ight. Sorry I wasn't able to love you. I'm sorry another man had to step in and do what I couldn't do. I'm sorry I missed out on sixteen years of ya life. I can't change what's already done. But I'm here now. If you'd let me be."

I don't say anything. Just stare at him.

I want my daddy.

Not this fill-in, this, this . . . imposter.

I close my eyes, then open them. "You're not ready to be responsible. Not for me." I pause, swallowing. "And not for *you*. I don't belong here, Omar. This isn't my life. It's yours."

In the flickering glow of the television, I think I see hurt illuminating from his eyes, maybe something more. "You right," is all he mutters, before silence creeps in and swallows us whole.

63

With the same backpack over my shoulder I came here with—what feels like forever ago—and my leather journal tucked under my arm, I make my way toward the gate, feeling freer than I've ever felt since Daddy's death.

I'm going home.

Crystal and her mom will be at the airport waiting for me with open arms, welcoming me back home, where I've always belonged.

I am leaving behind every bad memory of being here in New Jersey. But I am taking back with me some good memories, too, like my brief time with Shawn.

He was my lifeline when I felt myself sinking.

He saved me.

And I can never, ever, forget him for that.

Oh, and that night on the beach, we'd kissed the sweetest kiss I'd ever experienced, then he wrapped his arm around me as we both stared out at the endless expanse of the shimmery Atlantic ocean under a full moon, and watched the waves crest against the shore.

It was a beautiful moment. One I will cherish, always.

But we both knew nothing would ever come of it. We're from two different sides of the world. And, honestly, he re-

minds me too much of Omar. His—uh, um, how do they say—
his *swag*, that is. I kept seeing my mother's face, and thinking
I don't want to end up in a romance similar to what she had
with Omar. That kiss on the beach was enough for me.

So much has happened since losing Daddy. I miss him
more than I imagine is humanly possible and I can't wait to
lie in the grass, kiss his headstone, and be near him again. I
lost both of my parents. And, yes, I miss my mom, too. But
not the way I miss Daddy. Maybe because I had sixteen years
of my life with him, ten years more than what I had with my
mom. The memories run deeper with Daddy.

I don't care what anyone says. Julian Daniels is the only father I have. *Have* as in the present tense, because, although
he's physically gone, he is still alive inside of me. His memory is stamped in my brain, inscribed over my heart.

Nothing can take that from me. Not a judge. Not a blood
test. Not some stupid ole adoption papers. Nothing.

Omar may be my biological father. But he will never be my
real father.

Ever.

He's not *built*—as they say—for parenting.

I only have one father.

One Daddy.

And he's gone. But never, ever, forgotten.

I look back at Omar again. He's not a bad person. He's
just not someone I wish to know. Not right now, anyway.
Maybe one day.

Still, I'm glad I know the truth. Aunt Terri—whom I still
haven't heard from—was right. I had a right to know. However, there's also a part of me that wishes I didn't know. In
knowing, it made me feel like I'd been living a lie. But then
Daddy's smiling face pops in my head and I know everything
about him is, and was, real. And the truth is, he loved me unconditionally. And, no matter what, I'll always be his little
girl. His butterfly.

As I glance back over my shoulder, and take Omar in one last time before boarding my flight, I wave.

He waves back, a sadness flooding his eyes as if he knows I am never coming back here. Ever.

I smile.

He smiles.

We both know.

There's nothing here for me.

I'd left my life *and* heart back in California.

And now I am going home to reclaim them both.

I hand my ticket to the agent, then disappear through the passageway leading to the plane. I let out a soft sigh as I slip my bag off of my shoulder and slide into seat 2C in first class, courtesy of Crystal's mom. I spoke to her this morning to confirm everything. And during our telephone conversation she mentioned that she'd gotten in touch with Daddy's attorney. He's drawing up papers and presenting them to the courts recommending she be granted physical custody of me until my eighteenth birthday, while he continues to oversee my trust fund until my twenty-first birthday.

I'm ecstatic.

When the plane finally ascends into the sky, it's as if my own wings are stretching. Spreading. I gaze out of the tiny window at all the bright, puffy clouds floating in the sky and imagine Daddy, Mommy, and Nana holding hands. I can almost feel their smiles on me.

My time in New Jersey, though brief, was one of the longest experiences of my young life. I'm not mad that I came, though. I'm actually glad I did. I harbor no regrets.

It broadened my horizons.

Gave me new perspective.

And has helped me evolve into my true self.

I really feel like I'm a whole other person because of it.

A new being.

Daddy said to never be afraid to spread my wings and soar.

And I'm not. I am jumping out of my storm.

Peeling back layers of skin, and metamorphosing into everything Daddy has always encouraged me to be. There's nothing (or no one) that can give me what I've always had. Love. God, I miss Daddy so, so bad. But I know, in time, I'm going to be okay. But, for now, everything I'll ever need lies within me, and all around me. Daddy's love and his memory live on forever inside of me.

I will never stop loving him. Or holding onto the memories of what the last sixteen years of my life has been like having him as a father. I know what unconditional love is because of him. That will always be with me.

I settle back in my seat and wipe tears from my face. But this time they're happy tears. But for some reason Sha'Quita's face appears in my head, then her mother, Kee-Kee's. Good or bad, they've both left impressions, prints in my sand. Taking a deep breath, I take a moment to pull my words together. Then open my journal, and remove the cap from my pen and write:

cherry-red lips
stretched hips
hormones on full throttle
lusting
craving
begging
for attention
starving for affection
looking for love
in the bottom of a bottle
Rollin' and smokin'
puff-puff
pass

puff-puff
pass
hoping the weed
and the drinks
fill a need...
trading in her dignity
for a love hangover
pledging her allegiance
to the streets
chasing butterflies
while her soul bleeds
to welcome
in the heat
of a boy
who doesn't love her
because he knows
she doesn't
love
herself
puff-puff
pass
puff-puff
pass
closing her eyes
white-hot
desire
burns
through her chest
and her heart
skips a beat
as he pushes
and
pushes
bursting through

the fire
stripping her
of hopes
and desires…
filling her voids
with dirty deeds
planting seeds
of
empty promises
polluting her womb
and
he's not the only one
they'll all take turns
and still she's incomplete
becoming his latest tweet
puff-puff
pass
puff-puff
pass…
'round n 'round
she'll go
used up
abused up
still searching for a reason
to give her mind
body
and
soul
to a boy who'll
never make her whole
puff-puff
pass…

Pen poised over the page, I stop writing, then do something I never imagined I'd do. I say a silent pray for all the

Sha'Quitas in the world, wishing, *no*, hoping, they one day find peace of mind, peace of heart, and, most importantly, self-love.

I inhale. Exhale. Then write:

And she'll always be chasing butter-flies...

CHASING BUTTERFLIES

Amir Abrams

ABOUT THIS GUIDE

The following questions are intended to
enhance your group's reading of
CHASING BUTTERFLIES.

Discussion Questions

1.) Most people take for granted what they have, like family and friends, while chasing after the things they think they need. What did you think of the book *Chasing Butterflies*? Do you understand the concept of chasing butterflies?

2.) What did you think of the characters in the book? Nia's friendships with Crystal and Cameron? Were you surprised that Cameron had a crush on Nia, instead of Crystal? And now that Nia knows, do you think she'll give him a chance to be more than friends?

3.) Nia seemed to have a very close relationship with her father, Julian. Did it remind you of your relationship with your own father? What type of relationship do you have with your own father? If you don't have one, do you wish you did? If not, why?

4.) At a young age, Nia suffered several major losses in her life. How do you think she handled losing the only man she'd ever known as her father? Then learning that she'd been adopted? Do you think her father was wrong for not telling her long before he died? If so, why? Have you ever experienced finding out that your father wasn't your real father? If so, how did you handle it?

5.) Why do you think Nia's aunt treated her the way she did? Do you think she ever planned to allow Nia to live with her in the first place? If not, why do you think she misled her?

6.) What did you think about Omar coming into Nia's life? Was she wrong for demanding a paternity test before going to New Jersey with him? Do you think Omar really wanted to be a parent?

7.) What did you think of Sha'Quita? Why do you think she was so mean and antagonistic toward Nia? Why do you think she was so promiscuous? What did you think of her relationship with her mother, Keyonna? They smoke and drink and fight like girls on the streets. Do you know of anyone who has a similar relationship to the one Sha'Quita had with her mother?

8.) At the end of the book, Nia refers to Shawn as a lifeline. Do you think if she had stayed in New Jersey that the two of them might have become involved? What did you think of him? Do you think Nia was right in her assessment of him; that he was a lot like Omar?

9.) How do you think Nia's experience being in New Jersey affected her? Do you think she and Omar will ever have a relationship now that she's back in California? Do you think he should have tried to stop her from leaving? Or did he do the right thing by letting her go?